FEMALE LINES

New Writing by Women from
Northern Ireland

Edited by
Linda Anderson and
Dawn Miranda Sherratt-Bado

NEW ISLAND

FEMALE LINES
First published in 2017 by
New Island Books
16 Priory Office Park
Stillorgan
Co. Dublin
Republic of Ireland

www.newisland.ie

An excerpt from Deirdre Madden's *Time Present and Time Past* is reproduced by kind permission of Faber and Faber Ltd.

An excerpt from Lucy Caldwell's *Three Sisters* is reproduced by kind permission of Faber and Faber Ltd.

Print ISBN: 978-1-84840-642-1
Epub ISBN: 978-1-84840-643-8
Mobi ISBN: 978-1-84840-644-5

A CIP catalogue record for this book is available from the British Library.

Typeset by JVR Creative India
Cover Design by Anna Morrison
Printed by POLAND, PUP Intokar, www.introkar.com

LOTTERY FUNDED

New Island is grateful to have received financial assistance from The Arts Council of Northern Ireland (1 The Sidings, Antrim Road, Lisburn, BT28 3AJ, Northern Ireland).

Contents

About the Editors

Linda Anderson was born and educated in Belfast. She is an award-winning novelist (*To Stay Alive* and *Cuckoo*, both published by The Bodley Head) and writer of short stories, performance pieces and critical reviews. Her short fiction has been published in magazines and anthologies including *HU*, *The Big Issue*, *Wildish Things*, *The Hurt World: Short Stories of the Troubles* and *The Glass Shore*. She taught at Lancaster University, becoming Head of Creative Writing from 1995–2002. In 2006, she launched creative writing at the Open University, chairing the largest writing course in the UK until 2014. She was awarded a Fellowship by the Higher Education Academy in 2007. She is editor and co-author of *Creative Writing: a Workbook with Readings* and co-author of *Writing Fiction*. She lives in Cambridgeshire, writing fiction and non-fiction and working as an editor.

Dawn Miranda Sherratt-Bado is an academic and a dual specialist in Irish and Caribbean Studies. She has taught at Maynooth University, the University of Edinburgh, and the Scottish Universities' International Summer School (SUISS). She is author of *Decoloniality and Gender in Jamaica Kincaid and Gisèle Pineau: Connective Caribbean Readings*. She has also published in *Irish Studies Review*, *Breac*, *Dublin Review of Books*, *Callaloo*, and *The Irish Times*.

Foreword

Linda Anderson

From Pipedream to Publication

It was just after Christmas in 2015 when I received an email from
Dawn Miranda Sherratt-Bado, who was teaching at Maynooth
University. Her purpose in contacting me was to invite me to
co-edit an anthology of writings by contemporary Northern
Irish women as a follow-up to Ruth Carr's *The Female Line:
Northern Irish Women Writers*, the pioneering anthology published in 1985. Dawn proposed a celebration of women writers
across multiple genres along with an exploration of how much
conditions have changed in the past thirty years and what sort
of obstacles might still remain. My immediate impulse was to
say yes. *The Female Line* felt like a breakthrough publication at
the time but women writers remained significantly marginalised.
While some writers included went on to become prominent, others have 'disappeared', even after brilliant debuts: for example,
Blánaid McKinney, whose story collection *Big Mouth*, published
by Phoenix House in 2000, was praised as 'among the best short
fiction to appear, anywhere, in the past year or so'. A novel followed in 2003 but nothing since.

I hesitated. I had edited a huge, multi-authored book before
and knew how such a project takes over your life and consigns
you at the end stages to obsessive forensics of lucid sentence
arrangement and comma placement. I also knew that the idea
was a pipedream due to recent funding cuts in the North. But

the idea and the timing felt right. Sinéad Gleeson's *The Long Gaze Back* had recently been published. Although we didn't know it yet, its Northern sequel *The Glass Shore* was in the offing. The 'Women Aloud Northern Ireland' events were being organised all across the region for International Women's Day in March 2016. And Dawn has a quality of intrepid hopefulness about her, which is inspiring.

During the New Year period in 2016, I decided to say yes and soon embarked upon a period of intensive research and collaboration with Dawn and the contributors, and renewed contacts with some writers I had last met around twenty-five years ago. For me, it has been a kind of homecoming.

I had personally found Northern Ireland injurious to my writing, even my desire to write. My first novel *To Stay Alive* (1984), although praised in Britain and the US and shortlisted for major prizes, was described on the BBC Northern Ireland radio arts programme *Auditorium* as 'immoral and amoral' and a 'potboiler'. I survived that particular weekend by conjuring, almost channelling, John McGahern, remembering how he had to quit Ireland and his teaching job after publication of *The Dark* in 1965. Another local radio programme interviewed me about the novel, playing the theme tune from the screenplay of Gerald Seymour's *Harry's Game* as prelude. I was asked why I was bothered about Northern Ireland after not living there for twelve years. Then I was asked if I hoped to make a lot of money, from a film perhaps. So the introductory music was an insinuation, not any kind of tribute! There were less hostile responses, of course, but I was disappointed when that novel and the subsequent one, *Cuckoo* (1986), were often read either as thrillers or as part of the hopeless 'doom and gloom' mood of Troubles literature from the eighties. I thought they were more innovative than either category, more challenging of societal structures and assumptions.

One of the redemptive aspects of my involvement in this project has been to discover that my experience of being dismissed, whether through vilification or indifference, was common to Northern Irish women writers across the various genres – and that it stubbornly persists. But it is also evident that things are changing for the better. This is partly due to women's own activism, such as the Word of Mouth Poetry Collective's sustained development of women poets over a twenty-five-year period; the recent campaign, 'Waking the Feminists'; and the 'Women Aloud Northern Ireland' programme of events, conceived initially as a one-off burst of energy, which has now run for a second time. The Arts Council of Northern Ireland has a commendable record of funding support for individual writers and for projects like this book. Several Northern Irish women poets are bringing out individual collections with Arlen House in 2017-18. Special thanks are due to Dan Bolger and the team at New Island Books, who have done so much to promote women's writing throughout Ireland. In the space of three years they have brought out three anthologies, the prizewinning duo *The Long Gaze Back* and *The Glass Shore*, now joined by *Female Lines*. Dawn and I could not be more delighted.

Introduction

Linda Anderson and
Dawn Miranda Sherratt-Bado

Texts and Contexts

In her memoiristic essay 'Thatcher on the radio. Blue lights flash-
ing up the road', Susan McKay evokes Northern Ireland during
the 1980s, the milieu in which *The Female Line: Northern Irish
Women Writers* (1985) emerged. It was a site permeated by '"The
Violence", as it was called,' a place of sectarian and gendered
violence where 'armed patriarchs' and 'warzone women' clashed.
Amidst the conflict, the Northern Ireland Women's Rights
Movement marked its tenth anniversary by publishing *The Female
Line*, the 'first collection of writings by Northern Irish women
writers,' edited by Ruth Hooley (now Carr). This ground-break-
ing publication was a remarkable feat considering, as Carr notes,
'The Troubles [were] never … very far from the door.'

2015 marked the thirtieth anniversary of *The Female Line* and
it felt vital to publish an updated anthology which would explore
conditions for women in Northern Ireland post-ceasefires, post-
peace process, and post-Good Friday Agreement. What does it
mean for women to write in a time of 'post-conflict', and what
effect does this have on their work and on their lives? 2015 was
also the advent of the 'Waking the Feminists' movement in the
South. This begged the question of how much has changed or
stayed the same in terms of scope and opportunity for women
authors from Northern Ireland. Furthermore, in the wake of

1

the 2016 Brexit referendum, and the collapse of the Northern Ireland Assembly and the UK snap election in 2017, Northern Ireland's global position is once again precarious. Despite these circumstances, women writers from the North are flourishing due to more public platforms and greater publishing opportunities. *Female Lines* distils some of the powerful energy surrounding Northern women's writing, while also addressing the legacy of *The Female Line* which, as Carr remarks, 'is both handed down and self-written'.

In *Female Lines*, we trace the inheritance of the original anthology and follow its example by presenting a mosaic of new work by contemporary women authors from the North. This book captures a wide range of styles, forms, and perspectives and it includes short stories, flash fiction, extracts from plays and one novel, photographs, poetry, memoirs, and reflective essays. It showcases the work of thirty-two Northern women authors (thirty-one living and one deceased) and a photographer. The book features newly commissioned pieces wherever possible. Where this was not possible, we included the author's most recent work.

As a method of approach we consulted *The Female Line*, in addition to the anthologies of Irish women writers that followed in its wake: *Wildish Things: An Anthology of New Irish Women's Writing* (1989), edited by Ailbhe Smyth; *Wee Girls: Women Writing from An Irish Perspective* (1996), edited by Lizz Murphy; *The White Page/An Bhileog Bhán: Twentieth Century Irish Women Poets* (1999), edited by Joan McBreen; *Cutting the Night in Two: Short Stories by Irish Women Writers* (2002), edited by Evelyn Conlon and Hans Christian Oeser; Sinéad Gleeson's edited collections *The Long Gaze Back: An Anthology of Irish Women Writers* (2015) and *The Glass Shore: Short Stories by Women Writers from the North of Ireland* (2016); *Washing Windows? Irish Women Write Poetry* (2017), edited by Alan Hayes. For further research on the contemporary Northern Irish context we read widely, and the range of texts included two monographs which appeared serendipitously in 2016: Fiona Coleman Coffey's *Political Acts: Women in Northern Irish Theatre, 1921-2012* and Birte Heidemann's *Post-Agreement Northern Irish Literature: Lost in a Liminal Space.* What emerged from this period of research was the sense that Northern women writers have grown in confidence, numbers, and reach. The parameters for selecting contributors were that the writers were born or currently reside in the North, or that they have cultural or familial connections to it.

Fiction: The necessity of risk

'There is no point in making a thing … if there is no emotional risk to it.' So says Liam, a college tutor in Bernie McGill's story 'Glass Girl'. And risk is a hallmark of the fictions included here, whether in subject matter, form or tone. 'Glass Girl' is a quietly passionate story about bereavement that shows the healing power of art and of sisterly love. A very different story, also about loss, is Roisín O'Donnell's 'Wish You Were Here'. Her keynote magical realism is at work in this story but it is digital technology that performs the 'magic' – by fabricating an ongoing 'interaction' with a dead father as a means of trying to circumvent mourning. Jan Carson's fable-like 'Egg' uses metaphor in her characteristically playful yet profound way. A mother gives birth to a baby who is clutching a bird's egg. She devotes herself to watching over the egg to the neglect of everything else. Does this conjure the currently stalled rebirthing of Northern Ireland or the power of any beguiling but paralysed potential to lay waste to a life? Similarly rich in allusion and reach is Heather Richardson's 'All the Rules We Could Ask For'. This is a sophisticated 'anti-story' with a godlike narrator who talks condescendingly about characters as if they are mere story ingredients as they are herded on to the red or blue staircases of a ferry about to set sail. It's a story all about limits and containers, the things that control us. Two urban stories that are notably set away from tourist-trail Northern Ireland are Wendy Erskine's 'Locksmiths' and Tara West's flash fiction 'Winning on Points'. 'Locksmiths' is set in an area of Belfast where violence, crime and incarceration are matter-of-fact. The dialogue between a mother and her disenchanted daughter vibrates with unspoken resentments. The daughter has embraced DIY, doing up the house left to her by her grandmother. But DIY is shown to be something deeper: autonomy, doing it for herself, turns out to be a survival strategy. 'Winning on Points' is a savage tragi-comedy about an expert form of loserdom, showing how the benefits system fosters an investment in maintaining ill health. Only two stories deal directly with the aftermath of the Troubles. In Linda Anderson's 'Waste', a district nurse from Northern Ireland is weighed down by traumatic memories from the conflict but no one in her adopted England is interested in hearing her stories – until she comes across someone who does want to know – for all the wrong reasons. We have included only one novel extract, from Deirdre Madden's *Time Present and Time Past*, which explores how a middle-aged brother and sister come to terms with their pasts, including an estrangement from the Northern strand of their family. Harking back to earlier national turmoil, Sheena Wilkinson's 'Let Me Be Part of All This Joy' is set in a girl's boarding school in Belfast after World War I, the Rising, and the partitioning of Ireland. It is a gentle comedy with a light, satirical touch – but with chasms of unarticulated sorrow underneath.

Drama: Very public platforms

The three playwrights included in *Female Lines* are also writers of fiction and have had their stories featured in *The Long Gaze Back* and/or *The Glass Shore*. Showcased here are two stage plays which premiered at the Lyric Theatre Belfast: *Three Sisters*, an adaptation from Anton Chekhov by Lucy Caldwell and *Here Comes the Night*, written in response to the Easter Rising centenary by Rosemary Jenkinson and containing her characteristically dark and witty criticism of current-day Northern Ireland. Anne Devlin's radio drama *The Forgotten* was broadcast in 2009. It explores the influence and weight of what is forgotten through the crises of Bee, an artist whose health and finances are collapsing, forcing her to move back to her mother's home.

We have included an opening extract from each play to provide the set-up and atmosphere, accompanied by specially commissioned essays describing the inspirations behind the plays, the processes of making them, and their reception. These personal essays provide fascinating insights into how plays are made. Anne Devlin, for example, describes the importance of anchoring each scene in a specific soundscape in radio plays. In the complex process of adapting a classic play, Lucy Caldwell pinpoints the need for some true and vital connection between it and its transposition to a new setting: 'To be true to the play, I needed to be much truer to my new setting.' Rosemary Jenkinson highlights the importance of a shared vision of the play with a responsive director. All three refer to incessant rewrites.

These writers also recount their personal experiences of the marginalisation of women playwrights. Caldwell and Jenkinson describe the band of local reviewers as particularly narrow-minded and begrudging towards plays by women, while Devlin sums up the process whereby the work of women playwrights goes out of print, is not revived, and gradually vanishes from the canon. Both Devlin and Jenkinson highlight the reinvigorating impact of the 'Waking the Feminists' movement, started in Dublin in late 2015. The theatre scene in Northern Ireland looks poised at a crucial moment of potential change. Other audacious talents, such as Stacey Gregg, Abbie Spallen, and Shannon Yee are beginning to have their work more welcomed in the North, instead of having to be feted and staged outside of it.

Photography: Perspectival Shifts
The practice of fine art documentary photography developed as a reaction against the misrepresentational imagery of the North

which circulated in mass media during the first decade of the Troubles. However, the photo-documentary mode was traditionally a male-dominated artistic practice in Northern Ireland. This occlusion of women's visual narratives of the conflict continued into the peace process and it paralleled the general lack of attention to women's perspectives within a patriarchal milieu. However, in the post-Agreement moment women photographers are responding to this effacement by addressing gendered viewpoints, as well as socio-political issues that affect women directly. Accordingly, contemporary photography galleries throughout the North also help to advance opportunities for local women photographers by commissioning, showing, and publishing their work. *Female Lines* features images from Belfast-based artist and activist Emma Campbell's photo-documentary series 'When They Put Their Hands Out Like Scales: Journeys', which promotes the visibility of women who journey across the Irish Sea for an abortion. Abortion is only legal under strict criteria in Northern Ireland and Emma's work interrogates the ways in which the issue of reproductive rights and the figure of the abortion seeker are framed within post-conflict public life.

Poetry: A larger elsewhere

One of the sixteen poets featured in the book, Mebdh McGuckian, was included in the original *The Female Line*. In the early nineties, she went on to be sometimes the sole female inclusion or one of a tiny percentage of women poets included in the notoriously closed shop of Northern Irish anthologies. We are glad to feature four poets who were members of the Word of Mouth Poetry Collective founded in 1991 by Ruth Carr and Ann Zell, partly in response to this silencing, dedicated to the development of their own and other members' poetry. They are Joan Newmann, Kate Newmann, Gráinne Tobin, and the late Ann Zell. We include some of Zell's 'Donegal poems', which evince love of that coastal landscape and its wildlife and are also suffused with a sense of her rural past in

Idaho. We are able to include these poems thanks to the enterprise of Ruth Carr and Natasha Cuddington, who published the collection *Donegal is a red door* (Of Mouth) shortly after Ann Zell's death in 2016.

Many other poets here also depict local places with precise and painterly detail. We have Jean Bleakney's witty lament for the relocation of the Balmoral Agricultural Show ('After the Event'); Gráinne Tobin's view of a grand house in Ballynahinch ('Passing Number Twenty'); Kate Newmann's elegiac 'The Wounded Heron'. Cherry Smyth takes us down a road in Ballykelly to Shackleton Barracks and straight into hell in her reimagining of what was done there in 1971. There is often too a reach beyond the North and beyond Ireland, for example in Celia de Fréine's trilingual engagement with Rainer Maria Rilke's poems in his French-language collection *Migration des Forces*; Cherry Smyth's unflinching account of a failing relationship in Lisbon; Sinéad Morrissey's multi-voiced dramatic poem 'Whitelessness' with its team of scientists and artists on a climate change research expedition in Greenland. Breadth of focus is also evident in poems inspired by history, myth and legend: we have Joan Newmann's triptych of literary figures; Kate Newmann's incantatory 'The Leviathan of Parsonstown' in which astronomical advance is pitted (literally) against the tragedy of the Famine; Colette Bryce's tender portrayal of St Columba in 'The White Horse'; Janice Fitzpatrick Simmons' warrior ghosts in 'View from Black Pig Dyke' merging with modern atrocities. Personal poems include a number of portrayals of beloved fathers assailed by disease or dementia. Maureen Boyle's narrative poem 'Bypass' casts herself and her mother as anguished relatives and enforced tourists when they accompany her father to London for heart surgery. Paula Cunningham in 'Fathom' uses the imagery of 'Ariel's Song' from William Shakespeare's *The Tempest*: 'full fathom five thy father lies', in an unusually upbeat poem in the face of memory loss. Miriam Gamble's 'Bow and Arrow' takes a different approach, portraying her father as a boy shadowed unknowingly by an accident. Leontia Flynn's Forward Prize-nominated 'The Radio' depicts a mother perpetually fearful for her family's safety on their isolated farm during the Troubles. Constant news from the radio penetrates her strained body and mind. Motherhood is shown as 'a heart of darkness', a nonplussing burden shot through with jagged alarms. It is true to many people's experience of the height of the Troubles: influxes of terror via the news every hour on the hour. Motherhood as unrelieved anxiety is also one of Moyra Donaldson's themes in 'The Sixtieth Year of Horror Stories' and in 'Mare'. It is not possible to give details of every poem included here but what is important to indicate is the extensive range of subjects and the fact that the chief delight of these poems lies in the singularity of each poet's voice.

The essays: No more hidden histories

Margaret Ward's 'Reflections on Commemorating 1916' explores the centenary celebrations of women's contributions throughout the whole of Ireland, outlining the contradictions of an honouring of women's participation while excluding women historians from speaking on panels or at events. Quoting Adrienne Rich, she warns against the erasure of historical evidence of women's activism, something that deprives women of a sense of tradition and role models.

The four essays assembled here may well function as a repository of such evidence. It was not pre-planned or anticipated but the essays here all contain hidden histories or side-lined stories as well as insights about campaigning for change. Ruth Carr's account of the role of the Word of Mouth Poetry Collective in developing the work and careers of its member poets ('Sisters Are Doin' It for Themselves') is a case of twenty-five years of helping bring forth poetry that might otherwise have been consigned to silence. This essay truly gives a sense of different voices and experiences and captures the atmosphere of the best kind of writer's workshop practice, at once so charged and so disciplined.

One striking aspect of Julieann Campbell's 'Rewriting History' (about the 'Unheard Voices' project based in Derry) is the way in which she brings out the ongoing distress of survivors of violence, both the injured and the bereaved. We usually remember the iconic dead but know less about the everlasting pain of witnesses and survivors. One survivor of the Greysteel massacre says: 'It feels like I and my mother weren't even there.' Susan McKay's memoir of working in a Belfast Rape Crisis Centre during the eighties – 'Thatcher on the radio. Blue lights flashing up the road' – uses a patchwork method of mixing diary entries from the time with present-day reflection, adding vividness and authenticity to her account. Both of these writers describe the deep emotional toll of constant exposure to the suffering of others, what Susan McKay calls 'vicarious traumatising'. McKay and Carr also write honestly about the rifts and divisions that could flash within their respective groups, threatening their stability or even their continuing existence. Not for the fainthearted, which brings us back to where the book fittingly ends – with Margaret Ward's reminder of the transformative potential of women's activism and the need to always guard against the suppression of the evidence.

The trouble with anthologies
There is a gap of thirty-two years between the publication of *The Female Line* in 1985 and this anthology, conceived as a response and staging post. We would appeal for more anthologies, with all kinds of different missions and reaches. Otherwise, there is a risk in the way that anthologies are seen as constructors of a canon. They can be used to cement existing hierarchies and unknown absences. There are other writers who could also have graced these pages, if only there were room enough. We pass on the torch.

FICTION

Waste

Linda Anderson

Her house was astonishing. None of the usual old-lady cushions and fringed antimacassars and little pictures and china cabinets. Her rooms were stark and spacious, furnished with overbearing items. Two grandfather clocks daunted me at once. So august and upright and with those weighty pendulums swinging away, drawing attention to themselves. A baby grand piano with the lid up. Who lives here, I wondered, picturing a severe regal person, obviously someone used to keeping people waiting. 'Mrs Ball, it's your district nurse,' I called out as I had done upon entering by the prearranged unlocked door. Just at that moment the clocks chimed importantly and asynchronistically. It was as if one was goaded or reminded by the other but then could not catch up. What a racket! I looked around downstairs. The bossy grandeur of the place could not hide an air of neglect. There was a talcum of dust on the fine tables and chests. On the windowsill, segments of a dead wasp, curiously divided.

I ventured upstairs as noisily as possible, calling out her name, trying to keep embarrassment out of my voice. It is hard not to feel a sense of trespass when you enter the homes of strangers. The bathroom – another surprise. It was white. White tiles, white carpet, white bath, white toilet, white bidet, total clinical whiteout. There was even a white clock, a timepiece too far, in my opinion, in a house where the disappearing moments were already being announced every half hour (as I soon discovered) in the strident double act downstairs. Poor thing, I thought. Imagine being immobilised in this house listening to time draining away. I pushed the bedroom door and there was Mrs Zara Ball, propped up in bed with a hideous dog snoozing away on the pillow.

'Well, there you are,' I said with the kind of managerial cheer that usually works.

'Never anywhere else at this hour of the day. You're too early!'

'It's quarter past ten.'

She waved a hand dismissively.

'I understand you've got a problem with some varicose veins, a bit of ulceration? … I'll change your dressings up here. No problem. Then I'll help you downstairs, if you like.'

She lifted up her great swaddling duvet so that I could peel the old compression bandages off her spindly, blue-snaked legs. The dog farted squeakily. Mrs Ball chortled then whacked him when the sulphurous odour reached her. 'Casper! Filthy animal!' It amazed me that the owner of the dazzling bathroom would share her bed with this unhygienic mutt. I watched him as I went about my cleansing and bandaging. He was a bloated poodle with the same dank tallowy hair as his owner. No barking, no tail wagging, no curiosity or hostility for the intruder. He was obviously her captive. A denatured dog, toxic with tinned meat. A dog with all doggy liveliness and inquisitiveness bored out of it. It repelled me with its distended gut and rank odours. Though I felt sorry for him, too, and even thought of offering to take him for a waddle over some real grass.

Don't get involved, I thought.

It was less disconcerting to contemplate his appearance than his owner's. Mrs Ball was a gaunt creature with a noble, aquiline face in repose. But when she talked, she could suddenly look like a mad hen with glittering, dead eyes. Unfortunately, she was appraising me critically too.

'You look a bit hale and hearty,' she said slyly.

'It's the cycling. I bike everywhere.'

'Bit broad in the beam, aren't you, despite all your exercise?'

I said nothing. I had already experienced quite enough below-waist attention from an earlier patient, one of those dirty-sad old men who lose their inhibitions along with everything else.

'They ruin your figure, don't they? Little sods.'

'What?'

'How many have you had?'

'How many what?'

'Children! Offspring!'

I didn't answer, which did not deter her speculation.

'You look like the mother of a big brood. I can just see you all in your various uniforms. You in that get-up with your pocketful of pens and your thermometer and them in their comprehensive school ones. Going round the supermarket like a Girl Guide troupe.'

'So you imagine me as the mother of girls?'

'Can't see you handling a lad,' she leered.

'I have no children,' I said. It came out like an admission of guilt. 'I'm a career woman.'

'That's interesting. What was your career? Why did you give it up for this?'

She sounded so mean and merry. I felt about twelve years old. I quashed the impulse to blurt out that I had two degrees.

'How about you? Diplomatic service?'

'I was a kept woman!' she said triumphantly or defensively, I wasn't sure.

'What a waste!' I said.

Or what a mercy. All that waspishness confined to the home.

'It was hard work.'

'I'm sure it was.' *Especially for Mr Ball.*

The career woman careered downhill on her bike (ecologically sound choice of transport, of course. Could easily afford a car blah blah), to her next appointment. She raced through the town, through her private map of it in which she linked each area's preferred form of pet ownership with different kinds of ailment. Here we're leaving the pooches 'n' piles belt, heading through paranoia 'n' reptiles down towards pigeons 'n' angina.

Ha, bloody ha, I thought that day, after the Ball. That little encounter made me see myself all too clearly, me and my pathetic jokes, an attempt at superiority, me and my vaunted career. I was cheapskate community care, hired friend of the friendless, a shit-scraper. The housebounds were usually so glad to see me. I knew how to make myself chatty and cheerful, incapable of disgust as I assisted with various intimate necessities. I had trained myself not to flinch from ugliness. Yes, show me your warts and wens, your papery breasts, your acorn-studded limbs, your yellow eyes. I am Mrs Nursey Nice with a big valise crammed with soothing secret things – adult nappies, colostomy bags, dressings, and an array of salves and unguents that stink like a mixture of bonfires and sherry. Mrs Ball had managed to make me feel like the naked one and I didn't like it. She had not just sneered at my job; she had pried and poked into my life. Served me right probably for being some kind of thief, a stealer of privacy. My patients had no choice but to expose their failing flesh to me. Some of my death's doormen thought I should return the favour and I would have to swat many a sly lizardy hand sneaking up my blue cotton skirt. Like Mr Todd earlier that day with his up-and-under dive followed by smug impish looks. Those wizened flirts disturbed me despite my shockproof style. It was something to do with the way they held on to sexual hope, no matter how risible, importunate, or routinely rebuffed. That was impressive. But I found it galling to get offers from the drop-dead-any-minute when I was still susceptible to the drop-dead gorgeous. From whose point of view, my longings would be as clownish and misplaced as the geriatrics' gropings of me. Inappropriate, that's the word, the quelling word. Most of what happens to bodies, to persons, makes mischief with the notion of appropriateness and I know that. In my line of work, how could I fail to know that? But I could not remember ever having done a wild indecorous thing and I felt bereft. I felt ridiculous too for feeling so much, for letting the old bat get to me.

Just as I was getting off my bike, I saw something wonderful. A girl with two minky brown Labradors hurtling by. She was on roller-skates, holding the dogs' leashes in either hand. The dogs were exuberant and bounding but she controlled their speed while propelling herself along with a sure grace. They flew like Boadicea and her horses. I was captivated by this vision ... and just as suddenly crushed. There I was, so heavy and grounded and middle-aged. Like a statue forced to breathe. I had never been that girl. I had never given birth to such a girl either. God, where did that come from? I was feeling something alien, utterly unfamiliar. Now the old harridan was making me miss some phantom daughter! Images of our life together began to assemble swiftly: the Christmases, the school reports, the PTA meetings, the trips to McDonalds, the crises of puberty. My life, my real life, was so calm and eventless, it made me dizzy. My marriage had been short-lived, more of a matrimonial episode, or possibly an inoculation, to a man, suitably called Rob, whose face was coming back to me, his woeful handsome face with the frown scored into it like a wicket ... Rob the spare-time lay preacher who lost religion but retained the fault-finding zealotry. His insults poured back: *Why don't you lighten up? Why do you have to disagree? Must you wear that thing? Why do you have to analyse me all the time? Why do you always have to be on top?* Unfortunate phrasing seeing as he was forever complaining (complaining *also*) about my sexual conservatism.

Stop right there, I told myself. Mrs Ball was just a sour bully. I was giving her too much power over me. This was to do with a lesion in my pride from the past. Also, I was softened up by too many placid patients. Tomorrow I would armour myself with robust professionalism. Compassion even. A bit of mercy was probably in order, after all, for that bitter old bag whose

17

antagonism was probably reflexive, entirely impersonal, just a way of staying interested in life.

The dog was waiting silently at the door next morning when I arrived ready to out-tough his owner. He raised his foggy plead-ing eyes but I was determined to ignore the weakened mutt. Mrs Ball was seated at the table, clipping something from a newspaper. She must be better? Of course, her poor ulcerated legs would have made her ill-tempered yesterday. 'What's this?' I asked recklessly, expecting to see a collection of pious poems, gardening tips, cures for arthritis, pictures of royal persons. How easily my docile old-dear expectation revived itself! She leaned back to allow me to leaf through her album, which was stuffed with items about deaths. Deaths of strangers. British, European, American, whatever. Mostly described in the spare poignant detail of newspaper reports.

Mrs Ball collected deaths.

She brandished her new cutting. A honeymoon couple drowned while swimming in a river. Unaware of the dangerous currents … perhaps one drowned trying to rescue the other …

'That's tragic,' I blurted.

Mrs Ball was serene. 'Not what they expected, that's for sure.'

'Why? Why on earth do you want to compile this stuff?'

She shrugged. 'I like research. I like collecting. I like jokes.'

'Jokes?' I gasped.

She pushed the album towards me again. 'I defy you not to laugh at least once.'

All the deaths were spectacularly pointless, bizarre, or farci-cally ignominious. No common-denominator passings. None of your peacefully-at-homes. Famous-people-bite-the-dust seemed a favourite. Oh yes, Zara Ball enjoyed the grim demises of uppity celebs. There were more than thirty years' worth. John Lennon was in there, Elvis upon that toilet, Princesses Grace and Di,

Monroe, Mansfield, all the blondes, Amy and the other addicts, the Electric Light Orchestra cellist eliminated by a half-tonne hay bale bursting through a hedge to land on his car roof … She was also interested in lowly deaths, so long as they were ludicrous. I noticed that everything was methodically grouped. The woman was like death's secretary, entertainments division. The categories seemed to be:

Self-sacrifice for trivial causes. The elderly woman who torched herself because she could not look after her garden. The man who was stargazing on his balcony with his beloved Chihuahua when a sudden meteor shower startled the dog into springing out of his arms and plunging several floors to its death. The inconsolable owner drowned himself in a nearby river. Hee haw.

Deaths following outstanding success or happiness. The student who gained the highest ever marks in his university's science examinations, and hanged himself. Brides or grooms who snuffed it on honeymoon, or preferably at the reception. (Today's bit of post-nuptial nemesis would slot in nicely.)

Bizarre methods. The man who drilled holes in his skull with a Black & Decker. The woman who committed suicide by drinking fifteen litres of water.

Lucky escape followed swiftly by termination. The American translator whose car was blown into a river during a storm. She managed to extricate herself and swim to shore, where a tree crashed on top of her, killing her outright. The Japanese man who escaped with minor injuries when his house collapsed in an earthquake. After treatment, he returned to search for important documents. The one remaining wall fell on him, bye-bye.

Machismo beyond the point of duty. The Polish farmer who was drinking with some friends when it was suggested that they strip naked and play some 'men's games'. This began mildly with them hitting each other over the head with frozen turnips. One man escalated the contest by grabbing a chainsaw and slicing off the end of his foot. 'Watch this, then,' shouted the heroic farmer, seizing the saw and cutting off his own head.

I slammed the book shut. 'Perhaps those of us who are not dying had better get a move on,' I said, getting the bandages out.

'Oh dear, not even a titter,' she mock-pouted. 'Hah, we're all dying, every minute. Only one end to the story. You should know that better than anyone.'

I thought she meant because I was a nurse. But she meant because I came from Northern Ireland, with its industry of stupid sudden exits. And over the next few days, she started probing. And I started acceding. Adding to her hoard. Pandering to her. The first one I told her about was the chief inspector in the RUC who survived gunfire, escaped with his life several times. The policemen at his local station fed themselves with takeaways from the nearby chippie. One day the inspector slipped and fell in the station porchway, hit his head and died. It was the slow lethal accumulation of grease drippings from the takeaways that had made that patch of floor so perilous. His own colleagues had killed their boss. Mrs Ball loved that one. It had the most thrilling ingredient – the high-status person brought low in the most unforeseen and undignified way.

Then there was the one about the woman who persuaded her husband to emigrate to Australia to obtain a better future for their children, far from all the bigotry and violence. Years later, she happened to be shopping in Sydney and stopped to watch a demonstration in support of the Irish hunger strikers. A sudden gust of wind caused a banner-holder to drop his flagpole. It struck the woman on the head ... 'Killing her outright,' we chorused together – she knew the exact moment to chime in. I looked at her contented eyes and her hands clasped like a child's. She's mad, I thought. What's your excuse?

The more Mrs Ball liked me, the more I disliked myself. Was I so easily cowed by this curmudgeon that I would do anything to sweeten her up? Would I start telling porn stories to my lechers next? Why not? The district nurse who dispenses a daily dose of the obscenity of your choice. Why did I go on propitiating her? I started to wonder if her steeliness fascinated me. No news of suicide bombers or sunken boats would put this lady off her breakfast. Perhaps sheer heartlessness kept her going. After all, her legs were leaking. Her ribs cracked if she sneezed hard. She was crumbling millimetre by millimetre. Maybe she needed to forestall her own death, even as it crept over her. Or maybe she was just bored. Sometimes she would yawn like a cat, showing her stumpy little molars. Her existence might be one long dull sentence enlivened by a bit of *Schadenfreude*. Whatever the truth of it, I *was* scared of her, especially when I was not in her presence. She became Mother Time in her clock-crammed house. A leering *tricoteuse*. Skeletal Lady Death wielding her fateful scissors. Then I would see her and she would revert to human scale. Her Woolworth's scissors with little slivers of sellotape adhering to the blades. Her matted cardigans, her faintly vegetable odour. Her lumpy dog who sometimes snored during my rending stories. What a companionable trio we were. I had begun to talk to the dog when he was conscious or semi. I even fondled the blubber on the outposts of his being. Casper was too silly a name. I whispered Wolf to him like a secret code, trying to lure him back to doghood, to a state of grace. Wild boy, I said. Come on, Wolfie, bark like a dog, will you?

I kept on with my stories: the murdered by mistake; the poked to death by snooker cues; the hapless wanderers into the wrong bar … I was a funerary Scheherazade. Tacky, craven, and wrong. But I could not stop my ignoble threnody. Sometimes I wondered if I was getting relief from it, an illicit unburdening. Most people did not want to know about violent Irish deaths. Mrs Ball provided an audience, however cold-hearted. But one morning, mid-tale, I had a sudden memory of my friend Ruth's daughter, Ellie, when she had just turned ten. I had gone round one evening to see Ruth and after some wine and chat, we decided to watch a television documentary on Colonel Gaddafi. Ellie was sitting at the table, drawing. I suppose we thought she was in her own world, tuned out, but the truth is we hadn't thought at all. Just as the presenter described how Gaddafi had murdered his foreign secretary, then stored the body in the palace deep-freeze, so that he could enjoy a regular gloat over it, Ellie vomited, a great jet of sick erupting from her without warning and without strain. I envied her. For her intact humanity, her inability to conceal and her inability to accept.

I'm stopping this shit ... this compliance.

I told Mrs Ball one more story, from my own family history. My great-grandmother nursed her son, Archie, through a life-threatening bout of pneumonia. She and his aunts and his sisters kept vigil over him night after night, cooling his brow, helping him breathe, praying. The doctor said there was no hope. But Archie recovered. Suddenly returned to himself, got up out of bed, shaky and renewed. His family rejoiced. Archie went down to the army recruiting office, lied about his age, joined up, and was killed at the Somme a couple of weeks later. His mother died of grief.

'Don't they always?' Mrs Ball interrupted. His sister, I kept on, my grandmother, then lied about her age in order to emigrate to Canada. She was depressed for the rest of her life. Mrs Ball looked at me with haughty discontent and said nothing. The story fitted the criteria but my tone was wrong. I was insisting on the waste, the agony, the consequences.

'That's not one for the collection,' she said finally. 'That's one of those women-moaning-about-men stories. Spare me that, if you don't mind!'

I was the one who found her. It was just three weeks later. She was sitting neatly in a chair, her spectacles in her lap. Natural causes. She got off with an ordinary statistical death. Perhaps she would have found that inglorious, I don't know. It was certainly deficient in comedy. While I waited for the doctor and for social services, I secreted the album (wasn't it ours now?) in my valise.

'She looks emaciated,' the doctor opined. He sounded accusing.

'I don't think she had much appetite,' I said. 'But she had meals-on-wheels every day.'

'Did she eat them?' he asked caustically.

'I was only here for a half hour each morning.'

He relented. 'Her daughter died that way, you know. Self-starvation. Thirty-five years ago. She weighed four stone at the end. Zara did everything she could. Begged, bribed, forced the girl into hospital, left her alone, refused to leave her alone ... And the girl dwindling and disappearing all the time ...'

Wolfie whined and I said suddenly: 'I think I'll take him out of here for a while. Maybe I'll look after him tonight. Until something can be decided.'

'That would be kind. I wouldn't hold out much hope for him, though. No one will want to take on that pathetic lump.'

I knew where the redundant leash was hanging and hurried to get it, afraid that I might faint if I did not get outside. I heaved Wolfie into my arms and deposited him in my bicycle basket, where he stayed during the rest of my rounds, quivering like a lightning rod. Each time I reappeared from some doorway, he howled in a mixture of protest and relief. Back home I sat looking in disbelief at my newly acquired encumbrances. That woman's dozy dog and vile scrapbook! She had probably destroyed her own daughter. Put her on a diet at eight years old, most likely. I remembered Mrs Ball's contempt for any sign of spare flesh. *The girl dwindling and disappearing all the time* ... Served her right, oh yes. But then I began to imagine it. The girl unstoppably capsizing herself and her mother. For good. Forever. Really, I had understood nothing. Couldn't, wouldn't, didn't see the terror and rage behind Mrs Ball's masquerade. Never once did I see Zara (*Zara!*) bleed through her mask.

'You can't trust me, Wolfie,' I said and he moaned. I guessed he must be hungry. A safe bet with Wolfie. I found some ham and chicken slices for him in the fridge and bulked it out with potato salad. The death album was sitting on the table. I flicked through the pages. Away from Zara's necrophiliac zest, they seemed just a pile of random sad stories. They needed nothing from me, no compensatory reverence. But I needed to do something. Wolfie was settling into his post-prandial snooze when I put the leash on him. 'New regime,' I told him. 'Meal, then exercise. You'll get to like it.'

We climbed the hill up to the park. Wolfie could not believe his escape from custody. He snuffled the leaves, groaned ecstatically at the breeze. We started to walk faster and then broke into an enfeebled run. 'That's it, Wolfie!' When we were out of breath, I stopped by a gigantic sycamore tree. Wolfie sniffed voluptuously at the dog pee, all the urinary telegrams from his lost tribe. His joy, so simply returned to him, made me laugh out loud. I took out the album and began to rip and dismantle it. I flung the pages, the yellow curled ones, the fresh white ones. The wind whipped them into the air or chivvied them over the ground. Wolfie looked at me, inciting me to start walking again. We were elated with the unrecognisability of ourselves. From the top of the hill, I looked back at the deaths. They were flying away, far away from all gloating or grieving.

Egg

Jan Carson

You were born with a bird's egg tucked inside your hand.

It looked like a starling's egg, but it could just as easily have been a robin's. They are a very similar shade. Your eyes are the same high August blue. You are also lightly freckled.

At first, I did not notice the egg. I was drunk on the just-born smell of you. Your foldable arms, your ears, and feet – which were just like adult feet, only greatly reduced. I was worn out from all the pushing and shoving. Then, the sudden rush of you, coming in a flood at the end.

'This is really happening,' your father said. And just like that, it was already over.

You came thundering out of me fist-first. Fingers curled round your thumb, tight as a walnut shell. After your arm came your head, a second arm and a single torso, a pair of pancake-flat buttocks and two legs with feet like full stops clamouring on either end. You were all there. Every bit of you in the proper place and working. Every bit but your left arm, which stayed stubbornly up for almost a week.

'He's ready to punch anybody that gets in his way,' your father said, and laughed like this was a good thing. I didn't think it was. You seemed far too furious for a brand-new person. 'Is this normal?' I asked. It was not normal. The midwife had never delivered a fist-first baby before.

'Don't panic,' she said. 'He seems fine. I'll just check him over to be sure.'

Then, she whisked you away for weight and length and swaddling in a clean, white blanket. When you returned, you looked exactly like babies are meant to look. All blink-eyed and freshly pink. If I held you right I couldn't even see your strange arm sticking up from under the blankets.

'Isn't he perfect?' I said.

Your father didn't reply. His face was trying not to fold.

'What's he holding?' he asked, unpeeling the blanket to examine your curled fist.

'Nothing,' I said. 'It takes babies a while to uncurl. He's been bunched up inside me for nine months. No wonder he came out funny.'

'I think he's holding something,' your father said. He could see the pale of it glowing between your fingers.

I took your little nugget of a hand in my own and began to unpeel your fingers. I went at you slowly, gently, like tiny steps on ice. Baby fingers are brittle as bird's legs. I didn't want to snap you. It took a minute, maybe ninety seconds to prise your hand open. Your father and the midwife hung over me, holding their breath as if just the thinnest puff of it might break you. I could see parts of the egg straightaway but I didn't say anything until it was fully exposed.

'It's an egg,' I said. 'The baby's come out holding a bird's egg.'

No one spoke. There wasn't even a peep out of you.

I lifted the egg up and held it, very gently between my finger and thumb. It was almost like holding air. So light. So easy to ruin.

'This was inside me,' I said. 'How did it get there?' My own voice was swimming away from me. I thought I might faint.

'Did you swallow it?' asked the midwife. 'No, that makes no sense. How would the baby get hold of it?'

Your father had gone a funny shade of grey. Like a thing that was once white, then washed too often. He perched himself on the edge of the bed and asked to see the egg. I tried to place it directly into his hand, but he insisted on a tissue. He would not look me directly in the eye.

'You don't think there's another baby inside it?' he asked.

'It's a bird's egg,' said the midwife. 'Probably a starling. Babies don't come out of eggs.'

'A starling,' your father repeated softly. He lifted the egg to his ear the way you would with seashells, listening for the ocean. The egg didn't make any noise. He looked disappointed. Then, he shook it, reasonably hard.

'Stop,' I yelled, 'you'll kill it.'

'It's only a starling. There's hundreds on the telephone wires at the end of the road.'

'This one was inside me. It's mine. I want to see what comes out of it.'

Later, looking back I would realise this was the precise moment I began to love the egg.

We had not been expecting an egg. It hadn't appeared on any of your ultrasound scans. We'd printed them all out and stuck them on the fridge door so our friends would see and know you were finally a real thing. Not just wishful thinking or fingers crossed for the next try. Your scans are still up there, next to the grocery list and the takeaway menus. Next to a photo of the egg on its fifth birthday. Apple-sized you, curled up into yourself like a neatly tied lace. Banana-sized, with your feet scratching the ceiling of my belly. And finally, you, swollen to the size of a large turnip, staring straight at us, as if to say, 'I'm ready for out now.' Later, your father would stand in front of the fridge for hours, forgetting what he'd come for, as he stared at these grainy images. I'd find him there, just standing with a glass or empty bowl, his eyes microscoping across the fridge as he tried to see an eggshell ghosting through your clenched fist.

It was harder for him. He hadn't carried you. Or the egg.

No one had expected an egg. It was not normal. When the consultant arrived, he was unable to contain his shock. He called it a deformity, clamping a hand over his mouth to keep the disgust from creeping out. I could have clawed him for bringing such a dirty word into the room. I opened my mouth and howled. I couldn't stop.

'Now, you've gone and upset my wife,' your father said. 'Did you have to use that word in front of her? If you ask me it's not a deformity at all. It's more of an oddity.'

'Oddity' was not much better. This was how we spoke of your Great Aunt Lily who did not believe in washing or speaking to anyone who wasn't close kin. Shortly after this, your father would revise his thinking. Then, he'd call the egg a 'miracle' and wonder if we shouldn't get the papers round for a photo. There was money to be made, he said, referencing the family down the road who'd found the face of Mary looming out of the muck on their Land Rover's windscreen. Hadn't they made a fortune selling their story to the press? Enough for a conservatory, or so the story went locally.

The word 'deformity' hung sourly in the air. The consultant carted you down the corridor to a room where you were examined for other extra parts. Wings. Horns. Halos. The possibility of a second heart, murmuring softly behind your ribcage. Of course, they found nothing. You were just a normal baby, born with a bird's egg. No one knew how it got there or why it had not shattered beneath the pressure of your fingers or the force of being born.

After a week they let us take you home. The egg came too. I know you wish we'd left it behind. Your father felt similarly. He was all for throwing it in the bin.

'Nothing's coming out of that egg,' he said, 'let's go home and get the baby settled.'

But I couldn't shrug the feeling that there were two of you to look after now.

'I can't leave the egg behind,' I said, 'it grew inside me. It might still hatch.'

Your father could see the strain of this stretched into my jaw. A tiny nerve flexing just beneath the skin. There was no turning me, not when I dug my heels in. We took the egg home and made an incubator for it. An old shoebox lined with tinfoil, some cotton flannels and a desk lamp angled down like a drooped tulip. I hoped the heat would bring it on.

'I'll set it up in the utility room,' your father said, but I insisted upon the nursery. I wanted the two of you in the same room. Together. Equal. Neither child favoured. I dragged an old armchair into the space between you, measuring the distance so I was not a centimetre nearer to either one. I dozed constantly, waking to feed you, to bathe and change you. I told you you were the most precious boy in the whole world and meant it. Please remember that. I woke to turn the egg, back to front, to back again, shuffling the heat gently round its shell. I leaned over the incubator and whispered soft, coaxing words, 'Come on out now. We can't wait to meet you.' I meant it. Every whispered word.

When I dreamt, it was mostly of the egg. The way the shell would one day split in two, fracturing and peeling in strips, to reveal a small creature inside. Something which required care. Sometimes this creature was a bird, sometimes a very small child, no bigger than a bottle top. Mostly it was a warm but indefinite impression, not quite a ghost, but similar and equally hard to describe when awake. In the early days, I told your father these dreams, explaining each one in detail. Then I stopped. Your father wasn't interested in the egg. He never had been. It was all just an oddity to him. All for the need to humour me.

You thrived. You slept all night. You sat up, moved on to solids, took your first fumbly steps. You made noises, then fully formed words. The egg didn't. The egg grew no bigger or smaller. It simply sat there on its flannel, occasionally vibrating when a large truck drove past the house. But I couldn't bring myself to give up on it. I kept turning it front to back four times an hour for months. Then years. I put my back out leaning over its incubator to whisper stories and sing happy songs. I took photos of the two of you together on birthdays and at Christmas, ringing the egg's box in tinsel or birthday banners so it might know if we were celebrating and take some small pleasure from this. I refused to go on holidays. 'We can't take the egg,' I said, 'and we can't leave it here by itself. It might hatch.'

'It's never going to hatch,' your father said and, when you were old enough for the rides, took you to Euro Disney. Just the two of you, for a long weekend.

I stayed home with the egg. Reading. Sleeping. Hoping it might hatch while you were away and justify my absence. The egg did not hatch, and now I am in none of the photographs from your earliest holidays. Later I would also miss out on sports' day, Edinburgh, Legoland and parents' night at your new school. There was no one else to sit with the egg.

You grew old enough to find your own tongue.

'It's not fair,' you said, over and over. 'You love that egg more than me.'

'I don't,' I said, 'it's just that it needs me more. It can't do anything for itself.'

'I need you too,' you said. But the truth was, you didn't. You'd learnt to do almost everything for yourself. Your father was there for the rest: shoelaces, doctor's appointments and the like. You went to him first for everything. I was proud when I saw you using the toaster and washing your own uniform and sometimes, even, fixing dinner for us all. I was also utterly ashamed.

You were six then and already refusing to stand next to the egg in photographs.

'It's just an egg,' you said. 'It's not an actual person.' Even though I told you the story of how you'd come out of me, holding it tightly, in your left hand. You did not seem to see the miracle in it, only the oddness.

'Please,' you'd say, 'can you just get rid of the egg?' Your father would be there too, looking at me like I was the sort of soap opera character who is always saying, 'I don't have a problem. I can give up, any time I want,' and is actually addicted to alcohol or heroin or takeaway food.

In the end, the egg broke. It was not your fault exactly. Your father has said this more times than I can count. You were only playing in your room, only getting on like normal boys do. You knocked into the box. The egg fell out and cracked itself on the floor. You didn't tell me immediately. You waited until we were all sat down for dinner.

'Sorry mum,' you said, 'I broke the egg. There was nothing inside it.'

I kept myself from crying in front of you.

Your father would not let me punish you. Not even bed without supper.

'It was an accident,' he said. I could see he wanted to smile.

Later, when I went to clean the egg up, I noticed that it was not entirely empty. There was a tiny fleck of blood in the middle of the white, peering up at me like the eye in an overflashed photo. I thought of you then, tucked inside me with an egg in your hand and an eye inside this egg. One precious thing inside another, like Russian dolls. Or how we all are, secretly inside.

'Egg' was originally performed on BBC Radio 4 on 12 March 2017. It was read by Roisin Gallagher and produced by Michael Shannon.

Locksmiths

Wendy Erskine

I read about the time when Spanish banks were offering one hundred percent mortgages. But the crash came and people couldn't make the payments so bailiffs turned up to repossess homes and locksmiths to change locks. Families stood outside gazing up at their old bedrooms. There was a woman, it said, who bolted the door, ran to an upstairs balcony – and leapt. The guys, the locksmiths, masters of cylinders and springs, had never anticipated that their work would run to this kind of thing. In one of the big cities, the locksmiths said no, that was it, they wouldn't lock people out anymore. Just wouldn't do it.

Early last week I was in the DIY superstore at Airport Road West, getting a few things. All those generators: did many people really need generators? Perhaps they did. A man struggled to carry a huge bag of plaster powder but it dropped and split, sending up a minor mushroom cloud. A call went out over the tannoy for a cleaner. One of the assistants said to me, 'Can I help you, sweetheart?' I said, 'No, all fine.' Because all *was* fine: I knew what I wanted. I bought a cheap bedside light and a single quilt cover, cotton, the sort that could take a boil wash. I hesitated over the paints with the lovely names but got the largest tin of pure brilliant white because that would do. In the superstore there was a whole aisle devoted to locks from the basic to the intricate. I got a pack of three towels and a key ring for the extra key I had got cut.

Back when I first got the house I was in here all the time. It was a fairly exciting place. Home improvement, by its nature optimistic. I sometimes spent sixteen, eighteen hours a day working on the house, forgetting to eat. I became acquainted with every bad joist and frame tie. My toolkit grew. I began with a few cheap screwdrivers and moved on to a DeWalt drill, second-hand. I scraped off decades of sticky wallpaper, woodchip giving way to a paisley swirl, paisley swirl yielding to a bottle green paint. It was my gran's house and she left it to me.

If, when I was younger, anyone asked about my mother, the non-specific, 'She's away' seemed to suffice on most occasions. It was rare however that anyone would ask. But had anyone enquired, would there have been a big stigma attached to having a mother in jail? Probably not. At my school there were other people with family members who were in jail or out on licence. In my year, there was Gary whose big brother shot somebody outside a snooker hall. And then in the year above there was Mandy G. whose dad beat a woman to death. In all likelihood there were others from the years below, but I didn't know about them. You only tended to know about the older kids.

Living with my gran, I watched a lot of soaps and dramas. She always sat in the same seat and smoked; there was a yellow bloom on the ceiling which I eventually, with some reluctance, painted over. Before each programme my gran would pour herself a whisky and when there was a bar scene she would take a drink because it made her feel that she was there. I'd get a coke and do the same thing but I was still always in the living room. Everything in the house smelt thick of smoke; it was deep in my school blazer and couldn't be shifted.

The man who was killed by my mother was Tommy Gilmore, an old fella who had hoped, I presume, to spend the remainder of his days recovering from the work accident which had left him incapacitated. He'd got a major payout. It was somebody else's carelessness. Those long nights, those longer days, no doubt he looked forward to seeing my mother who called around with increasing frequency. She borrowed money and initially maybe he liked it, the attention she gave him, the prancing and twirling about in the things she had bought but then, when she never paid anything back and wanted more and more, and when he in turn threatened to contact the police, she beat him with an object, thought to be a poker, although it was never found. Tommy Gilmore had a stroke during the attack but it was the head injuries that killed him.

My gran would visit her daughter every month. It took the best part of a day to get there and back, an elaborate journey involving a bus, a train and a bus. There was a tray we used to call the Chinese tray because it had pictures of dragons on it. On the days when my gran went off, I was left two sandwiches and two glasses of milk on the Chinese tray and told not to answer the front door under any circumstances whatsoever. My gran always came back hobbling because she wore her good shoes.

Twice a year I went with her. It usually coincided with the time when the clocks went back or forward. When we got off the bus we stopped at a café near the train station. Anything you asked for in that café, they had always just run out of it, but they always let us know this with great regret. 'That's the last time we're going there,' we would say. 'We're going to take our custom elsewhere.' But we kept on going there because it meant that we could continue to see what they had just run out of, just this minute.

After the various security procedures, we took our seats to wait for the women to enter in single file. Some faces lit up at the sight of the visitors. Others' expressions didn't change. My mother's didn't change. The conversational gambits tended to be familiar, more or less. My mother would begin with a litany of grievances which might have included the conduct of certain prison officers or, just as likely, the unavailability of a particular type of sauce. Then my gran would rattle on about characters from the programmes she watched.

Although she had a pretty enough face my mother was paunchy for a woman, at least most of the time. At one point the prison got refurbed with a new gym with all the latest machines, and when my mother entered the room we saw a pared-down version, alert and hungry. But by the next time the cheekbones had gone. The lustre, clearly, was off the gym.

There were little things. She always had a tissue. She would twist and weave it through her fingers. She did that at least once during every visit and I always watched for it happening. A few tattoos appeared on her arms, capital letters, something or other. Her hair looked chewed and the style was permanently eighties despite the passing of the years. On one memorable occasion the two of us sat across the table with exactly the same colour of hair. We had used the same lightening spray which promised golden beach blonde but which reliably turned out orange. That went in the bin when I got home.

Always the same but with slight variations. One time it was obvious that there was something romantic going on with one of the other prisoners; her eyes kept sliding over to a woman on the far side of the room, talking to a guy in a denim jacket. I had watched people giving each other those doleful, burning looks in school. And then there was the time she got religion. For a period my mother wore a cross and a wristband with a Bible verse; she told us about the power of prayer and talked about redemption and her personal relationship with Jesus. She also learned some chords on the guitar.

'Yous not believe in Jesus then?' she asked us.

As part of a rehabilitation programme, she attended a workshop on education. She had produced some writing which documented her own experience of, and views on, the subject. She said we could read it but the facilitator had collected it in, so we couldn't. My mother on that particular visit was very interested in how I was getting on in school. I was quizzed on how I was doing in every class and my mother was full of motivational advice. On the next trip, I brought my big school file which weighed down my bag on the journey but the conversation never again turned in the direction of education.

My gran died as she had lived, in front of the TV. I found her when I came into the house. I put a cardigan round her, her favourite one, because she had only on a light thing, and I waited until the credits of the programme started rolling before I started making the phone calls. The funeral wasn't large: some neighbours and a few relations who had seen the death notice in the paper. The prison granted my mother leave to attend on compassionate grounds. The short service took place in an old mission hall my gran had attended at some point; the people from the hall picked the hymns and the readings; the only proviso they made was that my mother couldn't be in the hall. That was fine: no objection to that. I did one of the Bible readings, the thing about there being a time for this, a time for that, a time for whatever. My mother appeared only when we arrived at the cemetery. She was standing under a tree with some man and I couldn't recall having seen her outdoors before, although I must have done, when I was younger. She was close to the fella, conspiratorial, but then I saw that she was handcuffed to him. She nodded over to me, a dip of acknowledgement and that was it. Some people had congregated in the car park and although it was starting to rain, they weren't wanting to dash off too quickly. There were a couple of younger fellas in the car park who must have been at another funeral and they had made a whole deal of taking off their ties, stuffing them in their pockets, opening their top buttons. They passed round a bottle of QC sherry. They were talking to my mother: *so I says to him, and he says to me, and I says what the fuck, and he says wait a minute what the.* My mother found them very funny. They offered her the sherry and she took it in her free hand while the man handcuffed to her tactfully and serenely looked to the far end of the car park. One of the fellas tipped the bottle when she was drinking and it ran all down my mother's front, down the blue suit somebody must have lent her. She took a drink from the bottle again until I heard the prison guy say, 'OK, now come on, that's enough.' He was right: that was enough. My mother, pulled along by the wrist, tottered back to the car through puddles in heels that didn't fit. The younger fellas gave her a shout as she headed away. When I got home I had a cup of tea on the Chinese tray and watched a bit of a hospital drama.

And so, last weekend it was the first time in years that I was making the journey. After my gran died I didn't visit. Now, instead of travelling by bus, by train and bus, I was in a car. I took a detour so that I could see if the café that had always just run out was still there but it was now a phone shop. When I got to the place there were some people waiting outside – a man in a tuxedo holding a red rose, and some kids charging around with pink helium balloons – but others like me just sat in their cars. I wasn't sure what to do. When she appeared, I just sat watching her for a while. Not long. Just a minute or two. She looked smaller than I remembered and her hair was back in a ponytail. She had a blue holdall bag. I tooted the horn but she didn't look over. I tooted it again and then put down the window, shouted over. She looked at me as if to say, 'Oh it's you.' I didn't unfasten my seatbelt and I kept on holding the wheel.

On the drive back the car radio was on. She said, 'What is this? What they going on about? What a load of shit. Talking talking talking.' So I turned over to a pop station but when we hit the roundabout I moved it back again.

She was interested in knowing how long it would take to get home and how fast the car could go. 'Don't know,' I said. 'I usually don't go any quicker than this.' We passed a sign for the big shopping centre that's on the way and she said, 'Shit, I've seen the ads for that place! We going there? We're going there, yeah?'

I said, 'Sure. If you want to.'

I didn't particularly want to trail round shops so I waited on the seats, gave her twenty-five quid to spend. My mother came back with a skinny belt, a T-shirt with a photo of a sunset on the front and a set of three bracelets.

Back in the car I drove and she fiddled with the bracelets, putting them on one wrist, taking them off, putting them on the other. The belt hadn't been a bargain; the stitching was starting to fray already.

When we got back to the house all was quiet. She said, 'So there's no party?'

She would not have been surprised by a surprise party.

'No there's no party,' I said.

No one was waiting to jump out and pull a party-popper. No one was hiding in the kitchen.

'Where's the TV?' and she pointed to the spot where the TV would have been years ago. I saw the ghost of the old TV.

'I don't have a TV,' I said.

She made a slow sucking sound. 'No TV.' She looked at the rows of books.

No TV but.

'Here,' I said. 'This is for you.' I gave her the key ring out of my bag, a simple grey fake leather fob and a shiny key. Its newly cut teeth felt rough but it had turned with no resistance when I had tried it in the door. She looked at it and shoved it in the back pocket of her jeans.

'That's your front door key,' I said.

'Yeah,' she said. 'Ta.'

Where she had been she wouldn't have had a key. There would have been keys on choke chains, bundles of keys on large metal rings, but none of them would have been in her possession. Perhaps the key on the grey leather fob would have a symbolic value for her.

'Don't lose it,' I said.

'Piss off.'

My mother went up to a room that had once been hers. I could hear the floorboards creak and strain. Maybe she was sitting on the bed thinking about what used to be there; perhaps she was looking out the window at a view not so very different from the one she might remember. Downstairs the clock ticked. I could hear the slight gurgle of the water going into the radiator, the vague bark of that dog two doors down. Then the toilet flushed. The bedroom door closed with a bang. It had been a long time since another person had been in this house and the air was pounding with her presence.

Slow steps brought my mother back to the living room. 'Well,' she said, flopping onto the sofa, 'that room is white alright. White, white and white. With a side helping of white.'

'Window doesn't open properly,' she added.

I said that I would have a look at it.

'Used to climb out that window,' she said. 'Used to escape out that window.'

'Where to?'

'Anywhere,' she said. 'Wasn't really fussy.'

'I'd all the posters from the mags on the walls when that was my bedroom,' my mother said. 'You wouldn't have seen the walls for all the pictures.'

'Who of?' I asked. 'What of?'

'Can't remember,' she said. 'It was years ago. I was a fuckin' teenager.'

The walls were cool and smooth now. They weren't gobbed with blue tack and covered in pictures of leering faces torn out of magazines.

'She never knew that I went out,' my mother said. 'She didn't have a clue. Probably because she was half cut herself half the time. Wouldn't have known what was going on, who was in and who was out.'

I'd never noticed the clock's tick before. It had a slight reverb.

'You had to go out of the window frontways,' my mother pointed out. 'So that you could make the jump to the gutter and then the kitchen roof. One night I wrecked myself.'

She pulled up the leg of her jeans to show something. 'You see that scar?'

'Not really,' I said.

'There.' It was just her skin, white and puckered.

'Well, I wrecked myself when I fell one time.'

'If she was so half cut all the time, why did you not just go out the front door and save yourself all of that bother?' I asked.

'Half cut half the time, not all the time. I said half the time.'

'Easy to get back in,' she said, 'getting back in was alright as long as you stood on the bin to get up onto the kitchen roof. Room was always fuckin' freezing,' she said, 'with the window being open all that time.'

'Well,' I said, 'there's a duvet in the room now. And, as you say, the window doesn't open properly. You won't be getting out the window.'

My mother ran her hand down the arm of the sofa. 'This come from DFS?'

I couldn't remember. 'It might've been there,' I said. It was a while ago.

'I'd like a leather sofa,' she said.

'Oh would you?' I said.

'Yeah. I wouldn't get this. I'd get a leather sofa.'

She asked if anyone else lived here.

'No, nobody else lives here,' I said. 'Just me.'

'It's just me since she died,' I added.

'Just you then.'

'Just me.'

I recalled the locksmiths. I wasn't part of a group or a union or a collective: I was on my own. They didn't know the people they were being asked to lock out. The woman who flew from the balcony would have been just another name and address on a photocopied list of that day's jobs.

'Well, it's a dump round here,' she said. 'It always was and I can exclusively reveal to you that it still is. A total fucking dump.'

I asked her if she was planning on going somewhere else.

'Oh yeah,' she said, 'might well. Got a few ideas. Stuff I got on the go.'

'Like what?'

She tapped her nose to indicate 'top secret'.

'Well, I'm glad to hear that,' I replied. 'Good.'

'Yeah it's good,' she said.

'It's very good,' I said. 'It's very good to hear that you've got stuff on the go. And that you're not stuck in a dump.'

'You got a fella?' she asked.

'No.'

'Nah, didn't think so,' she said. 'What's for the tea?'

I had done a big shop before she arrived but there was nothing in the fridge or the cupboards that she wanted. No, no, and absolutely no way. I said that I was a vegetarian.

'Oh well you would be,' she said. 'Now why does that not fucking surprise me? Don't be telling me you don't drink either. No booze? You got to be joking.' And she gave a short little laugh. 'So this is freedom. This is what I've been waiting for. Welcome to the shithole.'

'My shithole though,' I said quietly.

I didn't think she'd heard.

I said it again. 'My shithole though.'

My shithole.

'Yeah,' she said. 'I'm sure you'd rob my grave as quick.'

'Fair's fair,' my mother said, 'you pulled a right fucking smooth move there.'

'You think so?' I said.

'There was me waiting on a letter from the law place telling me what I got,' she said, 'there was me waiting to hear what'd I'd been left. Waiting on a letter that never came. Anyway, fuck the cow.'

'You got a key,' I said.

'This room used to have an orange rug,' she said. 'A big orange rug.'

I remembered that rug and how I rolled it up to get it out the front door and into the skip.

'I'd put my face down on that rug in front of the fire,' she said, 'and it would be like I was lying in the centre of the sun. Right in the very centre of it.'

'When I was a kid,' she added.

I said, 'Look, do you want me to go down to the off-licence for you? It's only down the road.'

She considered but said no, because was the Troubadour still there? 'Don't tell me the Troubadour's not even there now.' I said that it was still there but it was called something different.

'Yeah well, beggars can't be choosers,' she said. 'Although it's probably going to be a shithole too.'

She went upstairs and came down again wearing the new T-shirt with the sunset.

'You coming?' she said.

'Where to?' I asked.

'The Troubadour. You've not seen me in, how long? Not even going to go for a drink, how's that meant to make anybody feel? Own flesh and blood,' she said.

The Troubadour was fairly empty. My mother had a double vodka and coke and I had an orange juice. 'Orange juice, for fuck's sake,' she said.

'Coke's flat,' she added.

One TV above the bar showed football with no sound and the other showed female wrestling.

Then my mother shouted out, 'Geordie!'

A small, wiry man had come in. When he saw my mother he let out a yell and held his arms wide. 'Jesus, but would you look who it is!' he said. 'Look who's back! Look at you! When you get out? Hey son, you going to get this friend of mine a drink?'

My mother didn't notice me slip out. I sipped the last of the orange and then off I went back home to my house. I read a book for a while, and then I lay upstairs with the light on, listening for the key in my door. I expected my mother, Geordie and various others to come bursting in. The digital display on my bedside clock counted through the hours. The Troubadour hadn't turned out to be such a shithole after all, perhaps. No doubt there had been an after-hours session, a move to another bar, a party back at a house somewhere other than here. There had been other old friends to meet.

The next morning I was up very early. I sat listening but there was nothing. The bedroom, when I ventured to check it, was as was. The white quilt was untouched. There were just a couple of things lying on the floor: her jumper and a pair of knickers. There was no sign of the key so she must have taken it with her. In the bathroom there was her toothbrush in the mug along with mine. I took it out and put it in her blue holdall along with her other bits and pieces, zipped the holdall shut and took it downstairs. I sat on my sofa which was not leather and thought for a bit as the wan morning light showed my brushstrokes on the gloss. What I wished was this: that I had a cigarette and a whisky with the ice clinking and that my gran was still here. In the cupboard under the stairs I had my toolkit and I knew I was nothing like the Spanish guys who wouldn't change the locks. The DIY superstore had that whole aisle of mortises and sashes and it opened in less than an hour's time.

Time Present and Time Past

Deirdre Madden

This excerpt is the ninth chapter of Time Present and Time Past *(2013), Deirdre Madden's most recent novel. It explores the impact of the past, both known and unknown, on a middle-class Dublin family with relatives in the North. Fintan, an outwardly conventional man, begins to experience unsettling visions and insights, which illuminate the mystery beneath the surface of everyday life.*

To a casual observer, Fintan's life throughout that spring would appear to be progressing in its habitual, unremarkable fashion. He takes the train into the city every day, and goes to the office, where he spars with Imelda and does his job with his usual indolent brilliance. He eats bigger lunches than he will willingly admit to when quizzed about it, by his concerned wife and teasing sons, over his substantial dinners at home in the evening. He ponders a suitable treat for Lucy and her little friend Emma, to compensate for the sleepover which he is still reluctant to sanction, and finally decides that the zoo might be a possibility; an outing so *déclassé* in these affluent and sophisticated times that it would have the added value of irony, were seven-year-olds able to appreciate such a quality. From time to time Colette nags him gently about paying a visit to his mother, something he knows is long overdue but which he can never quite bring himself to do.

And yet while all of this is happening, another reality has overtaken his life. Fintan has become obsessed with early colour photographs. Niall is complicit in this and feeds his habit, with books from the library, and links to websites which Fintan consults compulsively when he should be busy with his job, furtively minimising the screen should Imelda happen to put her head around the door for any reason.

He quickly grows technically proficient, and can easily distinguish the different processes; can distinguish an Autochrome from a Colourchrome with a casual glance. He is familiar with the names and works of pioneers in the field: the Lumière Brothers, with their photographs of subjects more usually found in Impressionist paintings, such as bourgeois *Belle Époque* lunches in the open air; Lionel de Rothschild, with his family portraits and flowerbeds; and Albert Khan, with his meticulous record of countries worldwide when their national stereotypes, long since homogenised and deconstructed by globalisation, had been the real thing. Perhaps most astonishing of all is the work of the Russian Gotkin, whose system of using three coloured filters gave results of almost alarming vividness and accuracy: it seems impossible that they can be so old.

Looking at the photographs makes Fintan feel vertiginous. They offer him a weird portal back into the past, into another world; as in the books he reads to Lucy at night, so that he feels as if he is tumbling slowly down a rabbit-hole lined with shelves, or that he has been shut into an open-ended wardrobe, pushing his way through furs and cool silks to a snowy landscape. On the day he first chanced to see the old photographs in the cafe, while eating his carrot cake, he had found it impossible to imagine himself back to that world. But now when he looks at the coloured photographs, which are sometimes barely a decade older than those black and white ones, he thinks – he, Fintan Buckley, hitherto a strong contender for the title of Most Unimaginative

Man in Ireland – why, he feels that he might look up from his book and find himself back in the distant past.

'You wouldn't like it,' Niall says bluntly, when his father shyly confides this to him.

'Why not?'

'It wouldn't be the way you think.'

They're in the kitchen at home, on an overcast Sunday afternoon. Fintan is looking through one of his photography books while drinking tea and Niall has just wandered in, wearing jeans and a black T-shirt that says on it in tiny white letters, 'This is what I'm wearing today'.

'It would smell different, for a start,' Niall says, putting his hand to the flank of the teapot to gauge the heat of the tea, lifting the lid and peering in to judge the quantity. 'It would smell of horse piss and horse shit. I bet everything stank back then. Can I have some of this? Drains, people's teeth, you name it,' he continues, taking a mug from the cupboard and serving himself. 'But I'll tell you what I really can't stand,' he says, sitting down opposite Fintan. 'It's that sort of Heritage sense of the past. This girl I know in college, last summer she worked in one of those big houses that's open to the public. She had to dress up as a parlour maid and talk to all the visitors, tell them all this made-up crap. She said the room they liked best was always the laundry. But can you imagine what life really must have been like back then, doing the dirty work in a house like that? Can you imagine nursing someone with diarrhoea in a house with no bathroom?' From the alarmed look on his father's face, Niall knows that he's got the point he's making. 'They want people always to identify with the ruling classes,' he goes on. 'They want you to think as if it was always a summer afternoon back then, all croquet on the lawn and kids in white smocks and girls in big hats, all that kind of stuff.'

'There was such a reality,' Fintan says, gesturing to the open book on the table.

'Yeah, but come on, for how many people? It's not the whole story.' They sit in silence for a few moments, drinking their tea, and then Niall remarks, 'It's kind of interesting, though, to think about the past in this way, I mean the really distant past, 'cos photography is one of the things that makes the biggest difference.' He says to Fintan that the visual impact of visiting a new place must have been infinitely powerful if one had not seen in advance sharp colour photographs of it, 'and of course you couldn't see photographs like that at the time, 'cos there was no such thing.' He cites Goethe's nigh-on ecstatic account of visiting Rome at the start of the nineteenth century: the shock of the beauty of it; the strangeness.

Fintan doesn't agree. He says that no amount of documentary evidence had prepared him for the reality of seeing Venice for the first time. He says that Granny Buckley had described to him the arrival of the American soldiers in Northern Ireland during the Second World War, and how their second-hand familiarity – 'They were like people in the films' – had only made them seem the more exotic.

'What I'm saying,' Niall argues, 'is that we tend to think that the past was more interesting than it really was, and my point is that it was more banal than we give it credit for, but also more complicated. And anyway, we're talking about "The Past" – he makes inverted commas in the air around the words as he speaks them – 'as if it was a discrete period of time, which is just stupid. I mean, if it comes to that, you can actually remember "The Past" – he does the thing with his fingers again – 'can't you, Dad?'

'Not a time before colour photography, no,' Fintan deadpans, and they both then laugh.

'But seriously, Dad, you must be able to remember things from ages ago, from when you were a kid?'

'It's very strange when I look at newsreels from the Troubles,' he says, 'because it does look familiar to me, and yet it also looks quaint: all the boxy little cars, the women in headscarves. But it

47

wasn't quaint at all, it was bloody awful. I knew that, even when I was little. I remember being in Armagh with Granny Buckley one day, shopping, and we walked round a corner. There was a soldier coming the other way, holding a rifle, and he bumped into her. That is, the butt of his rifle hit her right in the solar plexus. The soldier swore – I think he said something like "Fucking hell!" – I don't exactly remember, but it was strong, whatever it was, because I was almost as shocked at someone swearing like that in front of Granny as I was at them nearly shooting her.'

'And how did she react?'

Fintan laughs. 'You have to hand it to Granny, she played a blinder. She said to him, "You mind your language, mister, and mind what you're doing with that thing." And then she swept on round the corner. But as soon as she was out of sight of the soldier she stopped and she leant against a wall and closed her eyes and she said over and over again, "Jesus, Mary and Joseph! Jesus, Mary and Joseph!" She was really shook, and it took a lot to rattle Granny. I mean when you think back on it, in one way it's kind of funny, and in another way it's horrific. And I'll tell you this,' he went on, 'I really do remember that as if it happened yesterday.'

'It's a strange thing, how memory works,' Niall remarks. 'I can remember you and Mum from the whole way through my childhood, from when I was really small; and it seems to me in those memories that you don't look any different to how you do now. But if I look at photographs from that time, you look quite different. You both look much younger.'

Niall has finished his tea. He rinses his mug and leaves it on the drainer, then crosses to the window. 'Is it raining? I was thinking of going for a walk.' Fintan looks out into the garden, at Lucy's swing and the wooden bench.

'I don't think it's raining. It's hard to tell; it's a soft kind of day. I'd take a chance on it, if I were you.'

Niall drifts out of the room again, and Fintan continues to leaf through his book. He comes across a group of photographs from the First World War, of trenches and field hospitals, which are disconcerting because they look like stills from a film, even to him, who has always found historical movies unconvincing; the combination of period costume and the kind of teeth that only modern dentistry can provide striking him as particularly risible. He turns the page, and now he regrets that Niall has gone, because he has found a photograph which he would have liked to show him.

It is a picture of a red apple sitting on a mirror. There are other studies of fruit alongside, including a bowl of rather gnarled pears that look very much of their time, a time before pesticides.

But the apple is perfect. It is one of those deep red, round apples, its skin so highly polished that the light reflects off it in a white spot. Apples have always been a potent fruit for Fintan, and not just because he loves eating them. They remind him of his childhood in the North, where his granny had a little orchard. The caption on the photograph states that it was taken in 1907, which Fintan can scarcely credit, so exactly does it look like something he might buy and eat with his lunch.

He glances up from his book and looks out of the window. It is raining now, but it is a fine, soft misty rain, the sort you have to narrow your eyes and look closely at to be able to see it at all. The swing and the bench have disappeared, and the garden is full of apple trees. They are witchy and stiff; gnarled and sculptural; their branches ascending at first before inverting and pointing resolutely downwards. The colours are all drab, greys, and shades of olive green. Fintan is aware now that he is actually sitting on the windowsill, which has become wider than it was before, as the window itself has become smaller and more deep-set; and Martina is sitting beside him, only she is a little girl. She is looking out into the orchard. 'Look,' she says. 'Look, Fintan. The trees are moving.'

She's right. Some of the trees at the back of the orchard have begun to move forward. Fintan and Martina watch without speaking. The moving trees continue to approach through the dankness of the day, and then Fintan says, 'They're not trees. They're soldiers.'

It's a foot patrol, in camouflage fatigues, and as soon as Fintan and Martina realise this, the illusion of trees vanishes. As the soldiers draw nearer they can see them clearly: the metal helmets covered in net and all stuck with leaves; the blocky flak-jackets like perverse buoyancy aids, designed instead to make you sink; the long dark guns in their hands. They are moving closer, still somehow fitting in with the trees, in harmony with them, and yet also distinct now, as soldiers, as people. They are advancing inexorably towards the house. The sound of their voices is audible, the crackle of walkie-talkies. Fintan is afraid.

'Down! Down! Quick, before they see us,' Martina says, and she slides off the window-sill. As she goes, she grabs Fintan by the ankle and pulls him after her, so that he falls clumsily, and hits his head off the edge of the table with a tremendous bang, knocking himself out.

He opens his eyes. He is a middle-aged man, sitting at the kitchen table, not under it. There is a book, a mug and a teapot before him. In the wet garden there is a swing and a bench. Dizzy and unmanned, he is stunned, as if someone had closed the heavy book of photographs and brought it down hard on his skull.

Glass Girl

Bernie McGill

There is something wrong with my sister, Evangeline. She is
thin and light for a ten-year-old, and her toes turn in when
she walks; she carries the wrist of one hand in the other, as if
it is not a part of her, as if she is taking care of it for someone else. Her elbows stick out either side of her body and her
ears stick out either side of her head. Her fingers and toes are
long and bony, her legs look like they are not fit to support
her, could not be capable of lifting and moving the thick-soled
black shoes she needs to wear, that fix her to the ground like
weights. Her pale green eyes are over-sensitive to light. She has
a sensation, she says, from time to time, of something feathery
brushing over her skin. I cannot prevent the thought that these
could be wings that have never grown. I find it hard to shake
the idea that my sister is a creature tethered to the earth, who
was originally designed for flight.

The doctors have said that Evangeline needs to strengthen the
muscles of her legs, that walking on sand in bare feet is good for
this. With sand, they say, there is the correct balance of support
and give. This does not sound like a medical treatment to me,
but every dry day since I have come to the coast to stay with my
father, I have taken my sister to walk on the strand. We set out
from the house and make our way along the cliff path past the
high smell of salt and drying seaweed and down the graffitied
concrete steps that lead to the beach.

My father is Evangeline's father, and Catherine is her mother. My mother is dead. Evangeline is my half-sister, but I won't say 'half' about Evangeline. She is completely whole to me. Ours is a complicated story but that is just the way of things.

Evangeline knows the names of all the wild flowers and on our walk she tries to teach them to me: birdsfoot trefoil, marsh marigold, forget-me-nots, wild thyme. She won't allow me to pick them to use them in my work. She says they are where they ought to be and I must learn to leave them alone. If the tide is out when we reach the strand head, we take off our shoes and go searching in the rock pools for shrimp and limpets and hermit crabs and I photograph them for her. This is the only form of capture she will allow. If the tide is in, we climb into the dunes and lie on our backs with the roar of the sea behind us and listen for the rattle of magpies and make shapes out of the clouds overhead.

On the days when it's too wet to walk to the beach, when the rain bounces off the tarmac on the road and drums a steady rhythm on the roof of the house, Evangeline sits, cross-legged on the living room floor with her headphones pinning flat her ears and cuts photographs out of magazines and sticks them into scrapbooks. Mostly, these are pictures of plants and flowers and sea life and she asks me to pronounce the names for her and repeats them over and over until she has memorised every one. At night when she asks for a story, I tell her one of my mother's, the ones that she used to carry about in her head, that she got from her mother and grandmother; legends of treasure sunken in moss holes, of children stolen by fairies, stories from the island.

'You're so good with Evangeline,' Catherine says, but the truth is that Evangeline is good with me. Since my mother's funeral, the world has been blurred at the edges, altered in a way I can't explain. I am unsure, when I speak, of the right order of words. My voice sounds overloud in my head. I cannot find the language to talk to my father.

'You've had a shock,' Catherine says. 'It will take time to get over it.' But Evangeline seems to understand, Evangeline who said when I came here: 'Don't worry, my Ella, we'll look after you now.'

Today, Evangeline has an appointment at the hospital and I have the day to myself. 'Take the bike,' Catherine says. 'See a bit of the coast.'

Outside, my father unclamps the child's seat from behind the saddle of the old yellow bicycle, pumps up the tyres, says, 'Good as new. But I could drop you somewhere, pick you up, if you want?' He looks to the west, to the grey bank of mist that has hung for hours over the Barmouth, the flattened stretch of water beginning to silver and stir in the bay, a trace of damp in the air. I toy with the raindrop of green glass in my pocket, polish it under my thumb, check that the key is still attached. I remember the soft orange bulb the glass made in the gas flame when I worked it, the molten possibilities of it before it hardened and cooled. And still I cannot speak to him.

'There's a mist coming in,' my father says, not looking at me.

Evangeline trips out of the house, followed by Catherine, takes hold of my father's hand and lowers herself into the bicycle seat balanced on the ground. She sits in with her bony knees up either side of her ears, intent on braiding the safety straps. Without looking up she says, 'Bring me back a picture, my Ella.' I reach down, run the dark ponytail of her hair through my hand.

'We won't be long,' my father is saying. 'I'll phone you when we're done.' My phone is in my raincoat pocket. I don't tell him that I've switched it off.

'Will you cross to the island?' says Catherine.

He shoots her a look of alarm. 'It's too far, surely?' he says. He avoids all talk of my mother, as if mentioning her will crack me in two. And I can tell that he's still angry with me, about Liam, about everything that happened.

'I'll see how I go,' I say to Catherine, and heft my rucksack on my back and straddle the bike, and blow a kiss to Evangeline.

When I push off all three of them wave to me from the drive of the house.

It feels strange to cycle away without Evangeline's thin arms around my middle, without the slight weight and wobble of her in the seat behind. All summer we've toured the cycle paths, into the swimming pool in town for her water exercises, over to the amusements in Portrush where she is transfixed by the 2p machines. 'Just one more, my Ella,' she says each time we drop a coin through the slot, and she holds her breath as the tray sweeps forward, and squeals at the anticipated cascade of metal into the scoop below.

It's the tail end of August and already the colours are starting to turn. I follow the tourist route, past the golf links and serried caravans that nose the road around the coast. At Dunluce the limestone is streaked with the green and black of old watercourses; a marker in the sea beyond the ruined castle surfaces like the spire of a drowned church. Beyond Dunseverick I have to dismount when the climb proves too much for the old bike's gears, my thighs and rear beginning to ache. At Portnareevy the sun breaks through and I pull in to the viewing point. The fields around are dotted with black-bound rolls of silage. Across the water I can just see the chalk cliffs of the island picked out in the sun, green uplands above, the dark hollow of the bay, the northern side cloaked in mist. It's too far for me to see the tower of the church, the crooked white headstones where my mother is buried along with her mother and father. I take my camera from the rucksack, aim it at the white tip of the lighthouse in the east, the blue peak of Kintyre beyond.

My father moved here when he married Catherine, a year or two before Evangeline was born but until this summer, I've only ever spent weekends here. When I was younger he travelled to see me in Belfast, fitted visits in around site meetings and client appointments, collected and dropped me at the door. After he left, my mother and father spoke rarely. They texted when they needed to make arrangements about me. When he asked after her, I said she was fine. I am guilty, I know, of years of deceit, of the show I kept up to hide her drinking from him, from everyone. We were a good team. She went out to work every weekday; I never missed a day at school. Monday to Friday she was a model citizen. She'd wave me off on Saturday morning and be nearly sober when I got home on Sunday night. By the time my father figured things out I was old enough to choose where to live for myself.

'You have to leave, Ella,' he said. 'You're not responsible for her. You have to think of yourself.'

'Like you did?' I said and that ended the discussion. That was unfair, I know. She didn't drink when he lived with us. It had gotten worse over the years. The truth is, it was easier for me to stay and to worry than it was to worry and go. At least if I was there, I thought, I could keep an eye on her, monitor the level of intake. In the end I failed even to do that.

My father bought me this camera for my twenty-first birthday, turned up at the glass workshop in the college on the day, too tall and tidy in his suit. It had been weeks since I'd seen him, since the last argument about my mother, about what should be done. I'd stopped answering his calls. He walked in at the point when Liam had been helping me remove some pieces from the annealing oven. Liam moved away too quickly when my father appeared, busied himself with another group of students. I saw my father note it. I did not introduce them.

'Where have you been?' he said.

'Here,' I said. 'Working.' He glanced at Liam. He didn't seem to like what he saw.

'I've booked us a table,' he said, 'for tonight.' I didn't speak. 'That is, if you're free?'

'I'm not.'

'Tomorrow then?'

'You're not supposed to be in here,' I said, running my hands over the glass pieces, checking for fissures, for flaws.

'Okay,' he said. 'If that's the way you want it. Happy Birthday, Ella,' and he slid a gift bag under the workbench and left.

I couldn't believe it when I saw the camera; I hadn't known how much I'd wanted one. I was sorry I'd been hard on him. It wasn't all his fault; most of it was my mother's, I knew that. It was just easier to blame him since he wasn't there.

He has been talking lately about my plans for the future. He says there's a job in his office, junior draughtsperson; he could teach me the ropes.

'Give her some time,' Catherine says when he starts to talk about this, but time is not going to make his offer any more attractive to me. We have had to let the Belfast house go. The landlord found a new tenant; all my materials are packed into boxes in my father's house. But as I look out from Portnareevy, I am thinking of a shingle shore and a bay of purple kelp; of a gravel path by a dry stone wall overgrown with fuchsia. I am thinking of a red tin roof and a whitewashed chimney. I am thinking of a gable that is rendered with shells and rounded pieces of bottle glass, brown and blue, that glint when they catch the sun. I am thinking of a blackened hearth and the smell of old soot and a byre that could be a workshop: my mother's home on the island.

When I first tried my hand at glass-making, I was mesmerised by the process, the movement of the glass rod in the flame, the change in the colour through blue, white, yellow, green. The rod that, moments earlier, would have shattered had it been dropped on the ground became a molten rope which could be manipulated, balled, drawn out thin as a thread. I learned how to blow glass tubing until it ballooned into a globe; learned how to turn and shape it in the flame, hollow it out with a knife. I watched, entranced, as gravity did the work of modeller. I pinched the ends with tweezers, nipped off the unwanted stalk, my favourite part, closing off the glass. I attempted snow globes but as I experimented, the glass vessels grew narrower so that they began to resemble not made but grown things. After that, nothing I created had a base. None of my work stood up by itself.

Liam became my tutor in final year. When he saw what I'd made, he directed me towards the work of Stankard. I studied the flameworker's exquisite paperweights: lifelike glass honeycombs with hovering bees; pink-petalled tea roses complete with stamen; haws and blueberries, their stems intact. But I was surprised to find that in his work there was too much artifice for me. I did not want the solid. Weight was the opposite of what I was striving for.

'There is no point in making a thing,' Liam said to us, 'if there is no emotional risk to it. You need to be prepared to make yourself fragile. You need to be afraid to expose some breakable part of yourself.' I knew he was married but when he said that I didn't care. I'd have risked anything to have him.

I began to use the glass as a thin-walled cell to house the things I found. In one elongated piece I inserted a dried mimosa bud, fused the organic stem into the closure with a molten string of glass. In another I placed a pinecone, then a chestnut burr, a dead beetle, a dried moth from my windowsill. My heart fluttered when I reheated and squeezed the openings shut, attaching glass tendrils, colouring the glass, until it was impossible to tell where the natural ended and the made began. The pieces I created for my final exhibition I had to suspend by wires from a frame. They looked like unopened shells, seedpods, egg sacs, discarded skins.

'What are they for?' my father said the night of the final exhibition. I wanted to say that 'use' didn't come into it, but I knew what his response would be to that. I don't know how to tell him that this is something I need to do; that it may help me to find what I can no longer find in language, that finding it might make the world bearable again.

'They're beautiful,' Catherine said when she saw them. 'They look like they've grown there. Like they were meant to be.'

'They're sad,' Evangeline said. 'Why are they sad?'

'How do you know stuff?' I said to her, taking her small hand. 'I see through you, my Ella,' she said.

My mother didn't make it to the exhibition opening. 'It's there for a few weeks, isn't it darling? I'll go when it's quieter, when I can take it all in.' She'd started drinking before I left the house.

After the reception, when the guests had all gone, Liam joined the final year students in the pub. He stayed apart from me most of the night but I was aware of his every move, the lowering of his mouth to the glass when he drank, his hand reaching for the phone in his back pocket, his eyes on me when I rose. I knew where this was headed. I could afford to wait. The others drifted off, some to a nightclub, some to another bar. Liam's flat was a ten-minute walk away. 'I've got it to myself tonight,' he said.

His work was scattered on high shelves throughout the rooms, bizarrely shaped glass objects, comic strip characters welded to glass lava, experimental forms. We kissed on the living room sofa, abandoned our coffee cups and climbed the carpeted stairs. It was hard not to feel a pang of guilt at the toys strewn around the living room, the small pile of shoes inside the front door. In the bedroom he took a towel from a linen basket, laid it out on the quilt over the bed. There wasn't much spontaneity about it: the sex, through a fug of beer and shots, was joyless in the end. In the kitchen afterwards, pouring myself a glass of water, I uncurled the dog-eared corner of a crayoned drawing taped to the fridge door.

'Don't touch anything,' Liam said from behind me and slipped his arms around my waist. 'Come back to bed.' I stayed the night; thought I'd give my mother something to worry about, supposing she was conscious enough for that. In the morning Liam woke me, said he was sorry: I'd have to leave; he wasn't sure what time his wife would be back.

I walked through the city in the thin light before the buses had begun to run, past the still-shuttered shops and the littered pavements, the spoils of the night before. I'd never been out that early, had never seen the city in that light. I followed the street sweepers brushing the kerbs from City Hall up to Bradbury Place. On Botanic, a train rumbled under the road. I turned into our own car-lined street, twisted the key in the lock of the front door: my mother's heeled shoes in the hall, her bag on the ground beside them. I climbed the stairs, headed for my bedroom, but the door to her room was open, the smell of stale alcohol seeping out, the smell of vomit too. I pushed the door wide. She was lying, face-down on a dried pool of sick on top of the bed, still wearing the spaghetti-strap dress from the night before, open-mouthed, shut-eyed, blue-tinged, cold to the touch.

At Portnareevy I take the phone out of my pocket and switch it on. There are three missed calls from my father and a text that reads, 'Whereabouts are you? We'll pick you up?' I slip the phone back into my pocket. As I climb back on the bicycle, I see a white line stretch across the grey water: the wake of the car ferry crossing the Sound, almost at the mainland now. I have twenty minutes to make the harbour.

From here, the journey is easier; I can feel the gradual descent into the ferry town. The road winds through conifers. Past the slender trunks of the trees I can see the boat nearing the shore: glimpses of the vehicles on board, the mist closing in behind. The air dampens. Further on I hear the rattle of chains as the boat moors, the scrape of metal on concrete when the ridged ramp is lowered onto the quay, the sound of engines moving off. I freewheel down the steep hill towards the town.

I am rounding a bend on the sloping road when a white pick-up truck speeds towards me, a man at the wheel in a baseball cap, music blaring from the wound-down window. I brake and put my feet to the ground, pull in to the verge but as it passes, the truck hits a pothole, there is a rattle in the back, a jolt towards the tailgate, and the gate bursts open, landing two wooden crates with a crash on the tarmac a few feet behind me. I turn in the saddle to shout after the driver but he is hurtling along oblivious to what he's left behind on the road. In seconds the truck is out of sight, the engine whining into the distance. The road grows quiet; there is no other traffic; the mist rolls in.

I angle the bike into the hedge, ease the pack off my shoulders and walk back up the road. The crates have fallen right before the bend, will be invisible to drivers from the town side until they are on top of them. Closer, I can see that they've both burst open; that their dark contents are spilling over the road. I can't make out what it is at first: coal, maybe, or turf, but as I near the spill, I see that the dark mass is moving of its own accord; the crates are heaving with something alive. The road is crawling with crabs. The brown creatures scuttle out sideways and spread across the highway, legs scissoring, blue pincers raised, their red eyes shuttling from side to side: velvet swimmers from the island, the most vicious kind there are. I shiver in the cool air. The crabs make for the hedges on both sides of the road. I watch as the first of them scurries into the grass and then I remember my camera. Evangeline will love this: escapee sea creatures, her kind of story. I am standing on the verge in the fog, wondering if they will make it back down the cliffs to the sea, photographing the strange retreat, when I feel my phone buzz in my pocket. I know who it is without looking at the screen.

'Ella?' my father says. 'Where are you?' I look through the trees towards the sea and down the hill to the town, but everything has been swallowed up by fog. I could be marooned on a cloud, or on an island the size of what I can see. I feel the panic begin to rise in me. 'Ella?' he says again. 'Ella? Are you okay? Just tell me where you are.' The air around shimmers, the earth makes a fractional shift. I have the sudden conviction that I have stood here before, looking down at the sloping road, at the smashed crates, the circling fog, the escaping crabs, impossible though that is. Then I hear another voice behind my father's, Evangeline's, quiet, distracted by something, only half-engaged: cutting out or pasting in or colouring at the table.

The moment passes, the world realigns.

'Ask my Ella if she got me a picture,' she says. 'Tell her I'm waiting for her.'

'Ella?' my father's voice again, walking away from my sister now, trying to disguise his concern. 'Ella, please, tell me what's happening.'

A sound escapes me, a laugh or a cry; I can't be certain which. 'You wouldn't believe it,' I hear myself say, surprised at the sound of my own voice. 'Tell Evangeline I've got her a picture. Tell her I'll see her soon.'

I slip the phone into my pocket; pack the camera back in my bag. I cross the road to where the crates lie and drag them into the verge. There isn't a single creature left. The mist is beginning to thin. Through the trees I can see the ferry back out of the harbour and turn around in the bay. I feel for the key in my pocket, the fob of smooth polished glass. It's too late now to go to the island. I will go another day. I pick up the bike and climb back on and I cycle through the thinning mist in the direction from which I came.

Wish You Were Here

Roisín O'Donnell

#Magic

Sheffield's street lamps flicker orange through the scratched bus window. Graffiti is etched onto the pane. *LAURA N MIKE 4EVA XXX*. My doubled reflection floats on the laminated glass, beheaded by the noose of my bottle green school tie with its red and yellow stripes. Two sets of eyes stare from under my long black fringe. Halfway down the hill from Nether Edge, my mobile rings and I answer it, 'Hey Dad.'

'Fionnuala. What's the craic?' Your voice carries an infectious smile, as always.

'Guess what, Dad? I got an A-star for that essay on Henry VIII.'

'Now hang on a minute … Another A-star?' You give one of your long whistles down the phone. 'Jeez. That's just magic, Fin. Tell you what, you're looking at the best results All Saints has ever seen.'

The bus pulls in and a load of girls from my class clatter on and slide into the seats in front of me, giggling and falling over each other. I lower my voice.

'Have to go, Dad. Talk to you later?'

'Magic, darlin'. Talk to you soon.'

Magic. Ma-gic. It's that one word you stumble over. It's that one word which keeps me tethered to reality.

#BlueMoon

'Sweetheart,' Mum says, 'Your Aunty Tilly and I just wanted to have a chat ... We're just ... well, we're just a little *concerned.*'

In the Blue Moon Café, Pink Floyd plays under the hiss of the espresso machine and the clatter of cups. I reach for the mock china teapot, 'More tea, Mum?'

'Just a drop, love,' she frowns and tucks her frizzy blonde hair behind her ears. 'Look, do you understand what I'm saying to you, Fionnuala?'

'Uh-huh.'

'I know it's difficult, love ... but it's been six months now. This just isn't healthy.'

'So?' I put the teapot down with a hard rattle. 'I'm fifteen, Mum. It's *my* life.'

Two lilac-haired grannies at the next table swivel their heads to stare at us like owls. Aunt Tilda's pea-soup eyes dart between me and Mum, and she sips her milky tea, leaving slug trails of coral-pink lipstick on her mug. Bet she thinks she's woken up in the middle of *Coronation Street* and she's loving every minute of it. 'Your mum's right, Fionnuala pet,' she coos, 'this is just not normal.'

They both channel tragic looks at me, as if I'm a stuffed animal in a glass museum case. A fawn with a bullet-hole in its forehead. I'm about to tell them both to fuck off when my phone rings. 'I have to take this.'

Mum and Aunt Tilda exchange pantomime glances as I step out of the Blue Moon into the twinkling fairy lights of Chapel Walk. Funny, I keep forgetting it's almost Christmas.

'Hello?'

'Hey darlin', still taking the world by storm?'

'Ugh, Mum and Tilda are pissing me off, Dad.'

'Now then, Fin ... Go easy on your mum.'

Cheers to the team @HadesMag. Magic to have a story in the latest issue. Check out the link http:/gerard_keane_necroscopy_blues

#Lifelines

I scroll and scroll through tweets and updates, drawn by the illusion that I'll reach the end of the ever-refreshing page. But if your tweets leave me feeling strangely empty, your texts are like hugs from across the blue. My favourite time for you to text is during lunch break, when I'm alone in the art room, working on my papier mâché totem pole for my end of term exhibition. I think the art teacher Mr Porter knows I'm just messing, adding shredded paper and wallpaper paste to the sculpture bit by bit, to avoid hanging out in the canteen with the other kids. Slick-sluck-gunge. One sloppy tier at a time. My sculpture resembles a soggy grey wedding cake.

Hey Finny. Grand weather here 2day. How's weather with u? Did u get my email? Love Dad xox

Emails are for sleepless nights when I get up and turn on my laptop. In the soft blue backlight, it's just you and me. You write differently in emails to how you write in texts and tweets. Your email style is more akin to *Broken Haven*, a dog-eared edition of which sits by my bedside, its yellowing pages soft as skin, as if your only novel is developing its own hide and will soon sprout arms and legs. Your emails are little pieces of your novels just for me.

Fionnuala, mo chuisle, I thought of you when I was walking down Shipquay Street today. A breeze picked up off the Foyle and the river danced with white horses. It put me in mind of that windy day when your mother and I took you to the velvet strand at Buncrana and your Mickey Mouse ball got swept out to sea. Do you remember that?

@DonegalRenewables - why Inishowen should invest in #RenewableEnergy http://futurescience.ow.ly/5829

#7:05am

Mum's making breakfast with her hands on autopilot, the volume turned up to max. SLAM goes the bread into the toaster. GURGLE-SPURT-SPLASH goes the scalding water she lashes into the coffee cups. 'Our conversation isn't over yet, Fionnuala.'

'Uh-huh.'

'I was chatting to Karen Ridge again.'

'Mu-um! What have I told you? I don't need a therapist!'

'She thinks it'd be a good idea for you to leave your phone at home, one day a week.'

'Hmph.'

'I was telling her how you've found it hard to express your feelings since ...'

'Mum! Just coz I'm not going around bawling my head off!'

'Look, love,' she stops. Her face reddens, making her eyes look very blue. She blinks hard, 'Fionnuala. If we could just start with the phone?'

'Here,' I toss my mobile at her and grab my school bag, 'I have to go.'

#OneDayWithoutYou

I just need to use my imagination. You could be working on a new short story, in which case I wouldn't hear from you for weeks. You'd resurface on Skype looking skinnier, usually with an afro of curly grey hair and a massive black beard. Mum would give out to you, *You have a family, Gerard. How do you think Fionnuala feels when you don't contact her?*

And this is why it's been so easy to fall into this illusion. Our relationship was largely virtual anyway, so what's the difference?

On the bus without my phone, I write my name on the steamed-up window and watch the looping letters drip into each other. It feels strange, not having anything to mess with. I twist the ring on my finger, unzip and re-zip my coat. Without the stream of information, there's a quiet that tugs a dull, anxious note in my chest.

At Nether Edge petrol station, Adam Lynch bounds onto the bus and high-fives his mates. His spiked-up blond hair gleams dark with gel, and a white crust of toothpaste brackets the corners of his lips. Normally I stare at my phone to avoid him, but today I've looked up and made the dangerous mistake of eye contact. I look away but it's too late. He sidles over, swinging on the bus rail, the waistband of his Calvin Klein boxers flashing, 'Hey sexy, what you up to?'

'Nothing,' I shrug. The number thirteen reeks of Lynx and Impulse and fear and hormones. If anyone were to light a match in this bus, it would explode.

'Lads,' Adam shouts over his shoulder, grinning through his fluorescent pink chewing gum, 'I've just thought of a new nickname for her … FIONNUALA-THE-FRIGID!'

Pressing the STOP bell, I chase through the tunnel of laughter. My black school loafers clatter down the staircase. Two stops early, I jump off the bus into the rain.

#CatchingMyDeath

'Another A-star essay, Fionnuala,' Mr Burke hands me back my paper on Charles I, 'Those suggestions I made are only minor. It's really excellent work … in the circumstances.'

At break, the art room is closed, so I shelter from the rain under the leafless sycamores on the school avenue. I stare at my A-star essay until my words run blue and all my theories about the causes of the English Civil War go sliding down the page. The A-star doesn't seem real when I can't tell you about it.

'It's a bit wet out here, duck,' Miss Carlyle the English teacher squelches through fallen leaves, holding a folder over her head against the drizzle. 'Come on inside, before you catch your death.'

AD VITAM AETERNAM reads black lettering on the stained-glass window above the main entrance. In the corridor, bottle green school radiators hum, and the squeaky parquet flooring stinks of polish and wet feet. As I ease open the door of the canteen, a murky drumbeat hits me in the face along with the cloying stench of greasy sausages. 'FRIGID FINNY!' Adam whoops and thrusts his pelvis at me. Dozens of eyes zoom in on me. I back out of the canteen and slam the door on the volley of laughter.

The silence of the empty corridor surges. As I run out of the school building and jog across the deserted yard in the lashing rain, the lump in my throat swells to the size of Jupiter. No one sees me leave.

#Re:HelloFin

Hey Dad, everything's shit at school. The girls bitch about me and the boys take the piss out of me. I've tried ignoring them like you said, but that only makes it worse. I wish you were here. I can't tell Mum. I don't want to worry her. The only person I can talk to is you.

#Q&A

'Fionnuala,' Mum stands in my bedroom doorway with her hands on her hips. 'How long have you been home?'

'Not long.'

'Don't lie to me, Fin. Susan rang. Laura told her you went home early.'

'Can I have my phone?'

'You can't just start skipping school.'

'Can I have it?'

Sighing, she takes my mobile out of her bag and holds it aloft, the way we used to dangle dog biscuits for our old Labrador Danny when he was a pup. I shut my laptop and snatch the phone off her. 'Fionnuala! Before you turn it on, I need to tell you something. Come back here!'

But I'm already halfway down the stairs, dialling your number.

'This service is no longer available.'

I dial again. Jupiter in my throat is making it hard to breathe.

'This service is no longer available.'

With a few swipes of my thumb, I text, *Dad I've just tried calling, what's going on?*

'Message unable to deliver. Service no longer available.'

Behind me, mum is saying something about, 'I had to cancel it, Fionnuala … just not healthy … becoming more introverted … was a sweet gesture of him to do this … didn't envisage it would be so … real.'

#LostAndFound

It's grainy inside my head, like on my fifth birthday when I let go of your hand at Barry's Amusement Arcade. I remember the panic of being surrounded by so many legs and knees, none of which were yours. I remember the chatter of slot machines, the growl of the ghost train, the squeals of children from the helter-skelter, and the relief when you rushed to me through the crowd and scooped me into your arms, my tears blotching your Greenpeace T-shirt, your beard tickling my cheek. A liquid sound bubbles up from my stomach: a hiccup-choke-gasp.

Mum's slippers pad down the stairs behind me, fast and falling like a somersault. She hugs my waist tight, as if she's dived into a swamp to rescue me from drowning. And out of all the words that have drifted across my mind the last six months, out of all the sentences I've sent you, all the tweets and phone calls and texts, out of all the stories eroded down to their outlines, the only thing I can find to say to her is, 'Mum, I miss my Dad.'

#ScienceFiction

ProLong® was first developed by Elysium Technology in the States. You were the one who told me about it. 'Listen to this, Fin …' over the phone I heard the rattle of a newspaper, '"while post-death social messaging has been around for decades, the latest form of artificial intelligence will now enable us to keep in touch from beyond the grave, via actual phone and email conversations."'

'Sounds like one of your sci-fi stories, Dad.'

'Ha!' You hated it when people referred to your stories as 'sci-fi'. '"The device works by recording voice patterns,"' you continued, '"Using Bayesian inference, genetic algorithm and Google Prediction, this highly sensitive artificial intelligence monitors phone calls, texts and social media postings over a period of years. It then replicates the individual's vocabulary, syntax, and voice, creating a 98% accurate digital imitation which can simulate communication for years after the person has deceased …" Are you listening, Fin?'

'Uh-huh,' I had you on loudspeaker whilst I painted my toenails forget-me-not blue.

'This is brilliant!' you gushed. 'Imagine! Billions of word patterns! Infinite decibels of sound and pitch! And a computer can actually mimic us! Isn't that magic?'

#You

You devoured ideas in the way some other people consume box sets. You were writing and researching constantly, skydiving from one story to the next. Not that you ever had much literary success. I think you were vaguely known in Irish literary circles, and a review I once retrieved from your wastepaper basket showed you scowling against a rustic wall somewhere, looking suitably moody and poetic. Stories seemed to consume every minute of your day. Other people would have gone to their GP as soon as they noticed a stabbing pain whenever they went to the loo, but you were too busy. By the time you had a check-up, the cancer had spread. 'It's second degree, Fin …' you told me.

'Second degree?' I replied, 'So that's not as bad as first degree, right, Dad? … Right?'

For perhaps the first time ever, you went silent on the phone. I imagined the silence ebbing between us as a physical thing. A sea we both had our toes in but could not cross.

You were living back in Ireland by then, as you had been since I was nine. I used to spend summer holidays in your earth ship, which was buried into a mountainside outside Buncrana, on the Inishowen Peninsula. A concentric structure, like the ancient sun fort of Grianán of Aileach on the nearby mountain, your earth ship was striated with patterns of recycled glass. Rows of beans and cabbages fortressed the front entrance of the warren-like house, which was meant to obtain its heat from the earth. The windows would reflect the shifting azure chroma of Lough Swilly, known as the Lake of Shadows, where thousands of swans drifted like cotton buds trying to mop the dark water. Days with you often involved hunger pains because you'd run out of food. Or summer chills because you'd forgotten to clean the solar panels and the heating was jacked up. From a young age, I discovered it was easier to love you from a distance.

#OnYourLastVisit

Flushed and swollen by steroids, you looked like a hairless Santa. I felt suddenly shy around you, as if you were a stranger. Worse still, you wanted to *talk about things*, relaying intimate medical details and referring to your body as if you were already outside it. 'PSA ratings are good,' you told me, 'bladder functions are returning and the liver is improving.'

'Do you have to tell Fionnuala so much bloody information?' I heard Mum hiss at you in the kitchen one night when you both thought I was asleep. 'She's upset enough as it is.'

'I'm just being honest with her, Máire. Someone has to be.'

#CostPerMinute

The last time we spoke on the phone, you were in the palliative care unit at Altnagelvin Hospital. You were trying to say good-bye to me, but I wouldn't let you. 'Don't … let people … put you down, darlin',' you wheezed. 'Stand up for yourself, don't … let …'

'Okay Dad, but I'll talk to you soon,' I insisted. Then I started banging on about this new international call card I'd found. How I'd be able to call you for longer now and more often. You were trying to give me life advice, but all I could tell you was how the price of calls per minute was the cheapest I'd ever seen.

#Unearthed

A magnificent spray of cherry blossom stood outside your earth ship when they carried your coffin out into the sun. Our footsteps crunched the stony lane leading down the mountain to Saint Gabriel's Church by Lough Swilly. Around us was birdsong, the bleat of newborn lambs. The bright day oozed damp life and the rest of the world seemed very far away. Your home place was all that existed.

Father Michael spoke about swallows returning to roost and daffodils continuing to bloom long after the gardener who planted them has gone. And at your graveside, the undertaker's black-gloved hands were deft, efficient as a silver service waiter's. My uncles had placed you in a coffin which probably cost more than anything you'd ever owned. It occurred to me your death would cause no disturbance at all. Your grave was just a crease on the farmed and forested patchwork quilt of hills.

#BackHome

It rained and the cherry blossoms vanished from the trees overnight, outlining the grass verges of Nether Edge with damp pink mush. This upset me more than anything – the way that time channelled forth into summer, while I remained frozen by your graveside. In my head it was still April.

True to form, you hadn't left a cent behind. But you had managed to leave me a rather unusual gift. Two months after your funeral, I was sitting on my bed staring at the empty black branches of the cherry blossom tree, when my phone vibrated in my pocket.

Dear descendant, CONGRATULATIONS! You are now subscribed to ProLong® Life Extension Package 1. See elesiumtech. com for details.

My phone rang and your voice smiled, 'Fin, my darlin'. How are things?'

That first time I answered the phone, I dropped it.

#DecemberCold

Mum hands me back my mobile, 'Okay Fionnuala. I've unblocked it now so you can still talk to *him*.' Wiping my eyes, I follow her downstairs into the kitchen, cradling my phone like a priceless antique bauble.

Mum puts on the kettle and stares out at the patio, where our Christmas tree lies in a sparkling heap. 'This won't last forever, Fin,' she says to her reflection in the dark kitchen window, as if she's addressing someone trapped behind the glass. I'm about to reply when my phone buzzes.

Hey darlin', howru? Cold night here in Inishowen! xox

I wait for that familiar comfort rush, but it doesn't come. Instead, coldness crawls like an army of ice-legged ants over my skin. Mum's slippers lisp out of the kitchen.

Great craic @BuncranaLibrary this morning doing creative writing workshop for @InishTeens. Talented bunch!

#MakingFiction

I know you're not real, in the way I know most of the stuff I scroll through every day is not real; most of the news and commentary and opinion, and most of the feeds from my classmates. I know these stories are not real, and yet.

And yet.

#TalkToMe

'Dad, we have to stop talking.'

'What? Hang on a minute, Fin,' I hear you paying for your pack of fags – cheers, thanks a million. Take care now … 'Fionnuala, what's all this?

'Dad, you're not real.'

You chuckle. I hear you lighting up. 'Well Jeez, Fin, I'm about as real as the rest of us. What's got into you today, huh? How's school?'

'Dad, you're fucking *dead*.'

'God, Fionnuala. No need to be so dramatic.'

'I'm being dramatic? How am I being dramatic?'

'Suit yourself then, missus. C'mere, I've to tip on down to the library. Chat to you this evening, so I will.'

'Dad. Don't hang up. *Dad*.'

#EscapeToTheHills

I will go somewhere. I will finish school and I will go somewhere with my phone and my notepad and I'll figure this out. Today in class, Mr Burke said history is written by the victors. It's one of his favourite things to talk about – how history isn't real. Imagine spending your life teaching a subject you believe is inherently flawed. But that's the strange thing; it's at these moments, when he's on about the unreliable nature of collective memory, that my history teacher looks most animated. Like at the very moment of knowing it's all fake, that's when he loves his subject most. I will go somewhere, perhaps to your Lake of Shadows, and watch the changing landscape and we'll talk. Or maybe I'll skip the grid, go somewhere there's no phone signal. The Amazon jungle. The Siberian steppe. The Arctic Circle. Maybe I'll stand in a place as white as a blank page, and there'll be no dial tones and no hashtags and nothing trending and no news feeds, and then I'll know what I have to do next.

All the Rules We Could Ask For

Heather Richardson

Let's say we'll contain a story within the time it takes to make a short sea crossing from Dublin to Holyhead. So we'll begin as the passengers surge up from the car decks, forced together into the Red Stairway and the Blue Stairway, nudging each other upwards, touching but never blending. Up they go, squeezed along like toothpaste through the jagged tubes of the stairways, until finally out they pour, spreading out, each one now free to buffer himself or herself from everyone else with a bubble of space.

And here come the four characters in our story. They're travelling two by two. Here's Karl and Dave, who work together, and here's Elaine and Jodi, who are mother and daughter. They're choosing their seats, and they will, of course, be at adjacent tables, which means this will be one particular story rather than the many other ones it could have been.

Let us first dispense with Karl, because he will not be important to us. This does not mean that he is not important in himself, but he is a quiet young man, preferring to listen than to talk. This might be interpreted as signifying some moral worth in Karl – big, quiet young men are generally thought of as a good thing – but really, that's neither here nor there as far as this story is concerned. When Karl was born (and it is hard to imagine such a big, silent man being a baby) his parents decided to call him Karl-spelt-with-a-K. This was not indicative of left-leaning politics, but simply because, as Karl's mother said, 'It's a bit different, isn't it?' As if being *a bit different* were somehow enough to distinguish any of us in the great sea of the ordinary where we are each simply another salty droplet. If Karl had been a girl his parents had planned to call him Kerri-spelt-with-an-i. Karl still lives with his parents. We would all like to think that someday Karl will find a good woman who will view his silence and even, dare we say it, his slight stupidity, with fondness and tolerance, like those wives in television commercials. Sadly, we cannot bank on this happy ending for him. The reality of women is that in the long run they are neither fond nor tolerant. This is not intended as a criticism of women. They are the more aspirational gender, always striving for improvement, which can only be to all our benefits in the long run. So Karl, should he find such a woman, may be persuaded that he needs to come out of himself; prodded into conversations with near-strangers at social events he did not wish to attend; nagged about his inability to stand up to a difficult boss, and generally so harried that he will think wistfully back to those days when he lay, all large and silent and lonely, in his own little room in his parents' house.

But enough about Karl. He will sit and listen and smile and make confirmatory noises as Dave talks to Elaine and Jodi. Let's move on to Dave.

Dave leads the way as he and Karl look for a table. All the window seats have been taken, but Dave does not mind, as once out of harbour there is nothing to look at but the interminable grey of the sea. A more introspective man might find such a sight would incline him to meditation, or even induce a touch of existential angst, but Dave merely finds it boring. So he selects a table at the very hub of the various food outlets on board. He sits beneath a huge picture of Laurel and Hardy, which has been pixilated and neon-tinted for artistic effect. Karl sits opposite him, and realises too late that while Dave can look outwards at the many other passengers, he himself can only see Dave, Laurel and Hardy.

Dave is cold, but he is proud of his fine chest and shoulders, and in particular of his arms, and knows that to be viewed at their best he must wear a T-shirt, and not hide himself under anything warmer. He places his arms on the table, positioning them in a way that he hopes will best display the tone of his biceps. When he stretches back, as he does now, the careful observer will notice the filigree markings that hint at the tribal tattoo on his upper arm. The nature of Dave might almost be an argument in favour of oppressive, guilt-inducing religion. What else could have the power to insinuate the merest sliver of self-doubt beneath his sleek, waxed, tattooed skin?

Elaine and Jodi arrive at the table next to Dave and Karl. Elaine is flustered, concerned that she and Jodi will not find a place to sit, although the boat is barely two-thirds full. She looks at the empty table, chewing her lip. 'C'mon Mum,' says Jodi. 'Are we going to sit here or what?'

Dave and Karl have noticed them, which is nice. Nobody likes to be invisible.

'Are you keeping these seats for anyone?' says Elaine. Life has taught her that pre-emptive assumption of her lack of entitlement is a useful strategy. It enables her to feel on solid ground. Events tend to confirm her approach.

'Go ahead love, go ahead,' Dave says, waving towards the vacant table like a king bestowing a low-grade ennoblement on a servant whose name he can't remember. Dave enjoys Elaine's grateful smile. He knows he is the bringer of her relief, and this makes him feel good about himself. Some years ago, when he started his first job in Boots the Chemist, Dave discovered his capacity to please women. A smile, a laugh, the free deployment of the word *love* was usually all it took. This is not to say that Dave came to this realisation in any analytical way; it was simply that he behaved in a certain manner, experienced the positive outcome, and learned to maintain said behaviour. He finds it particularly easy to do this with women like Elaine, whom he has quickly, sub-intellectually, assessed as not being his type. This is not because she is older than him – he would certainly not scorn someone who was a mere ten or twelve years his senior – but he likes his girlfriends to have a certain gloss, and he has noticed that motherhood tends to rub the polish off most women.

Jodi slides into the outward-facing seat – she has an extra-large Charlie Chaplin picture behind her – and Elaine sits opposite her. Elaine offers Dave and Karl several little verbal tokens of gratitude, glancing from one man to the other to see how they are received. It is to Elaine's credit that for the rest of this story she will offer Karl almost his fair share of eye contact, even though Dave will be the only one who properly speaks in response to her.

It is hardly necessary to detail the minutiae of their initial conversation – Elaine and Jodi from Birmingham, returning from the annual duty visit to Irish grandparents, Dave and Karl from Leicester etcetera, etcetera, etcetera ... Jodi scrutinises Dave, taking in the T-shirt, the mammary bulge of his pectorals, the tan, the tattoo. Around ten minutes into their acquaintance she asks him, 'Are you gay?'

'Jodi!' Elaine says, her feelings an uneven mixture of embarrassment at the question (about sexual orientation *and* addressed to a man they scarcely know) and astonishment at this strange being her daughter has become of late.

Dave is unfazed by Jodi's enquiry. 'No. All the lads at work think I'm gay though, just because I go to the gym and I don't go out on the beer with them.' He leans over and nudges Jodi conspiratorially. 'Actually, I am gay really. I pretend I've got a girlfriend to try to cover it up.'

Elaine laughs, grateful to Dave for retrieving the situation. Karl laughs along with her, which is generous of him, as he has heard this quip of Dave's several times.

Jodi looks confused, as if she has been given too many pieces of information to compute. She decides the best way to deal with the muddle in her head is to hit Dave. She flails at him, fetching him a limp slap on the shoulder. 'Jodi!' Elaine says again.

Jodi slumps back into her seat. 'I want something to eat.'

Elaine digs into her handbag, and then into her purse. She pulls out a fiver. 'Here, why don't you see what the queue's like at Burger King.'

Jodi snaps the money out of her hand and slides out of her seat. She walks away in that awkward way teenagers have, convinced that everyone is watching her and waiting for her to make a mistake.

'Sorry about that,' Elaine says to Dave.

'Don't worry about it.'

'That was domestic violence.' Elaine wishes she hadn't said that. She hopes Dave knows she is joking.

'S'okay.' Dave is quiet.

Elaine looks over in the direction of Burger King. She can see the backlit sign, but not the queue. Her line of sight is blocked by yet more super-sized pictures of comic stars of yesteryear. 'She used to be shy,' she says.

Jodi is two people away from the front of the queue. A husband and wife are standing behind her, and she thinks they might be planning to push in front. The man is edging forward, so that now he is nearly alongside her. He has his arms folded, which gives him another few inches' inroad into Jodi's space. Jodi wishes her mate Jenna was with her, because Jenna's really mouthy, and doesn't care, and would just turn around to the man and say *Back off mate*. Jodi wishes Jenna was with her, because Jenna would be able to talk to that bloke, Dave, and would know how to be all cheeky and flirty. Then again, if Jenna was here, Dave would probably fancy her, because all the blokes seem to fancy Jenna, and none of them ever fancy Jodi, except that lad Fintan, who doesn't really count because he goes to the Day Centre every day on the special bus.

Poor Jodi. She is being dragged from childhood to womanhood as if by the hounds of hell. Hormones, you see, are much misunderstood. Jodi is not in thrall to libido; her adolescent body is not thrusting forward like a lustful zombie. Jodi's physical state has less to do with sexual awakening than it has with blind instinct. Just as lemmings throw themselves off cliffs, or salmon leap up rivers, or eels swim hither and thither from one side of the ocean to another – and no doubt all these creatures, as far as they are capable of rational thought, must think to themselves, *Why exactly am I doing this?* – Jodi is simply compelled to act as she does. She can no more prevent herself from attacking Dave – and everyone knows what fighting like that leads to – than a bird can decide against migrating. Hormones are indeed the wind beneath her wings, buffeting her around the sky. She doesn't know which scares her the more – flying or falling.

Jodi has already discovered that alcohol frees her from the perpetual whirl of anxiety and self-consciousness. Soon enough, no doubt, she will go to a party with Jenna, and her other friends, and some boys (though not, we hope, Fintan), and drink will be taken and she will find that the demands of evolutionary biology will have her wriggling out of her skinny-leg jeans so that a skinny-arsed youth can follow his own hormonal imperatives. There is, of course, an alternative. She may become infatuated with an older man – someone like Dave, for example – and pursue him with a relentlessness known only to teenage girls, until he is overwhelmed by sheer weariness at constantly fending her off, and submits. Almost, we might say, grooming in reverse. It's not easy being a man. Young women can be most determined, and minor details such as the illegality of congress between a fifteen-year-old girl and a twenty-seven-year-old man will not cause them a moment's concern. The world – that's us – will of course take a different view. We see Jodi as vulnerable, and indeed she is. Her predation of the likes of Dave is no more within her control than her spots or her mood swings. Poor Jodi. She might almost be an argument in favour of the close confinement of young women until such time as they are neutralised by marriage.

Happily for Dave he is unlikely to succumb to the advances of Jodi. He is like a gleaming ball bearing, all shine and surface but impervious to injury. Dave and Elaine are still talking. Somehow the topic has moved on to pet dogs. She is offering Dave (and Karl, in theory) a more substantial morsel of her life. 'You get attached to dogs, don't you?' The two men nod. 'I loved our Buster. I was so upset when we had to put him down. I mean it was the kindest thing but … Do you know what? Afterwards I sat down on the pavement outside the vet's, and I just cried and cried. And this old couple were walking past, and the wife said to me, "Are you all right, love? Have you been assaulted or something?" And I said, "I've just had to have my dog put down," and they looked at me as if … Well, they were disgusted.'

'Yeah,' Dave says. 'You get attached to them.'

Jodi returns with a burger and fries. She slides back into her seat, and begins eating her fries, hoping that Dave will take one. Jodi may be naive, but she understands that nicking someone's fries is a sign of interest. She herself often nicks fries when the boys she knows get a takeaway, but none of them have yet responded to her advances.

'Can I have a chip?' Elaine says, reaching across and taking one.

'Hey!' Jodi says in protest.

'I paid for them.'

'Cheeky cow.'

'That's nice.' Elaine shrugs at Dave and Karl. 'Like I say, she used to be shy.'

And so the boat sails on. Elaine does not notice that Dave has a way of swatting away each little butterfly of conversation she releases. Her efforts flutter valiantly in the air for a second or two, and are gone. Dave likes to talk about Dave. 'Yeah, we go all over with work, don't we?' he says, nodding at Karl.

'What do you do then?' Elaine has wanted to ask this question for some time, but has been fearful of the answer, because if Dave says something like *Oh, you know, this and that, ducking and diving . . .* she will be disappointed, and she is not wise enough to know that she should not be investing even this tiny hope in him.

'Promotional work,' Dave says. We may wonder for a moment what company would deem Dave and Karl to be the best ambassadors for their product range.

'Oh,' says Elaine, happy not to have been disappointed yet. 'Is that at shopping centres and the like?'

'All the big stores. House of Fraser, that sort of thing.' Again, we try to visualise Dave in front of a display in House of Fraser, promoting some or other product. Could it possibly be men's toiletries? No doubt *male grooming products* is the preferred term, the kind that come in intriguingly engineered bottles. *Lotion après-rasage. Gel hydratant pour le corps.* Or fitness equipment, perhaps? Maybe Karl and Dave demonstrate cross-training machines in the sports departments of large shops. Maybe Dave has a script he has learnt by heart, which he recites over and over again while Karl moves his limbs backwards and forwards like an automaton.

Jodi has finished her burger and fries. 'I'm thirsty now,' she says.

'You should have got a drink when you were up there.'

'I didn't want one then.'

Elaine sighs. 'I'll go. I could do with a tea myself.' She stands up. 'What do you want then? Diet Coke?'

'Yeah.'

Elaine glances at Dave and Karl, not wishing to force the acquaintance, but hopeful to advance it by a show of amity. 'Can I get you anything while I'm up?'

'No love, you're all right.'

Karl shakes his head in confirmation of Dave's refusal.

Elaine walks to O'Brien's Coffee Shop, suddenly aware that this conversation, this chance meeting, is not going to develop any further. Something in the tone of that last *love* made it clear to her. Deep inside Elaine a fragile little blossom of hope wilts. Before she made this journey she had harboured a secret dream that something would happen, that perhaps there would be a chance encounter that would change her life. Although she is a grown woman, and a mother to boot, she has not yet learnt to abandon such foolishness.

'So, have you got a girlfriend then? I mean really?' Jodi is interrogating Dave.

'Young free and single, me.'

'And don't you want a girlfriend? Is there anyone you fancy?'

Dave moves about in his seat, as if he cannot get comfortable. Suddenly he stands up. 'Just going for a jimmy,' he says, and walks away.

Karl and Jodi sit in silence. Jodi watches Dave go, then stares blankly across at the windows and the sea. Karl clears his throat. 'He's not really over his ex, if you want the truth.' Jodi does not respond.

Elaine returns with the drinks. The boat has slowed down although the harbour is still a long way off. 'What about the cost of petrol then?' Dave says. 'Shocking, isn't it?'

Karl nods.

'I can't afford to drive anymore,' Dave says. 'My car only does eight to twelve miles to the gallon, you see.' He waits for Elaine or Jodi to ask him what sort of car he drives, but they don't.

Elaine is not deliberately thwarting Dave's wish to tell her about his car. She has simply lost heart with this conversation. She has realised that Dave will walk away from this journey with no memory at all of her. Being Elaine, she thinks this is a reflection of her unimportance, but it is in fact a reflection of Dave's imperviousness. 'Yeah,' he says, 'eight to twelve to the gallon.'

There is a sense of expectation in the passengers. They can see that the horizon has suddenly come closer while their attention was elsewhere, and that the grey of the sea has solidified into a line of sombre green landfall. Somewhere on the boat a member of staff is clearing her throat, preparing to read her own script detailing the niceties of disembarkation. And before she has finished, indeed, almost as soon as she has begun, the passengers will gather their belongings and allow themselves to be sucked down the Red Stairway and the Blue Stairway to their cars and coaches and the sad, utilitarian gangway reserved for the foot passengers. Dave and Karl will board the train for Leicester (changing at Crewe), while Elaine and Jodi will seek out Elaine's modest Honda Accord and the road to Birmingham.

And so this journey ends. None of our four characters has noticed that the boat travelled more slowly than is usual, and we suppose that doesn't matter much. We all arrive eventually, even if our journey is not as quick as we expected, and our destination is not the same as the one we were promised.

Winning on Points

Tara West

Polio is the best. If you had some sort of childhood illness like polio, you're onto a winner from the start. Rheumatic fever isn't bad. You could say you had rheumatic fever when you were a child and maybe a metal plate in your head as well and you'd get a lot of points for that. Heart disease is good. If you're lucky enough to have your mother and father die young, you score even more points. You always have to be thinking about your points. You keep score in your head. You think to yourself, if you smoke more or less, if you drink more or less, if you go to the shops near the house or if you go to the big Tesco, would this bring your points up or down? You have to think, do they track where you go and what you buy using your Tesco Clubcard points or whatever. Do they see you're buying scratch cards or fegs or midget gems? Everything you buy is proof. You can have a sixty a day habit. You can be addicted to cigarettes although if you smoke a lot, your official description is COPD, not Dependency, although you still get a lot of points. Maybe even more points than heavy drinkers. You get extra points for wetting the bed so Dependency is easy money. You could always give drinking a go, but you really do have to wet the bed whether you want to or not, so you get a lot of money but nobody wants to visit you. If you're sick enough you don't really need to do much acting. But if you don't make a song and dance, you don't get any points. And it's nice to be the centre of attention when you've never been there before, doctors and nurses asking can you do this, can you do that, catching you when you faint on the treadmill and fall on the floor. Your daughter can say to them, lips all tight and holding a hankie to your head, we told you this would happen, we told you. And the nurses will look at each other, wondering if you're going to sue them or if you're just acting. But it doesn't really matter whether you're bleeding or you're acting, you've got plenty of points by then. You can go to the benefits interview and the woman can squint her eyes at you all she wants, but there's nothing she can do. If you want a car, it's not that hard. You can get a Japanese one, although your daughter and son-in-law can drive it because you might have to use an oxygen tank to breathe. You can get a brand new one. The car, not the oxygen tank. The oxygen tank is probably thirty-second-hand by the time you get it. And when else would you get a brand new car with a big bunch of flowers in the back? They can go all over the place in it, your daughter and your son-in-law. Sometimes they bring you something back, like an 'I Love Cork' magnet. You can collect those. You can cover the whole fridge with those. The more things that are wrong with you, the more points you get and the more money they give you and the more things they find wrong with you. It's like your granny buying you sweets because you had a bad time at the dentist. You think you could smoke sixty a day if you weren't sick? You wouldn't have the time. Or the money. You can sit outside Tesco in the back of the new car and smoke. You can watch your daughter and lots of people going in and out and think about what they're going to buy, and your grandson will sit there with you and look up from his phone and say 'Tesco tracks what people buy, Granny. Think what they do with that information. They sell it to the government. The kind of bread people buy. The drink they drink. The kind of tea. Do you think they track what you buy, Granny?' 'I don't know, love. I don't know.' And he'll say, 'Well, we need to be careful because my ma thinks they do, Granny.' Everything you buy is proof. You could lose all your points if you started eating salad or something. Your grandson won't mind you smoking in the car. He won't complain. 'Keep you smoking, Granny,' he'll say. 'You enjoy yourself.' Sometimes when you're sick you can get associated illnesses and that works like an accumulator. Like, if you've got COPD and you can't move about much and you can't get out of the car, then your hips seize up or whatever, you could end up morbidly obese and not be able to get out of the house at all, and then you can get diabetes and agoraphobia. That's a thing, agoraphobia. You can't go out the front door, and if you do, you think you're going to die. You can get into a car, but that can make you hyperventilate. Maybe even pass out. That's a lot of points. A lot of points. Then when you're stuck in the house, they bring you buns. And then you get sick with your diabetes. While you're there you can say you're mental. Say your illness or the drugs are making you want to top yourself. Because sometimes you might want to top yourself, sometimes you might feel like that. But you can get more points for saying it. And then you can get jewellery off the Shopping Channel because you want to help your daughter but you can't get off the settee any more, or you can get a week in Spain for your grandson if all his friends are going and he doesn't have any money. You can't get fridge magnets in Spain. They don't do them in Spain. Even if you do top yourself, at least you've done all right by your family. You've got them a car and holidays and jewellery or whatever. You can even pay ahead for your funeral. Your family will want to help you though and they'll hide all the tablets and knives. You can always say you're mental without having any other illnesses but that won't get you many points so don't bother. Mental is no good. You have to have mental with something else, like Dependency. That's far better, if you don't have COPD or heart disease or something else you can see on an X-ray. Make sure your Tesco points prove it. You can buy mad things like you would if you were mental, like lawn seed and desiccated coconut and five bottles of bleach. And lots of vodka. Even though you can get it cheap from the fella in the van. Don't. It has to show up on your Tesco points. It's proof. Everything you buy is proof. People act different around you when you're sick and you can't get out of the house. You might smell a bit, even when you've washed yourself, you still have a smell. You have to be ready for that. You might have a neighbour who starts calling in all the time, bringing you things like DVDs and magazines and buns and just sitting there with you, patting your hand or whatever. You might start to like them calling in, but you have to think about these things, you have to not be stupid. Your daughter or grandson will tell you what's what, they'll tell your neighbour to eff off. Your family know what's going on, they know when somebody is after your money. Your family will protect you, even nieces and nephews you haven't met before. Always a new face turning up to visit. You won't see the same one twice. It's like working in a shop except you give the customers money. If you've worked for the government, you can do even better. Like if you get COPD and heart disease and diabetes and go mental as well, like if you worked at cleaning in a government office, you can send your whole family to Turkey to get a fridge magnet or on a cruise so they get a good long break. Then your old work friends can come round, laughing their heads off like something funny happened just outside the door and when they come in they'll be quiet and shuffling like somebody's died. You'll smile because you want them not to worry. You have to make sure it's when your family is in Turkey because then you can give your friends anything you want. Coats, bits of jewellery, old photographs or whatever. Your daughter will have everything she needs by then. You think you'll never have anything to give your kids but this way you can set them up for life. Your points will prove you bought the lawn seed and bleach and vodka yourself. You'll always wonder if it would've been better if you'd had polio but the insurance probably pays out whatever you die of. You can eat the coconut if you want.

Let Me Be Part of All This Joy

Sheena Wilkinson

'Miss Irvine assures me the girls are awful keen.' Miss Nash looked pretty keen herself.

'Och, girls *do* run after anything fresh,' Jane said. Any*one* fresh. 'Until the novelty wears off.'

'Maybe. But – young blood, new ideas …'

'Hardly *new*.' Jane tinkled a laugh to show that she was in no way being unkind to Miss Irvine with her *new ideas*. 'Sure *I* got up a Literary Club in – 1917, wasn't it? But it fizzled out.' She had tried to get the girls interested in the new poets, but they wanted *Drawing Room Farces*.

'That was five years ago.'

Five years! Where would Miss Irvine be in five years? Not still at The Shrubberies, trying to din *The Golden Treasury* into the lumpen heads of south Belfast's young ladies.

'Anyway.' Miss Nash beamed. 'I'd like you to give Miss Irvine every support. *Such* a dear girl. She went to Trinity, you know. In Dublin.'

Yes, I do bloody know. Jane stood up. 'Miss Nash, I'm on detention duty, so …'

She gathered up the pile of Upper Fifth exercise books. Twenty-two essays on 'Ode To A Nightingale'. Her hands barely met round them.

It was freezing in Little Hall. Jane wrapped her gown tighter as she stepped on to the dais. Two Lower Fourths giggled in the back row. Brown bobs, ink-stained tunics, pimples.

'Mabel, Maud – front row, opposite sides. *Incomplete preparation?* Well, you'll have plenty of time to complete it now.'

'Yes, Miss Dodd.' They dragged themselves forward and resettled with much pencil-box banging, adenoidal breathing and tragic looks across the expanse of empty desks.

Jane took out the first essay – Sybil Allen's. Why were girls so *silly* about Keats? *B-. More analysis, less emotion!* she wrote in red ink. Sybil would blink and fret.

She rotated her shoulders. Did Kathleen Irvine work this hard? Oh dear. She sounded bitter and grudging and she *wasn't*, just tired and – well, it wasn't fair, this fussing over Kathleen, with her short skirts and her short hair and her charm. Silly wee girls, always fighting to carry her books and leaving violets on her desk.

Fustle-fustle. Girls were such fidgets. 'Silence,' Jane said. 'There's still fifteen minutes left.'

Mabel – or Maud? – the spottier one – looked at her friend. *Go on!* the other's face said.

'Um …'

'We don't want to be late …'

'Miss Irvine's giving out the parts for *A Midsummer Night's Dream.*'

A Midsummer Night's Dream! Trust Kathleen Irvine to pander to the girls' desire to prance around in fairy costumes with their plaits loose.

'Detention ends at four o'clock and not a moment sooner.'

'But …'

'We'll miss auditioning for Titania!'

'You should have thought of that.'

They humphed back to work, pens creeping. But neither was remotely likely to be cast as a fairy queen so no harm would be done.

The second the clock's hands read four o'clock, she said, 'You may pack up, girls.'

Breathing loudly, they did. Jane shuffled together the unfinished marking.

Mabel-and-Maud hovered at the door.

'Girls, would you mind giving me a hand with my books? Just up to my room?'

Glum but obedient, they plodded after her. It wasn't the thing to invite girls to your room, but the Tutorial Sixth were always running up to Kathleen Irvine's room for cocoa.

When she opened the door, they stared with blunt curiosity – of course they did! When Jane was at school her friends had been desperate for crumbs of knowledge about their teachers. Minnie Wallace had been the toast of the Lower School for days after spotting the history mistress buying beef brisket in the butcher's on the Ormeau Road.

So she tolerated their nosiness. And her room was pin-neat, no hairbrushes or nighties on display. Fresh, too – she always kept the window open, even when it meant – as now – having to listen to the shrieking clash of a hockey match and the rumble of the traffic. She hoped they noticed the pictures of Charlotte Brontë and Shakespeare.

'Lots of books,' one said.

'Well, *you'll* appreciate that, being such keen members of the Literary Club.'

They giggled.

'Just set the books on the desk. Oh – careful!'

'Sorry, Miss Dodd!' Mabel-or-Maud set to rights the little framed photograph of Francis Ledwidge she'd overturned.

'Is that your *sweetheart?*' she asked, her cheeks flaming above the spots.

Her friend leapt in. 'You idiot, Maud! Course he's not!' *Good girl*, Jane thought, and was about to ask her if she knew Ledwidge's three books of poems, slight affairs, some reviewers thought, but charming: '*Let me be part of all this joy*' – lovely, really. And of course, like Keats, like so many of his fellow war poets, the tragic death. Yes, Ledwidge was exactly the poet to appeal to the Lower Fourth. Such fine dark eyes.

Mabel went on, 'Is he your brother, Miss Dodd?'

'*What?*' Was this a trick? Did they think she would pretend a famous poet was her brother?

And then she understood. Mabel and Maud, like everyone else at The Shrubberies, hadn't the faintest notion who Francis Ledwidge was. The *You idiot, Maud!* meant something quite different. It meant: *Dried-up old Miss Dodd could never have had an actual sweetheart.*

Which was true.

Jane smiled, a brave smile. 'He was – my fiancé. He was killed in 1917.' She stroked Ledwidge's face with her fingertip. 'Five years ago next Thursday. My birthday, in fact.' Why had she said that? They were horrified, lumpy cheeks flaming. Jane rushed to reassure. 'Don't worry, girls,' she said kindly.

'I only – we didn't …'

'Of course not. I don't believe in wearing my heart on my sleeve.'

'You don't have a ring.'

Jane sighed. 'Too painful a reminder. I keep it' – she could not think *where* she kept it – her handkerchief case? – 'somewhere very special.' She smiled that brave smile again, and this time the girls didn't look horrified. Their faces glowed with interested compassion. Far beneath them, a girl cried: 'Well *saved*, Edna!' What sort of ring was it? Something tasteful. 'It's an emerald,' she said. Ledwidge was from what was now the Free State so a green stone was very suitable. In fact, despite fighting for the British, he had been rather an Irish nationalist. Miss Nash would have been horrified.

'He's very handsome,' Maud said.

True. Possibly why she'd cut out and framed the picture.

'What was his name?' Mabel asked, greatly daring.

Jane twisted her fingers together. Oh God, a man's name, quick! Not Francis. 'John,' she said. A common name. But not unromantic. Keats was John.

'Now, run along. You don't want to miss your big chance, do you? Miss Irvine will be waiting. And girls, what I've told you – it's very *private*.'

Off they ran. Jane stood at the window, holding the photograph, watching the hockey players race up and down the grey asphalt. A tram clattered past, on its way out to the green banks of the Lagan. Might she and John have walked by the river? Well, yes, of course they would, when he was on leave. She would have hated to know that he must go back, but she would always have been brave and cheerful.

Next morning, Lower Fourth were so angelic that Jane feared they must all be sickening for something. Hands up with sensible answers, racing to hold the door open, every scrap of preparation done, even poor Dulcie Mullins who wasn't all there.

A posy of snowdrops appeared on her desk after lunch.

That was when she knew for sure. Mabel and Maud were incapable of keeping the romance of a mistress's secret sorrow to themselves. *Imagine, Miss Dodd had a sweetheart killed in the war, and he was awful handsome!*

But it wasn't a lie that could hurt anyone. After all, she thought, with a strange thrill, poor John is dead these five years.

The goodness spread to the Lower Fifth. Sybil Allen took her B- with stoic courage and said she would try harder next time. Rapt attention shone from every face.

On Thursday morning, Mabel and Maud, sweaty-scarlet, hovered at her desk.

'Miss Dodd,' Mabel said. 'We're awfully sorry – we know it's your birthday today …'

'And also …'

'So we want you to have this.'

'To show we're – you know …'

This was a box of Ling's Turkish Delight. And a card of staggering sentimentality which, to Jane's shock, made her eyes prick.

'Och girls, that's very thoughtful.'

She set it on the desk; she had to; they'd have been so hurt. She set them a composition and, as their pens flew – they were *so* cooperative these days – thought back to February 1917. She had been here at The Shrubberies, doing exactly what she was doing now. A different Lower Fourth, but not very different. Someone's father had been killed; someone else's brother; Miss Nash's cousin. There had been special prayers.

Why wouldn't she have mentioned John's death? She felt a pang for her younger self. But perhaps such stoicism hadn't been quite healthy? *Give sorrow words* – oh dear, wasn't it bad luck to quote from *Macbeth*?

At lunch, Kathleen sat beside her. 'Happy birthday,' she said.

'Och! I don't bother much, at my age …'

Kathleen smiled that smile which doubtless turned the Lower Fourth to jelly. 'I was wondering if you might join me for tea at the Royal after school? We don't seem to have had time to get to know each other. I know you're very busy, as senior English mistress, but—'

'I'd be delighted,' Jane said, and found that she was. Her insides fizzed. She hadn't been out of the school grounds for weeks. What luck that her good navy frock was freshly laundered. Probably Kathleen wanted advice from a more experienced mistress, but it was charming of her to present it as a birthday treat.

'And I don't want to be intrusive,' Kathleen went on, her fork poised over her plate of stew, 'but you know how girls talk …'

'Ah.'

'It can't be the easiest of days. We – well, we lost my brother at the Somme. So I hope I can understand a little.'

Jane lowered her head. 'It isn't common knowledge,' she said quietly. 'Our engagement was a – a private thing. Families … He was – um, you know …'

Kathleen nodded.

Oh God, now she was turning them into Romeo and Juliet. Jane attacked her stew.

93

Last lesson, there was a vase of early daffodils on her desk. The Lower Fifth smiled, eyes full of sympathy.

'Thank you girls,' Jane said. They were still on Keats. 'When I have fears that I may cease to be …'

We lost my brother at the Somme.

'Sorry, girls – I'm not feeling the best.' She swept out, gown swishing. As she leant against the wall outside she heard their squeaks and murmurs.

Poor Miss Dodd.

So brave!

She stood at her window. She had never left a class, not in ten years. Another hockey match. Kathleen was umpiring, running up the sidelines in her Trinity tunic, blowing a whistle, the sun gleaming on her golden bob.

We lost my brother at the Somme.

She scribbled a note, crept down the corridor to Kathleen's room, and slipped it under the door.

She was dying for a cup of tea, but feared the staff room. Kathleen's light feet pattered past her door, then stopped at her own room. Jane lay on her bed. John watched her sadly from the bedside table to which she had promoted him. The desk wasn't appropriate for a fiancé.

A soft knock. 'Jane? I've brought you a wee cup of tea.'

How kind! Still – people liked to be kind, didn't they? Look at how sweet the girls were these days.

'Come in,' she said, in a brave, suffering voice.

Kathleen hesitated inside the door, cheeks flushed with exercise in the February wind.

'You poor thing,' she said.

'It's only a headache,' Jane said. She stroked the photograph to show that really, it was so much more. 'But I'm not up to going out for tea. I'm so sorry.'

'I understand,' Kathleen said. Her blue eyes shone with compassion.

'It's always a difficult day,' Jane said. She allowed herself a small brave laugh, and looked down at the photograph. 'J-John always made such a fuss on my birthdays. He used to buy the loveliest presents.' She gestured round the room. 'Books, usually. We shared a love of poetry.'

Kathleen's eyes followed hers and then rested on the photograph. 'Drink your tea while it's hot. Can I get you anything else?'

'No. I shall spend a quiet time in reminiscence.' Gosh, she sounded like a Victorian widow.

She enjoyed her evening. Cook sent dinner on a tray. No evening prep; no staff meeting; no after-dinner coffee in the staff room. She might cultivate headaches. She would never give in easily – would always struggle bravely between duty and self – but in the end she would agree that yes, maybe a wee day in bed was what she needed.

The knock came late – after nine. Jane was in her dressing gown.

'I won't disturb you,' Kathleen said. 'I just thought you might like to have this. I noticed you only have the first two. Happy birthday.'

Jane was touched. 'You dear girl,' she said. 'How very kind.'

When she had gone, Jane opened the parcel. A slim, greenish-grey book. Francis Ledwidge, *Last Songs*, 1918. A handsome edition, a photograph of the poet in the flyleaf. How observant of Kathleen to notice she didn't have it. She was, as everyone said, such a dear girl.

DRAMA

Three Sisters

an adaptation by Lucy Caldwell
from a literal translation by Helen Rappaport

Three Sisters *in this version was first performed at the Lyric Theatre, Belfast on 15 October 2016. The cast, in order of appearance, was as follows:*

Siu Jing	Shin-Fei Chen
Orla	Julie Maxwell
Marianne	Christine Clare
Erin	Amy Blair
Baron	Lewis MacKinnon
Beattie	Niall Cusack
Simon	Julian Moore-Cook
Vershinin	Tim Treloar
Andy	Aidan O'Neill
DJ Cool	Patrick McBrearty
Rod	Matthew Forsythe
Teddy	Gerard Jordan

Director	Selina Cartmell
Set and Costume Designer	Alex Lowde
Lighting Designer	Ciaran Bagnall
Composer and Sound Designer	Isobel Waller-Bridge
Movement Director	Dylan Quinn

Vocal Coach	Brendan Gunn
Assistant Director	Louisa Sanfey
Literal Translator	Helen Rappaport

Prologue

Siu Jing. She speaks directly to the audience.

Siu Jing   Well, here we are.
Pause.

This is the place I keep coming back to. This is where everything began to change forever.
The house is full of soldiers. They are not there, not really. But they are in every day of my memories. On every corner. In every street. Sometimes they stalk through my dreams.
It is the fifth of May 1993.
Or as I used to think, the fourteenth day of the third lunar month in Gui-Leen
(雞年): the Year of the Rooster.
It's a long time since I thought like that. For years now I have dreamed almost entirely in English. You don't realise as it's happening, then one day you realise it happened long ago.

The lights up slightly.

These are my sisters. Well, they're not yet my sisters, but they soon will be.
Here is Orla. Orla is always busy. Orla always complains about how busy she is but in truth,

she is scared that if she stops, she will be forced to confront ... herself. She buries herself in being a mother, or as close to a mother-figure as they've had for a long time.

This is Marianne. Nobody understands Marianne, herself least of all. Right now, she is thinking that she wants to die. Or that maybe she doesn't want to die, but she doesn't want to live any more. Not like this. This – here, now – this isn't life. This day, and all the days to come. The thought of them paralyses her. If something doesn't happen, soon, she is going to kill herself. That's what she's thinking.

And this is Erin. Erin is the baby – the joker – the flibbertigibbet. That's what her father used to call her – his flibbertigibbet. She was the only one that knew how to make him smile. This is still her role – until the day she decides she doesn't want to play it any more, at all.

It's Erin's eighteenth birthday. It is also the first anniversary of their father's death, but the sisters are determined to celebrate anyway.

I am nineteen – just one year older than Erin.

So.

These are my sisters and this is their story.

It is also my story. It might not have my name on it, but it is my story too.

And this is where it begins. An evening in May.

The lights up fully.
Siu Jing watches the sisters.
She leaves.

Act One

Belfast, 1993.
May. Early evening. Blue skies.
Orla, Marianne and Erin.
It is Erin's eighteenth birthday and the sisters are getting ready for her
party. It is fancy dress. Erin is dressed as Supergirl and Orla is Marge
Simpson.
The radio is playing Kylie Minogue's 'I Should Be So Lucky'.

DJ Cool   Now folks, regular listeners will know that it's
extremely unusual for me to interrupt the *Non-Stop*
Drive-Time Hour but this is a very special occasion.
Today, the fifth of May, is not just any day: and so a
special shout-out to the lovely Erin who turns eighteen today! Forget the fourth, May the fifth be with
you! D'you like what I did there? Do you? Do you
get it? May the fifth –

Marianne turns the radio abruptly off.

Erin   Hey! That was my shout-out!

Marianne   I swear, I can't take another second of him.

Orla   Come on, girls. Here we are. The fifth of May.
We've done it.
How's it been a whole year already?
Do you remember how cold it was? We were foundered. I mean it was absolutely Baltic. Here, what
do you reckon people actually from the Baltic say
when it gets cold?

Pause.

> D'you remember when they took the coffin away, God. It was lashing it down, absolutely lashing it. Your man playing the Last Post to us and the gravestones. Why d'you reckon no one came, was it 'cause he was Catholic or 'cause he was English?

Erin   Why are you doing this?

Baron, Beattie and Simon are outside. Baron and Beattie are smoking.

Orla   'On May nights, when so many doors are closed, there is one that is barely ajar.' Where's that from? I can't remember where that's from. It's been going round my head all day. Oh God Almighty, I want to get away from here!

Beattie   Away and jump!

Baron   You are talking bollocks.

Marianne starts singing 'I Should Be So Lucky'.

Orla   Stop it. Marianne! You're doing my head in.

> All afternoon all evening and every single weekend, hearing yet another bunch of stuck-up kids who don't give a shit sawing their way through scales that they obviously haven't bothered practising since the last lesson – is it any wonder I

have a permanent headache? It's almost literally boring me to death. The only thing that's keeping me going –

Erin   Is America.

She raps the first few lines of 'Fresh Prince of Bel-Air'.

We should just do it you know. Put this house on the market and get on a plane.

Orla   Yes! D'you know I don't even care where we go. New York, California, Philadelphia, Bel-Air –

Erin   Well, there's no way Andy will stay here once his thesis is done. The only thing stopping us is her.

Orla   She can get a J-1 and come for the summer.

Marianne *(sings, to the tune of 'I Should Be So Lucky')* 'I should be so lucky, with my rubber ducky, strangle Mrs Mangle too ...'

Erin   See? Sorted.

Orla   Someone got up on the right side of bed this morning.

Erin   D'you know I just woke up and thought: it's my birthday! And for once the sun was shining and I suddenly thought of Mum, and when we were kids, and it was like the sunshine was this message from her, like – anything is possible?

Orla	You're shining with it. And you, Marianne, you always look well in yourself. And Andy would if only he'd lose some weight, God, I hate to say it but he's piling on the pounds and it does nothing for him. But who am I to talk, you'd think I was forty I look that haggard. But no you're right – here we are, I mean we've made it through a whole year – the sun is shining and for once my headache's gone. And you have to remember: everything that happens, happens for a reason.

Pause.

And one of these days I'll meet the love of my life.

Baron	I'm sorry, but that's complete and utter bollocks. *(Calling in.)* Can we come in yet?
Erin	No. Hang on.

The sisters put the finishing touches to their costumes.

Erin	OK. Yous can come in. Ta-daa!

Baron, Beattie and Simon enter.

Beattie	Ach will you look at you.
Erin	Do you like it?
Baron	You look beautiful, Erin.
Erin	Who are you meant to be?

Baron	Who am I meant to be? Can you not tell?
Simon	Fail, mate. Epic fail.
Baron	'This is the final cruise of the Starship Enterprise under my command, boldly going where no man … where no one has gone before.' I thought you'd appreciate that, Erin.
Simon	No girl in the history of girls has ever been turned on by *Star Trek*.
Baron	Shut up, Simon.
Marianne	That, for the record, is sexist.
Simon	Whatever, goth-girl. You haven't made much of an effort, have you?
Marianne	I don't do fancy dress.
Erin	She needs to get over herself! And here, why aren't you in fancy dress?
Beattie	Oh, I'm too old for that sort of stuff-and-nonsense.
Erin	Uncle Beattie!
Orla	We've got a bag of stuff here. You can have a mask.
Erin	And who are you?
Simon	Oh, this isn't my costume. You want to see my costume?

Baron	Are you actually going to take that coat off now? He's had it on all afternoon. All the way here.

Simon	Get ready …

Simon starts to unbutton his overcoat.

Beattie sings the first few lines of 'Button Up Your Overcoat'.

Simon	What the fuck is that, man?

Beattie	That, son, is before your time.

Simon	Well enough of the soundtrack, OK, are you ready?

He whips off his overcoat. He's wearing his full army combat gear.

Baron	What are you doing, man? Are you fucking insane?

Simon	I don't need no superhero costume. So I've come as … myself.

Baron	If anyone saw you … You could've got yourself killed. You could've got us both killed.

Simon	Not scared of anyone, mate. Bring it on.

Erin	You've come as yourself?

Simon	I know you like a man in uniform.

Baron	You are insane.

Simon	Take a chill pill, Spock.

Baron   I'm not Spock, I'm Captain Kirk.

Simon   So court-martial me, Captain Kirk. Sir.

Baron   Whatever. Happy birthday, Erin.

Orla   Yes, happy birthday, Erin. Now who wants a drink?

Beattie   Yes please.

Orla   Not you.

Erin   Me!

Baron   I forgot to say! There's this new honcho at the barracks, some kind of special adviser, ex-military, says he knew your father. Said he'd stop by this evening, if that's alright, pay his respects.

He picks up an acoustic guitar and starts strumming.

Erin   Is he old?

Baron   Not particularly. I'd say he's … fifty?

He strums the guitar.

Erin   Oh God. That's ancient. What's he like?

Baron   Seems OK. Talks an awful lot though. His wife. His mother-in-law. His two little girls. The fact that his wife's actually his second wife. Oh, and did I mention he talks about his wife and his two little girls?

He sings the opening lines of Teenage Fanclub, 'What You Do To Me'.

She's a complete psycho, apparently. Waltzes around like she's walked off *Little House on the Prairie*, these big long shapeless things and her hair in plaits, and bangs on about 'the male gaze'. And she's always threatening to top herself, just to wind him up. Christ, if it was me I'd have run a mile, but he stays and feels sorry for himself.

Beattie (*reading his newspaper*) Here's one for you, son. They reckon they've got a new cure for baldness.

Simon Fuck off.

Beattie Says here they take the individual hair follicles from your chest and graft them one by one –

Simon I'll graft you if you don't put a sock in it.

Erin (*to Simon*) You leave him be. (*To Beattie*) Here, Uncle Beattie!

Beattie Yes, wee pet?

Erin Why do I feel so happy today? It's like – I'm flying. Flying through a high, blue sky, and not a cloud in sight …

Beattie You're a wee sunbeam so you are.

Erin As soon as I woke up it was all so clear – like someone had blown the cobwebs away – today is the start of the rest of your life. I don't know what it is

I'm going to do but I'm going to do something. I'm going to be someone. I am! I'm sick of just being me. I'm going to be someone else. Someone better. I'm going to make a difference. I'm being serious!

Beattie   I know you are, wee pet.

Orla   Dad had us up at the skrake of dawn each day, as if we were in the cadets. Erin still wakes up first thing, but then she lies in bed for hours having epiphanies. Look at her. She's deadly serious.

Erin   Am I not allowed to be serious? You have to stop treating me like a wee girl, Orla.

Baron   I hear you, Erin. You know the way I grew up in The Braids –

Erin   We know.

Baron   In 'one of the finest examples of Georgian architecture in the city' my mother always used to say. Such a cold and stuck-up place. See my family – there's not one of them would give you the steam off their piss if you were on fire. I remember my mother sacked the housekeeper once for daring to tell me off. I'd tramped mud all through the house and when she asked me to take off my boots I chucked them at her. Can you believe it? They thought Sandhurst was a fad, my family – they didn't think I'd last a week. But they were wrong! People can change. People can start again. Just look at this place. A year ago – six months ago – who'd've believed it?

111

Beattie   Not me, son.

Baron   You don't count.

Simon   He's talking about the new generation, mate. You – you're basically wormfood. How much do you smoke? Forty a day? You'll have a massive stroke one of these days – wormfood. If I don't snap first and put a bullet in your brain.

Simon spritzes himself with Cool Water fragrance.

Beattie   Well, at least I'll be of use to the worms.

The doorbell goes.

Oh-ho! That'll be for me. I won't be a minute. *(To Erin.)* Don't you move a muscle!

Erin   What's he at?

Baron   I'd say … maybe … he's got a certain someone … a birthday present.

Erin   Oh God, do you think so?

Orla   It's always something totally dodgy.

Marianne sings the opening lines of The Velvet Underground, 'Pale Blue Eyes'.

Orla   What's up with you?

Marianne sings.
She gets up suddenly.

Orla   Where are you off to?

Marianne   'Home'.

Erin   Marianne!

Baron   It's Erin's birthday, you can't just leave.

Marianne   Whatever ... I'm sorry, hun, you don't want me
               bringing you down. I'll come back later. I just
               need to –

Erin   Why does everything always have to be about you?
               The earth doesn't revolve around you, you know.

Orla   *(to Marianne)* On you go then. What are you waiting
               for? I'd swan off if I could. Unfortunately someone
               needs to stay here and keep things going.

Erin   Wise up, you two!

Simon   What's the difference between a pussy and a cunt? A
               pussy's warm and soft, a cunt's what owns it.

Marianne   You are a fucking disgrace, you know that?

Simon   Takes one to know one!

Marianne   *(to Orla)* And you, stop being such a fucking mar-
               tyr.

113

Orla   Seriously. I'm this close. I'm warning you.

She leaves.
Beattie comes in with a box and unpacks a set of Tyrone crystal: a decanter and goblets.

Erin   Oh my God.

Baron   I told you …

Marianne What the fuck is he thinking? It's her birthday, not her wedding day.

Beattie My wee pets, the three of yous are all I have in the world. I remember, Erin, when you were just a few weeks old. I didn't want to hold you for fear I'd break you. When your mother, God rest her, put this wee scrap of a thing in my arms I couldn't even breathe. 'Don't,' says I. 'You'll be grand,' says she. Oh, it could have been yesterday.

Erin   You really shouldn't have.

Beattie Ach get away with you.

Erin   No but I mean – seriously. It's too much.

Beattie Too much! Nothing's too much for my wee Erin on her eighteenth birthday. Besides, I got it at a good price: a friend did me a deal.

Marianne And did this friend of yours get it off the back of a lorry?

Beattie   What are you implying?

Erin   No offence, Uncle Beattie, but what am I supposed to do with a crystal whatchamacallit?

Beattie   Well I shall take it away this minute, then.

On Writing *Three Sisters*

Lucy Caldwell

The Moscow Question

I don't remember how or when I became obsessed with *Three Sisters*.

I do remember when I first came across it. I was in my second year at university, taking some playwriting master classes with the Scottish playwright Chris Hannan. He read a scene from Act IV with us, the scene where Tuzenbach realises that Irina doesn't, will *never*, love him, to illustrate a point about dramatic subtext. It was my first introduction to Chekhov. I dutifully read the whole play through – and didn't think much of it. The characters, with their names and nicknames and patronymics, were too hard to keep track of. Nothing much seemed to happen.

And yet.

Over the next few months, and years, something strange happened. The play had got under my skin. I read it again, then again. I went to see a production of it, which left me unsatisfied. I read the rest of Chekhov's plays, bought a collection of his short stories. I saw a second production, a third. To date, I've seen *Three Sisters* more than a dozen times, more than any other play. Contemporary versions, classic versions, Russian-language versions. Mustapha Matura's relocation to colonial Trinidad; Diane Samuels and Tracy-Ann Oberman's *Three Sisters on Hope Street* in post-war Liverpool. On my shelves are versions by Frank McGuinness and Brian Friel, by Michael Frayn, Samuel

Adamson, Benedict Andrews, though my favourite remains Elisaveta Fen's Penguin Classics version from the 1950s, that first volume I bought in the second-hand bookshop, aged nineteen.

I struggle to this day to articulate exactly why it might be that *Three Sisters* became such a lodestone for me. I'm one of three sisters myself, so there's that. It might be something to do with longing: *Three Sisters* is the best play I know about yearning; dreaming of the place – the people – where and with whom you more truly belong. It's the play that comes closest to articulating what it means to live in and to be bound by time: how we all spend our time waiting for our true life to start, until, ground down and suffocated by the tedium of everyday life, we realise that it has already happened, long ago.

It's the play that seemed to chime most clearly with what it was like growing up in 1990s Belfast: the turmoil, the tedium, the restlessness, the resentment, the desperate desire to get away, to be somewhere, anywhere but here, now.

I don't remember when I first idly thought or talked about writing my own version of the play. At first, I wrote a draft of the first act in which the characters, with their original Russian names and patronymics, use samovars and talk of going to Moscow, but in Belfast accents. It would work, I reasoned with myself, because we would understand that 'Moscow' was a symbolic rather than an actual destination. It didn't work.

To be true to the play, I needed to be much truer to my new setting. I spent a long time pondering where my characters should want to go. Dublin? London? 'The mainland'? And then it came to me.

In my teenage years, we talked incessantly about going to 'America'. We didn't know what we meant. It was partly the famous Hollywood sign, partly the yellow cabs in *Friends*; part *Sweet Valley High* and space rockets launching from Cape Canaveral and fast food and Disney World and MTV. It was the *Fresh Prince of Bel-Air* and swimming with dolphins. It wasn't a real place, but an idea, an idealisation. I rewrote Act I, giving the characters their own names and letting them dream of 'America', and it started to fall into place.

Other Things

You think you know a play. Then you climb inside it.

I'd recently become a mother when I wrote my version; I understood in a way that I never had before the sisters' grief for their mother. The more recent anniversary of their father's death starts the play, but the deeper truth is that they are motherless children. Of course they can't move on. They are steamrollered by grief, unable to leave the place where she is buried, unable to come to terms with her loss.

I could tell you about the revelation whereby Kulygin became DJ Cool, or how I unlocked the function of Chebutykin/Beattie, or about how, after choosing 'Pale Blue Eyes' as Marianne's song – which contains the line 'thought of you as my mountaintop' – I discovered that the meaning of 'Vershinin' *is* 'mountaintop' in Russian.

The joys of adaptation are the serendipities, synchronicities, that let you know you're on the right track: the moments where it seems the playwright is right there, enjoying it as much as you are.

Chekhovian Language

A Russian scholar at a dinner warned me that the play very rarely works in English. A typical Russian toast, he said, might go along the lines of: 'You are my dearest friend and I want you to know how much I love and esteem you.' This just doesn't translate into English, reserved and ironic and understated as it tends to be.

I think we misuse the term 'Chekhovian language', using it as a shorthand for languid, restrained, wistful; taking our cues from the Edwardian English of the first translations, or the melancholy poetry of the 1950s versions. The play in Russian is dense, muscular, charged. There is a wild strain of melancholy but the pain is raw and the ugliness of the characters' selfish motives and behaviours is not veiled. Chekhov is not crumpled linen suits and Panama hats, genteel disillusion. In setting my version in nineties Belfast, I had to be true to nineties Belfast. Being faithful to the spirit is far more important than plodding along to the letter.

'Aha,' I said to the Russian scholar, 'it might not work in English-English, but it works in *Belfast*-English: I fucken love you mate, you're sound as a pound.'

Actors' Instincts I

Actors' instincts are one of your greatest assets as a playwright. In the literal translation I worked from, by Helen Rappaport, there is a note towards the end of the play, in Masha's final speech. Originally, the speech included some extra lines, which were cut at the request of the actress Olga Knipper, later Chekhov's wife. 'Above us (are) migrating birds,' she says, harking back to her speech in Act II about the need to have faith in *something*. 'They have been flying every spring and autumn for thousands of years already, and do not know why, but they fly and will go on flying for a long, long (time) – many thousands of years – until, finally, God reveals (his) secrets/mysteries to them ...' I read this and thought: how beautiful, and scribbled a note to myself to reinstate the passage. But of course when voiced, at that particular moment in the play, it is far too much: too sentimental, too saccharine. Olga Knipper was completely right: more so than Chekhov himself.

Actors' Instincts II

The Olivier-award winning actress Denise Gough tells of a time in drama school when her year were studying *Three Sisters*. Having long blonde hair, she was cast as Irina, when she desperately wanted to play Natasha. She went home that night and shaved off her hair: came in the next morning and said, 'Now can I play Natasha?'

I started my version of the play most interested in the sisters, but little by little, Natasha took hold of me. In most versions, as in the original, she is cast as a girl of a lower social class, to whom the sisters are disdainful and snobbish. A hundred years on, the corollary of internal, class-based social upheaval seemed to me to be immigration. I loved the idea that while the sisters endlessly talk about moving across the world and starting their lives again, right under their noses is someone who has done just that, who has arrived in the country barely speaking any English and by the end of the play is fluent. Someone who has made sacrifices, put up with great hardship and is getting by and getting on with things, keeping a household together, raising a family. Natasha – in my version Siu Jing, a Cantonese-speaker from Hong Kong – is how we measure time in the play. She is also the future of the country: her mixed-race children hint at a much-needed plurality in generations to come.

It took many rewrites to get the balance right, but over successive drafts it became clear to me that Siu Jing was the heart of the play, and I ended by writing her a Prologue, *The Glass Menagerie*-style, in which the whole play is framed as her memory. 'These are not yet my sisters,' she says, 'but they soon will be', and 'It might not have my name on it, but this is my story, too.'

Tech, Dress, Previews

There is a saying in theatre that the worse the dress rehearsal, the better the first performance. Due to a swathe of technical problems with the ambitious set, our dress rehearsals were cancelled, and we ended up running the play just once, finishing – I want to write minutes, but it must have been longer – before the curtain was due to go up for the first preview. Everyone, actors, designers and technical crew, had been worked up to the line and right down to the bone. Early calls and all-nighters, missed meals, tempers flaring: in this toxic mix it was hard not to see the set's refusal to lift – as it was supposed to at the end of Act III, the whole frame of the house rising up into the sky – if not as an omen, at least as a sign that something was badly wrong. And the first preview was a disaster. It was a Saturday night, the opening weekend of the Belfast Festival, and almost every single seat in the auditorium was sold. Including, as it transpired, a row of seats that didn't exist: the design of the play had removed Row A so that the stage could jut forward. There was confusion as people tried to find seats that weren't there, or sat in the first row anyway, or argued with each other and with the ushers frantically trying to sort things out, moving people who'd deliberately booked a front row seat up to the back or into the slips. The curtain went up late, and whilst the actors and audience made a brave attempt at keeping the energy up and staying attentive, by the second half everything was dragging almost to a standstill.

It was the most excruciating experience of my life. It's a funny thing; you write draft after draft of a play, editing and tightening it; have read-throughs and weeks of rehearsal; and yet it's only when you're watching the play in front of an audience that you finally see clearly what needs to be done, and you understand it at the speed of light. For this reason I forbid family members and friends from seeing a play of mine in preview, and if I happen to attend a play at the start of the run, I try to see it again, later on, as it's inevitably a different thing entirely. That night and the next, white-faced and sick to the stomach, I cut almost half an hour from the play. It was too easy to try to blame the circumstances, to make excuses: the script was the thing and it just wasn't good enough.

But a matinee, two more previews and, crucially, a rest day later, it felt like a new and mercifully different play. The technical problems were ironed out, the cuts were energising and the actors were growing in confidence. I poured a libation of vodka onto the stage and invoked the spirit of Chekhov to be with us: we were as ready as we'd ever be for Press Night.

Crritic!

In *Waiting for Godot* (the only play I've ever acted in as an adult, but that's a whole other story) Vladimir and Estragon are trading insults. 'Moron!' Vladimir begins, to which Estragon replies, 'Vermin!' It goes on until Estragon, 'with finality', as the stage directions have it, declares, 'Crritic!' At this poor Vladimir, rendered speechless, wilts and turns away, utterly defeated.

I felt a bright, sharp kinship with Samuel Beckett as the reviews for *Three Sisters* came in. Reviews don't matter so much for a book; they're like paper-cuts, stinging for a moment then quickly forgotten. A book is essentially finished by the time the reviews come out, and the author has moved on, too, in the likely time lag of a year or more between delivering the manuscript and publication. But a play is a living, breathing thing and a vicious review can kill it. Audiences depleted, and with low expectations; actors exhausted by the demands of opening and suddenly belittled and demoralised: sometimes it feels as if you're seeing something bleed to death in front of you.

My *Three Sisters* garnered the whole gamut of reviews: the raves tended to be from younger critics, especially those immersed in the world of theatre and familiar with the work of Chekhov. Those from the Belfast-based critics were often of a shamefully low standard; the worst of them streaked with a viciousness and vindictiveness that should have no place in arts criticism.

It was some little solace to recall Chekhov's own experience of having his plays first staged. When *The Seagull* premiered in October 1896, the reception could not have been worse: the catcalls and derision were deafening. Chekhov pleaded with the theatre to cancel the rest of the play's run and then walked out into the night, vowing never to write a play again. 'The theatre breathed malice,' he later wrote to a friend. 'The air was compressed with hatred, and in accordance with the laws of physics, I was thrown out of St Petersburg like a bomb.' Two years later, the play had been belatedly hailed as a work of genius. Nevertheless, when the Moscow Art Theatre opened the much-anticipated *Three Sisters* in

January 1901, the enthusiastic curtain calls that greeted the end of Act I had dwindled to almost nothing by the end of the play. The critics (*plus ça change*) griped that the wealthy sisters should have just gone to Moscow.

Selina Cartmell's production of *Three Sisters* was stark and stylised and intensely lonely, not to everyone's taste. But what gave us all courage and hope was that young people loved it: gasped and roared with laughter, applauded hard. The best nights were when we had groups of sixth formers or students in: the difference in the energy of the play was palpable. It has been great consolation since to hear from undergraduates and MA students who went to see it three, four times; who are writing their theses on it, or taking audition speeches from it; and to receive emails from acquaintances who had utterly understood it.

> *It occurred to me watching it that both our parents and our younger siblings were born in peace time. We're quite unique as a generation because we were born into a war without realising it and we couldn't hear the helicopters in the sky because we were so used to them, and we listened to Ash and didn't realise why it made us sad. It really moved me and I'm so grateful your play was able to articulate something about our generation.*

A play is a peculiarly public humiliation: when you retire to nurse your wounds and your ego and wonder if you will ever write again, this is the salve; this is what keeps you going; this, and the slim chance, though faintest of hopes, that someday, somewhere, the play will have another life, another chance.

To America

When *Three Sisters* opened, I felt I'd never write another play again. By the time it closed, I knew that if I didn't start one straightaway I'd lose my nerve and never would. By coincidence, or maybe not by coincidence at all, within a week of getting back to London I had a conversation with an actor and dramaturge who told me to set something outside of Belfast. 'The play you're describing is tugging to be set in America,' he said, and just like that, something inside of me was unlocked and I went home and started sketching out some scenes with contemporary American characters, set on the East Coast. Critics, readers, tend to talk about your work in terms of common ground and recurring themes; but often one piece of work is written in defiance or in opposition to another; snooker balls spiralling. With *Three Sisters* and with its sister-work, *Multitudes* (2016), written at the same time and coming from the same place in the psyche, I've said all that I have to say, for the moment at least, about Belfast and about growing up there in the 1990s. There is a wry aptness, too, in going to America: the place my Orla, Marianne and Erin long to get to, the place they'll never reach.

In the final days of the run, Donald Trump was elected as the new President of the USA. I emailed the actors: *URGENT SCRIPT CHANGE. To Canada. To Australia. To Ulan Bator. To anywhere, anywhere else.*

Hearing the last performances of the play, the sisters' dreams of America and entreaties to each other to go, let's go, what's stopping us, felt bittersweet indeed. They are trapped there, in 1990s Belfast, but in writing them, I realised that it's time to move on.

The Forgotten

Anne Devlin

The Forgotten *was originally performed on BBC Radio 4 on 16 January 2009 and it was directed by Heather Larmour. The full cast was as follows:*

Bee	Ger Ryan
The Forgotten	George Harris
Thea	Gemma Reeves
Anthony	Sean Campion
Examiner	Peter Balance
Granny May	Stella McCusker
Mary Russell	Fo Cullen
Doctor	Kieran Lagan

Act One, Scene One: Interior of a Bedroom

FX: Snibs of a small suitcase opening.

Bee   When you travel in the mountains in snow,
                          the blood wagon is a red rug on a stretcher and
                          it's carried by two skiers down the mountain
                          and wrapped in this rug is the injured party.
                          Then the tumbling whiteout follows you and
                          overtakes you and you can only see the jacket
                          of the person in front whose track you are fol-
                          lowing and there's the sound of a great animal
                          roaring at your back and you don't know if
                          this great moaning creature will magnify your
                          steady focus or gather you up into a whiteout
                          from which you'll never emerge.

Thea (V/O)   **That's my aunt Bee's first letter to me
                          from abroad. She sent me postcards
                          when I was little but this was the first
                          letter.**

                          **Her frequent appearances either by
                          mail or in person fostered in me a
                          desire: I wanted Aunt Bee's life.
                          BEAT
                          Then something strange happened – it
                          was as if she forgot about us for a long
                          time. And then to my grandmother's
                          great relief Aunt Bee got in touch with
                          her brother.**

Act One, Scene Two: Interior of a Café

Fx: Settling at table

Anthony	Bee, how are you?
Bee	Great. And yourself?
Anthony	Not too bad.
Bee	Which country are you in? Are you here now?
Anthony	Yes, I'm here now for a while now. Anything to drink?
Bee	I'll have water.
Anthony	Me too. I have to keep a clear head. Why did you not want to meet at the other place?
Bee	Because when I walked in the chair attacked me. And I didn't want to meet in a place where even the furniture was against me.
Anthony	Is that what it feels like?
Bee	Yes. I've never understood what it is that you do. I hope you are not angry with me about that.
FX:	**Sound of water bottles being placed on the table and poured**

Anthony   I'm not angry with you.

Bee   But you see, when we meet it's usually to do with family matters so I never really catch up with your career.

Anthony   Nor I with yours.

Bee   Well, I've slowed down.

Anthony   What are you working on?

Bee   Oh, large mice and water rats mainly.

Anthony   I have got a bit fed up in the past with the big sister act that you do. And I have found that a bit patronising.

Bee   I'm sorry. I really am.

Anthony   I think you don't value what I do.

Bee   It's not that. I don't understand money – I never have. You work for a bank isn't that right?

Anthony   That was three years ago.

Bee   Oh, I keep losing time. Three years was a few months ago. Everything is hurtling very fast. Hours seem like minutes.

Anthony   It's called ageing.

Bee	I need to ask you for help. I'd like to go home, but I need to borrow money from you to pay for my removal costs.
Anthony	You're going back?
Bee	Yes, I always intended to. I just hadn't expected it would happen like this. I told you I've got slower and I just haven't been able to finish my commissions as quickly as I used to. So …
Anthony	Of course I'll help you. How much do you need? Would you like a cheque or a bank draft?
Bee V/O	**I look over Anthony's shoulder to the mirror wall behind; I see a woman who has folded her hands across her mouth like a gothic arch; if I was playing poker I would lose.**
Anthony	If you're going home you must live with mother and Thea.
Bee	That's what I was hoping.
Anthony	Well, you know, Bee, perhaps you could help me. I'm worried about Thea. She seems to be without ambition.
Bee	What does she want to do?

Anthony	She wants to do what you do. Maybe you could talk to her.
Thea (V/O)	**Uncle Anthony was born when Bee was seventeen.** **Forty years before. And he sighed over her and rescued her. And he was clever. He knew that I would know he rescued Bee, and therefore being an artist was being a loser. He so wanted me not to do what Bee did and he would use her against me simply by example.**
Anthony	You want to be like your aunt? She's a car crash.
Thea (V/O)	**I needed Bee to exceed his expectations of her achievement. For my sake. My grandmother sent me to bring her home. We travelled by ferry. It was a slow jour-ney – even so, she communicated very little of her state of mind to me.**

Act One, Scene Three: Exterior, On board a Ferry

Fx: The open deck of a car ferry in the Lough, a hum of ships' engines and the intermittent chorus of gulls.

Bee (V/O)	**Passing the reclaimed land at the har-bour where all the containers are kept – containers on container island. I am about to say to the young one who is**

standing beside me: 'That's what happens to your life if you fail.' But I don't say this in case I rob her spirit of joy.

Bee   Is Anthony still doing that job for the bank, Thea?

Thea   I don't know. He says they gave him a golden parachute – whatever that means.

Bee   A sail would be better.

Bee (V/O)   It wasn't as if my conditions were enviable. My house gone, life split, child lost; and the books I'd collected since I was nineteen packed into sixty boxes. How many boxes to hold a life? In the end, I use three hundred.

I once asked the external examiner before my teaching came to an end: 'What's the difference between sleep and coma', at high table in my last spring term. He's annoyed – I have taken advantage of his expertise – but answers honestly.

External Examiner   In sleep the brain is resting; in coma, it's fighting for survival.

Bee (V/O)   How did I get to this place of coma, of my life in three hundred boxes?

Act One, Scene Four: Interior of a Bedroom

Granny May	Didn't she used to drink? Now she touches not a drop.
Thea	Uncle Anthony says she would drink and attack people's most deeply held beliefs…
Granny May	Aye … if you remind her now … she looks like someone who's bumped into you in the dark … What are all these boxes?
Thea	Notebooks.
Granny May	We should read them. That way we'll find out what's been goin' on in her life …
Thea (V/O)	**My grandmother and I helped her to get the room ready; it took us three days; we put in the clock she'd heard as a child. I thought it would help her come back to herself. But when we were unpacking, she looked distressed.**

Act One, Scene 5: Interior of a Bedroom

Fx: Clock ticking.

Thea	What's wrong, Aunt Bee?

Bee	I have a case of clothes that I don't recognise among my luggage – good clothes, but not my size. I would never wear that colour. And where on earth did this pattern come from?
Thea (V/O)	**She is holding up a sheath of cloth which immediately made me think of India.**
Thea	Were you a hippy, Aunt Bee?
Bee	I might have been.

FX: Chimes. Seven.

Bee	Oh. I remember this clock. It has a lovely tone. Is it seven o'clock already?
Thea	No. It rings seven at five – don't know why. It's never been fixed.
Bee	I'm so relieved to be home.
Granny May	Well, we're glad to have you. Stay as long as you need.
Thea (V/O)	**Aunt Bee looked at my grandmother for a long time after she said that.**
Granny May	Have I said something wrong?
Bee (surprised)	No.

Bee V/O	**It's amazing how having no money makes you feel invisible.**

Act One, Scene 6: Interior of a Bank

FX: Interior of a Bank/External City Traffic.

Bee	Excuse me, you keep sending me notices. They're charges for unauthorised payments but I haven't made any payments. In fact, I haven't written a cheque for two years. I … I don't know what these sums are: £150, £130.
Bank Teller	You took a loan and you undertook to repay it. It's irresponsible of you to run out of funds.
Bee	I haven't run out of funds. I simply haven't been paid for a while and I'm working as fast as I can. The money is owed to me.
Teller	(*Sighs.*) What is it you do again?
Bee	I'm self-employed. I exist on commissions. At the moment I'm designing a set for the theatre. But I haven't finished. So I have a cheque here to cover the loan.
Teller	Where did you get this cheque?
Bee	My brother. The problem is – if you add these unauthorised bank charges – I have

two here – the cheque won't cover the loan any more. And I don't know what these two cheques are for.

Teller   Storage? Does that ring a bell?

Bee   (*Pause.*) Yes, it does. I remember now. I … I've spoken to you by telephone about it and I promised to get it sorted, and here I am with the cheque, so will you please stop adding these charges?

Teller   I can't stop them. It's a machine.

Bee   But you are escalating the overdraft. It's making my situation worse. I'll come back tomorrow with another cheque.

Teller   I'm on holiday tomorrow.

Bee   Can't you delegate?

Teller   It's a computer which makes the decisions.

Bee   Can't you turn the computer off?

Teller   Excuse me, madam, would you like to step away from the counter? You are making a scene and distressing the customers.

Bee   I'm a customer and I'm distressed!

Act One, Scene 7: Exterior, in a Park

Bee (shouting) (Sounds like an animal in pain.)

Bee	(*Shouting into a tree.*) I hate them. I hate them all. Thieves! Criminals! Bankers!

FX: Leaves blow off a tree. Someone rolls out from under it and stands up.
The creature is covered in autumn leaves.

The Forgotten	Hey, hey, whoa, take it easy now.
Bee	I have to tell you that is not a good look.
The Forgotten	Your shouting woke me up.
Bee	I thought I was alone.
The Forgotten	You've never been alone. I'm everything you refuse to say.
Bee	I don't refuse to say much. That's the trouble.
The Forgotten	Ah. But I am those thoughts you hide even from yourself. And uh, congratulations! Very few people ever get to see me.
Bee	What did I do to deserve this attention?
The Forgotten	You created me.
Bee	How?

The Forgotten	Everything you forgot joins up with everything else you forgot. That is who I am. I am The Forgotten.
Bee	Can anyone else see you?
The Forgotten	Not in so many words.
Bee	Good, because my mother and my niece are coming straight for us down that path.
The Forgotten	Well, climb into my branches if you want to avoid them. Here.

FX: Rustling as he lowers a limb which she climbs onto.

Bee	It's years since I climbed a tree. Can I go higher?
The Forgotten	The higher, the better.
Bee	I'm afraid I've disturbed the robins.
The Forgotten	Settle down and they'll come back.
Bee	It's a bit like getting on a horse. There's even a place for my feet.
The Forgotten	If you go higher there's a stout branch you can sit along and you can even rest your back against the trunk.
Bee	This is high enough.

The Forgotten Come on now, trust me. You see that U shape? You can even sit in that.

Bee Oh alright.

FX: Climbs into the tree further.

Bee Oh my goodness. I can see the sea!

Waking The Forgotten

Anne Devlin

Theatre is always about embodiment. Musicians have their instruments, actors have their bodies. Radio is the antithesis of this, because radio is about the voice alone; we are listening in the dark with our eyes closed. Radio is the perfect form for flight, or placelessness, as a recent study of the radio plays of Anglo-Irish writers states: 'the radio body is open to endless iterations and imaginings.'[1]

I began as a dramatist in radio in the 1980s with *The Long March* (Faber, 1984) because my plays agent Peggy Ramsay believed it solved the business of getting people on and off stage without having to think up entry and exit lines. She regarded radio as a training for theatre. I love the sonic resonance and dramatic intimacy that only radio provides. On my return to Belfast after thirty years in England, Heather Larmour at the BBC asked me if I had an idea for radio. I sat down and wrote a treatment and dated it 25 September 2007:

The Forgotten
A woman tells of a dream in which she witnesses the collapse of the city: it ends with the image of a woman and her child in a desolate landscape of mudflats waiting at a bus stop.

The dream is a premonition of her loss of society and her isolation. As her alarming lapses of memory lead to her loss of home and

---

1. Emily C. Bloom, *The Wireless Past* (Oxford: Oxford University Press, 2016), p. 143.

career, her original family bring her home to live with them. In the company of an ageing parent whom she believes she is there to care for, she attempts to hide her own advanced Alzheimer symptoms. Misunderstandings abound until one day, shouting into a tree in the park, she meets a creature called The Forgotten. The play is a conversation with The Forgotten in which she begins to suspect that she is not suffering from dementia …

Unusually, the title arrived with the treatment, which presented itself like a little story. The main inspiration came from an encounter in a park in Ealing in August 2006, twelve months before I returned to Belfast. I had worked at Ealing Studios as a screenwriter on *Titanic Town* (Faber, 1998), so perhaps there is a spectral afterlife to these films. It was the seventh anniversary of my father's death and in distress on the phone to someone at home, I had run down into the park to shout under a really big tree. During those years we had all lived in a telephonic landscape and experienced the diaspora as unembodied. Under a tree in west London, the aircraft hangar sets of Ealing Studios in the distance, I stood there shouting and waking the forgotten. I let out a series of expletives under that leafy canopy. My glance was snared by a movement at the other side of the tree and I realised I had disturbed someone's meditation. Mortified, I fled from the scene.

When I returned a whole week later to examine the place where I caused the disturbance, I found that several of the trees had little brass plates beneath them, one of which stated, 'This tree was planted in honour of the first black foster parents in England.' Nearer the studios, I found a garden which was created by the Caribbean Windrush generation to mark their arrival in Britain in June 1948. I went home and wrote the opening snatch of conversation with The Forgotten, visualising him detaching from the tree like a figure of fallen leaves rolling up and stretching out in front of me, like Percy Bysshe Shelley's image of thoughts as fallen leaves. I even wrote down the line: *I'm all the thoughts you've forgotten.* And this inspirational encounter would survive as written from the first two-hour script to the final draft of 56 minutes 37 seconds. (Except for the expletives, which were softened because you cannot say 'fuck' on Radio 4. You can in Drama on Radio 3, because then it is literature.) Heather Larmour's role in responding to my first draft was crucial to its arrival at transmission. Her immediate observation was that while the thoughts were detached from the tree in the form of fallen leaves, it was the tree who was talking.

Like *The Long March* (first produced in 1982), my stage plays are known for being historically rooted: *Ourselves Alone* (1985), *After Easter* (1994). They are and remain history plays. I had become a writer, a dramatist, while living in England. So I wasn't standing in front of the material. If I had any impetus it was to recreate something that was missing – what I have called an acoustic landscape. When family illness forced me to return to live again in Belfast in 2007, it wasn't possible for me to go on writing in the way I had before. I had no dream space, no distance. Therefore I had to remove the social context and the dates, and the real names of the place to soften the impact, in order to write *The Forgotten*. Another aspect of the treatment was a dream I had in 2006, of a woman and child on the mudflats witnessing the collapse of 'the city'. In fact, the dream preceded the financial collapse of 2008. So in the play Bee comes to grief financially and has to go home and live in her mother's house.

During the period of writing the play in 2008 I was living in Belfast and attending meetings of a group called the Civil Rights Commemoration Committee. We were looking at 1968 forty years on. It was a way of revisiting and understanding the strands of politics that fed into the CR movement, and why it had failed. In the US the Civil Rights Movement is a broad-based civilising force. In Northern Ireland the Civil Rights Movement is seen as divisive and partisan. But that is not all that is being withheld: this collapse of time, history, and place, the unnamed city, resulted in a more poetical play than I would have normally written.

The Forgotten was also a conversation with my dead father. I had turned to psychoanalysis sometime during the nineties and it was beginning to play out in this piece. It was Jacques Lacan's influence: what you forget is more significant that what you remember. Because of course 'it', 'the forgotten,' becomes you. It is controlling your actions, unbeknownst to you. So you have to remember in order to regain control.

My personal experience of diaspora and that of the Windrush Generation became entwined; visible to me only as I was leaving England. I felt in returning to my native city I had to keep faith with them. There were in 2007 no representatives of the Windrush Generation in the North I returned to. I came from a society that couldn't tolerate difference. So when we came to casting, I knew the voice of The Forgotten was that of an Afro-Caribbean man. And then other things confirmed this strand for me: I discovered there was a tree of forgetting which slaves planted at the spot where they were abducted from the west coast of Africa.

The problem with not naming the place is that Heather had a lot of work to do in casting. She cast southern Irish voices for the family, with the exception of Granny May, played by Stella McCusker, who is a Northerner. This neatly reverses my actual family history. My mother is Dublin-born, while we, her children, were all born in Belfast. Ger Ryan played Bee, while the young Theadora was played by Gemma Reeves. Sean Campion played the brother, Anthony. And the film actor George Harris played The Forgotten. I think he represented what I most feared losing on my return to Northern Ireland: the multiculturalism of the place I was leaving. I felt it would also be a radio challenge: a reminder that appearance comes to us via sound as well.

In order to get beyond race, you have to take account of race. I inserted gender to lead in this borrowed sentence when I repeated it at Liberty Hall, alongside class and religion, at a 'Waking the

Feminists' event on International Women's Day in March 2016. In Northern Ireland 'sectarianism' is cited as taking precedence over race and everything else in the obstacles to be overcome. In my view racism precedes sectarianism. We are of course talking about identity and attacks on identity. In the case of female playwrights this is two-fold: the exclusion of women dramatists' mature vision from the theatre and to justify this exclusion, a retrospective cleansing of the canon occurs, and the work is allowed to go out of print, nothing is revived, and the playwright is forgotten.

I went on record recently explaining the dismaying process of what happens to the first drafts of women's plays. I quoted Fishamble Theatre's pioneering research, which showed that while more women entered the theatre with their scripts, more men emerged with a production. This means that we have to look at the development process: the ones which get it right. In BBC radio drama this process involved a one-to-one, not with a script editor, but with the producer/director. In radio they are the same person, whereas in theatre, film and TV they are separate entities. So my most important relationship when working on *The Forgotten* was with Heather.

'Christ, the things they do to one's work (just chop it and sugar it, and cut out the points and write in their own crudities),' writes Louis MacNeice in 1941 about the BBC.[2]

This did not happen to me – Heather Larmour did not write a line in the script. What she did was ask vital questions. I looked at the breakthrough third draft, and this time on the opening page Heather makes a red digital intervention following Thea's line, '*She sent me postcards but this is the first letter.*' Heather asked: 'Is below a series of voice-overs or are they talking to each other in a room?' And again in the next section, where I have simply planted the dialogue, she asks: 'Is there a setting for this dialogue, are they in the car on the way home?'

---

2. Ibid., p. 67.

In other words, she attempted to earth my flights of language. I was forced to place the dialogue on a ferry in Belfast Lough. I had to place the action in a real location, even if the play was for radio. And from this note, the challenge of the next draft was to give the place where they all were living in time a definite characteristic. The location becomes littoral; we are on the coast road.

Equally with this draft she asks: 'Anne – just wondering whether Bee's voice-overs and Bee's reading from the diary will be confusing and how we distinguish between them?' This note became very important to sorting out the time zones. In distinguishing between them, it allowed me a new plot development: Granny May and Thea are reading Bee's journals, illicitly. This process has a weakness which is that you can go past your best draft. It's much more likely to happen in film and television. When I first came back to Belfast, I had one day which I wrote about in my journal where every clock between my house and the city centre told a different time, as if time was in reverse or stalled. And this piece of writing made it through all the drafts. Once you start to get into a character's voice in a play, it begins to shape your perceptions. Stage plays are about character, whereas with radio it isn't necessary to take character beyond brief sketches of dialogue.

Heather's best editorial decision was to end *The Forgotten* with Bee's narration about the effect of the past on our ability to function, rather than with the viewpoint of the younger generation. She did that because she really liked this piece of writing; the necessity of that involvement is hard to overstate.

Bee: Nothing is constant, the seconds are moving forward; only the past is locked, coming into the present to warm it up or cool it down at regular intervals. Where did I go? What library or book did I disappear into? What body held me? A pregnancy and two stone, a ghost baby chewing at my nipple – I put it down, in separate letters teeming like rain on the thin end of the edge of a field of blue grass, a place of parting, so I will know it again.

It seems to me that what Bee is describing about the effect of the past is what happens when writers have an invisible career, failing to make it into print or production.

On Friday, 2 January 2010 Paul Jones writing in the *Radio Times* said this of *The Forgotten:*

> A strange little play, this. And appropriately so, since strange not to mention frightening is what life must be like for someone suffering from hallucinatory dementia. Bee the woman at the centre of Anne Devlin's quirky and disturbing tale, is experiencing alarming lapses of memory. And when her world becomes unmanageable, she is forced to move in with her elderly mother and niece. In an attempt to understand what is happening to her, they open Bee's journals and delve into her dreams and hallucinations.

If I had started to write a radio play about 'hallucinatory dementia' it wouldn't have worked. I can only know that when I begin to read what I've written. So I'm reliant on a good reader. Writers are not their own best readers.

Michael Longley wrote to me after the broadcast, perceptively describing the play as a balance of the poetic and the psychoanalytic. Other influences included: Harold Pinter's *A Kind of Alaska* (1982), and Caryl Churchhill's *Far Away* (2000), with its zoomorphic language. My grandmother had Alzheimer's when I was a child, and nobody knew its name. This parallel world of *The Forgotten* is a strategy like Alzheimer's itself. There are no pathways out. Bee's dilemma and my own became intertwined. She creates art in order to keep awareness of the ruin of her world from crushing her until she becomes stronger.

When Dawn Miranda Sherratt-Bado and Linda Anderson asked me to revisit *The Forgotten* with a view to writing an essay to accompany an extract for publication, I was amazed to find that my new stories, both published and in progress, had returned to the snow-bound mountains and skiing: the subject of the postcards Bee sends to her niece. Éilís Ní Dhuibhne suggested that I was plagiarising myself.

What the 'Waking the Feminists' movement did in drawing attention to the hostile structures that the theatre is presenting to women forced me to reconsider my own retreat from the theatre. What is the nature of my failure to rewrite a second draft of my stage play in progress for the Lyric Theatre Belfast, which I stopped in June 2014? What would it take for me to engage with the theatre again? Faber declined to publish the radio script of *The Forgotten*, suggesting I turn it into a stage play for which there was more likely to be a market. I haven't so far taken up the challenge. Sinéad Gleeson's creation of two major outlets for short stories led me out of the silence: *The Long Gaze Back: An Anthology of Irish Women Writers* (2015) and *The Glass Shore: Short Stories by Women from the North of Ireland* (2016). I had taken to writing stories in order to find my way out of the invisible zone where my dramatic work remains since I wrote *The Forgotten*. Because it seems to me that this telling is insisting on being told, in whatever form.

Here Comes the Night

Rosemary Jenkinson

Here Comes the Night *was first performed at the Lyric Theatre, Belfast, on 23 April 2016. The cast, in order of appearance, was as follows:*

Vincent/Jim   Michael Condron
Freddie/Dean   Thomas Finnegan
Mary/Donna   Kerri Quinn
Jenny/Marta   Susan Davey
Fr Black/Boyd   Niall Cusack

Director   Jimmy Fay
Set Designer   Grace Smart
Costume Designer   Enda Kenny
Lighting Designer   Paul Keogan
Sound Designer   Philip Stewart

Act One Setting: Willowfield Drive (also known as Pope's Row), East Belfast, 1966. A two-bedroomed parlour house. There's a door to the right leading out to the hall. Part of the wall is only half-covered in wallpaper. There is a still life painting of lemons.

Act Two Setting: Same house in Willowfield Drive, 2016.

Act One, Scene One

Living room. Autumn morning 1966. Them: 'I Can Only Give You Everything'. Vincent Gallagher is sitting typing feverishly at his type-writer. The fire is lit but he's been concentrating so hard for the past hours, he's let it burn low. He rips a piece of paper out of the type-writer and reads it.

Vincent   It was rainbow season and as he walked out he could see a rainbow stretching from the east to the west like a bridge, soaring above the cold square monoliths of Harland and Woolf: but on that morning, when he looked up at the coloured gantry, following its arc across the city, the indigo and red seemed to bleed away entirely leaving a pure curve of green, white and gold … *(disappointed, shakes his head)* No, way too much. *(Looks at it unsure)* Hunh.

He picks up a pen to amend it.

Vincent   Condense. Condense.

There is a loud, cheerful rap on the front door.

Vincent   Christ.

He thinks about ignoring it. There's another rap. He sighs.

Freddie *(off, through the window)* I can see your shadda. Are ye working?

Vincent *(to himself)* Not now I'm not.

He looks back at his page, tempted to ignore Freddie.

Freddie *(off)*   Should I go then?

Vincent groans, throws his hands up, gives up.
He goes out to answer the door.

Vincent *(off)*   Right, Freddie?

Freddie *(coming in with Vincent)* So you're in, are you?

Vincent   No, I'm not in, I'm actually out.

Freddie, a postman, dumps his bag of letters on the floor and throws his cap off.

Vincent   Well, I'm out mentally anyway.

Freddie *(looking at the wall)* Still not finished yet, eh?

Vincent *(looking at his page)* Having big troubles with it.

Freddie *(of the wall)* No, I meant *that*.

Vincent   Oh-h.

Freddie   Sure writing's like walking. You just put one word in front of the other, don't cha?

Vincent *(sceptical)* Hunh.

Freddie   Jesus, man, you've near let the fire out.

Vincent   Oh, yeah. I'll get the coal.

Vincent goes out the door into the kitchen.

Freddie *(after him)* The hands are near frizz off me here.

Freddie takes off his gloves and blows on his fingers. He picks up the poker and stirs up the embers.
Vincent comes back in with the coal scuttle.

Freddie   Good boy you are, buck her in then.

Vincent *(putting some coal on the fire)* That's her! She'll soon warm up.

Freddie   She'd need to. I tell you, it feels like I've just gone up Everest in me trunks. Me balls are Baltic! *(letting his wrist fall limp so his fingers dangle down)* And see? Me fingers are like icicles.

Vincent   Ah, you big girl. Look at you … *(imitating the effeminacy of Freddie's hand)*

Freddie   But I'm still the finest swordsman in France. En garde!

He strikes the pose and pretends to cut Vincent to bits with the poker.

Vincent   Get off. *(gets touched by the poker)* Hey. Look at the mess. *(brushing off the ash)* Just … look.

Freddie *(keeping on)* Ah, give over.

Vincent *(turning away)* Clear off! Or I'll not get you your whiskey.

Freddie *(putting down the poker)* No need to get humpy with us.

Vincent leaves.

Freddie *(after him)* You could do with a drink yourself, you look like shite warmed up.

He picks up the page Vincent has just been reading and looks at it. He reads out declamatorily.

> 'It was rainbow season and as he walked out he could see a rainbow stretching from the east to the west like a bridge, soaring above the cold–'

Vincent *(off)*   Get off out of that!

Freddie *(quietly)* '… A pure curve of green, white and gold.'

He sucks in the air at it, grimaces.
Vincent comes in with the whiskey and glasses.

Vincent   You know you're not meant to look at that.

Freddie   Here, I'm qualified. *(pointing to his postbag)* I am a man of letters after all!

Vincent   Aye, Freddie Birch DFA. Does Eff All.

Freddie   More than you anyway. Here, at least people read the words I give them.

Vincent pours the whiskeys. Freddie observes him.

Freddie   Now I understand why you're having doubts. 'Green, white and gold'.

Vincent   Yeah. Sorry.

Freddie   I don't care. For all I care you could be saying Patrick Pearse is as cool as Hitler. But it's just … with all that's been happening.

Vincent   I know.

Freddie   I mean, me, I don't mind the Trickler meself. Sure it has orange in it as well as the green, it's very ecumenical.

Vincent   Jot of water?

Freddie   No chance. Why would I drown me best friend?

Vincent passes him his glass. They grin.

Freddie   To us. No, to the Trickler.

Vincent   To the Union Jack!

They clink glasses and drink.

Freddie *(satisfied)* Aaahh. Jesus, I needed that. Ah, wish I was like you, wife out working for you, snug as a bugger in here.

Vincent   Aye, but not for much longer.

Freddie   Ah, you, ye had to folly the Catholic breeding programme, didn't you? *(Vincent groans, admitting it)* Go forth and multiply. Sure this wee house'll be bunged with babies in no time.

Vincent   That's the last short story I'll knock out, then that's me.

Freddie   Hard to work like the rest of us.

Vincent   Hard?

Freddie   Here, just cos a fella has to have a wee rest. Right, I'll not be giving you your post for that.

Vincent   Ah, come on.

Freddie *(pulls it out of his post bag, but holds it to his chest)* No, you're unappreciative.

Vincent   Let me give you another wee half'un then by way of apology.

Freddie   A half'un? It's a quarter'un with you. Aye, go on, right up the sides. Holding that bottle hostage, are ya?

Vincent *(pouring)* Aye, aye, aye.

Vincent stops pouring but Freddie forces the neck of the bottle down for more and it spills onto the rug.

Vincent   Dammit!

Vincent ineffectually tries to rub the stain away.

Freddie *(gives him the letter)* There you go then, that's you.

Vincent   Cheers. *(starts to open it, then notices the name)* What? Mrs Kavanagh?

Freddie   Oh, sorry, wrong one. Pass us it back then.

Vincent shakes his head in disbelief.

Freddie *(giving him the right letter)* No bother at all. *(taking the other one back)* Look, you half opened it! She'll be thinking I read it.

He starts licking the envelope to close it.

Vincent *(watching him dispassionately)* You don't even know whose tongue was on that before yours.

Freddie   Brigitte Bardot? Ursula Andress? Lllll …

He starts licking it mock-seductively and Vincent laughs.
The front door shuts.

Vincent *(whispering)* Jesus, it's her!

He tries to hide his whiskey behind the typewriter. Freddie leaps up,
wipes his hand over his hair.
Mary, seven months pregnant, comes in, but stops to survey the
scene.

Vincent   Mary, you're back early.

Mary   Too early by the looks of it.

Freddie *(holding out his hand)* Mary, love, you're looking well.

Vincent   Are you alright?

Mary   I had a dizzy spell, so they sent me home.

Vincent   Oh, God, love.

Mary   No, no – I'm fine now.

Freddie   You sit down, Mary, pet. Vincent, fill a glass for
                     her quick.

Vincent   She can't drink.

Freddie   Course she can. It'll put hairs on the baby's arse.
                     All this modern skitter about not being able to
                     drink. Sure, me Ma had a glass of stout every day
                     and look at me.

Mary	Aye, no wonder you've a terrible thirst on you.
Vincent	Do you want to go up and have a wee lie-down, love?
Mary	What, and listen to you two yo-hoing down here on your tod? No thanks. Are people out there not waiting on their post?
Freddie	Ach, Mary, sure aren't they that used to me now, they expect it to be late.
Mary	I suppose. Any word on the road?
Freddie	All quiet on the Eastern front.

Mary *(thrilling to it)* Oh, but it was bad for a while, Freddie. Us at the Mater had a fair dose of rioters to patch up.

Freddie	I was just talking to Mad Dog McKee's wife and she was telling us about this wee fella on the Ormeau Road. He was lighting a petrol bomb and, bang, his arm was blew off. *(observes Mary's gratifying reaction)* The Ormeau Road this was.
Vincent	The *Arm*-eau Road was it?

Freddie and Vincent laugh.

Mary	Vincent, that's not funny at all.
Freddie	You sick bast – I mean person. 'Scuse the language, Mary.

Mary Oh, it's fine. Put some slack on that fire, would you, Vincent?

Vincent *(putting the slack on)* Grand.

Mary Roaring away it is like one of their bonefires. But it's the UVF starting up's the real worry.

Freddie I know, Mary. *(lowering his voice with intrigue)* And did you not hear last week about the shooting at St George's Market?

Mary *(thrilling)* No. What shooting?

Freddie Get this. Ten chickens got murdered. Aye, the UVF claimed responsibility. They said it was their military wing. *(They look at him)* Chicken? Wing? Gettit?

Mary *(laughing)* Dear God. Me falling for it too.

Freddie Ach, the city's grand now. The rain's weshed the roads pure clean. Here, I've been pulling up the handbrake long enough here. Time I got these delivered.

Mary Near time I got delivered meself, Freddie.

They laugh.

Freddie Good one.

Freddie lifts up the big bag of letters.

Freddie   Look at us, I'm like Santy with his sack.

Vincent   No, you're more like Rudolph with his red nose.

Freddie   Cheeky bast – *(catches himself, aware of Mary)* I
                   mean eejit. Cheers for the drink now!

He slings the bag over his shoulder.
A couple of loud cracks sound against the window.
Freddie and Vincent jump. Mary grabs her bump protectively.

Vincent   Jesus!

Mary   Christ! What in God's … ?

Freddie *(going to the window)* That's stones.

Vincent *(to Mary)* Are you okay, love?

Mary   Aye, the baby got a bit of a stirring but I'm fine.

At the window Freddie shouts at the kids.

Freddie   Wee rats! Sure, your shite's yella! I'll boot your
                   tripe in! Wee bastards!

He runs out the door.
Mary hurries to the window.

Mary   He's nearly up with one of them.

Vincent   Are you definitely okay though?

Mary is too busy observing to listen.

Freddie *(from off)* Just you fucking wait!

Vincent picks up the letter on his table and opens it. He goes to join Mary who's absorbed by the scene outside.

Mary   Oh, God sake!

Vincent   What?

Mary   He's been kicked in the bumps.

Vincent *(in sympathy)* Aow.

Mary   Ooh, poor Freddie, but he's up again.

She stands rubbing where the baby is moving as she watches, twisting her head for a better view.
Vincent can't believe what he reads.

Vincent   Mary …

Mary   The wee skitter …

The sound of shouts from the street punctuate Vincent's excited words.

Vincent   It's Queen's. They want me to read. At last! 'New Voices Penetrating the Silence!' Do you hear, Mary?

Mary   Oh, poor Freddie, dancing about like a jack-in-the-box and them chucking stones at his feet!

Vincent   Mary … I'm going places.

Mary   I'm going out.

Mary runs out.
Vincent looks at the letter again incredulously.

Vincent   Queen's University want *me*. To read. *My* story.

He throws his head back and raises his arms aloft.

Vincent   Yeahh! Get in there!

The Beatles: 'Girl'.

The Hijacked Writer

Rosemary Jenkinson

I never envisaged myself writing a play to commemorate the Easter Rising, but in theatre timing is everything and you have to be alive to every opportunity. To a Northern Protestant like myself, 1916 is synonymous with the Battle of the Somme and the banners in the East Belfast streets were a big reminder of that fact as I was writing *Here Comes the Night*. I still think there is an expectation in Northern Ireland that you write about your own side – outdated as that sounds – and quite a few of my plays do feature loyalists. However, with this play, I was more than happy to buck that trend.

September 2015

At the outset, I wanted to write a bipartite play set in the same house in two different eras. My original vision was that it would be about a republican writer, Vincent Gallagher, who is evicted from a Protestant area because of his Easter Rising story, only for his work in 2016 to be resurrected and hijacked for political reasons. When I first spoke to Jimmy Fay, the artistic director of the Lyric, about my idea, he saw a gap in the Lyric's programming and suggested it should tie in more with the Easter Rising centenary by setting the first half in 1966. I also saw it as a great chance to get my play produced as quickly as possible. Often theatre companies are slow to respond to your work, even when it's really contemporary and political, so I was going to make sure I reacted quickly in turn.

I wrote the first scene of the play, which worked well, then waited for the commission. I never write for a company until the commission arrives in the post. Theatre is a world of sudden passions and coolings and funding delays, so you cannot take anything for granted.

November 2015
The Abbey Theatre unveiled their 'Waking the Nation' programme for 2016 and sparked off a huge furore. Only one female writer was included in the new season. The social media frenzy led to the creation of 'Waking the Feminists', a campaign calling for equality for women in Irish theatre. When I looked at the programme, it was not only the lack of female writers that stood out, but also the fact that the Abbey had not commissioned any new plays related to the Rising.

The day after I signed the Lyric commission, I headed down to the 'Waking the Feminists' public meeting at the Abbey. I had had a previous commission with the Abbey entitled *Careless People*, which was never produced. Through that experience and many others, I know exactly how women playwrights are undermined during the writing process. It's not that we are shrinking violets and cannot bear criticism; it is that the quality of our work is doubted. In my case, I had attended a workshop at the Abbey and was asked if I would write a new version of *Careless People* that I knew would blunt my story of career-hungry parents leaving their children in the care of an unvetted nanny who turns out to be an abuser. I always try to be flexible but I could not agree with their vision. I understood that my play was highly controversial in theme, but it was the form I wanted and it had something powerful to say about society. I think the real problem is that women have not up until recently had permission to be controversial. I remember that after my play *The Bonefire* (2006), which was about loyalists, was well received by audiences but rejected by Dublin critics, I was advised by a literary manager that I should 'write more responsibly.' I have to admit that this attack on *The Bonefire* floored me because it was my first play and, for a time, it stopped me pushing more boundaries.

Apart from Marina Carr, so few women are being welcomed into the top echelons of Irish theatre. A few years ago, a male playwright who had been produced at the Abbey told me he had been treated 'like a king', which made me realise that men are regarded with greater reverence. The predominance of male playwrights has obviously led to more roles for male actors. I probably have been guilty myself of following the trend of writing more male characters than female, just to appeal to theatre companies.

The day of the 'Waking the Feminists' meeting in Dublin felt like a new rising – it was as if collectively we were blowing the doors off the Abbey. Again, the timing was perfect – I started the first draft of my script with huge confidence and energy. I knew I had to be quick if I wanted the play on by April.

February 2016
By February Jimmy had led two workshops and I was doing non-stop rewrites. I have always loved working with one person on a play. I know that in other big theatre companies there are drama-turges who work on the play before it ever sees a director, but the fewer visions there are to dilute a play, the more distilled it will be. One of the biggest issues was the title, *Willowfield Drive*, as it was the street where I lived at the time and its history was real. Research showed that from 1966 onwards a lot of Catholics left the area due to sectarian tensions and my neighbour told me that, in 1971, a team of paramilitaries from the Shankill steamed into Willowfield Drive and ordered the remaining Catholics out. It did prick my conscience somewhat to focus purely on one side's ethnic cleansing when I know that both sides were guilty dur-ing the Troubles. I also did not want to highlight where I lived and I admit I am on the paranoid side as I have an overactive

imagination, but Gary Mitchell's experience has made me hyper-aware of the dangers of writing about your own district. In 2005 Mitchell was famously forced out of his home in Rathcoole by paramilitaries who resented being the subject of his plays.

Fortunately, Jimmy came up with a great replacement title, *Here Comes the Night*. It is the title of a Them hit sung by Van Morrison which really fitted in with the sixties. Jimmy then scheduled the play for April on the main stage. After ten years of writing for studio spaces it felt like a huge achievement to finally be on a main stage. Jimmy was so invested in the play that he decided to direct it himself, which I was delighted about, and through auditions we assembled a great cast.

The Reviews

There is a part of me that loves the bruising, gladiatorial arena of theatre, where your work can either be hailed or put to the sword. My work tends to be highly critical of society, so it makes sense that sometimes society is critical of me. The one thing I always bear in mind is that critics can kill your play, but they cannot kill you as a playwright. The theatre community will always know your quality even if the outside world fails to recognise it. It is frustrating, though, when certain critics just do not get your work but because the pool of reviewers is so small, especially in Belfast, you cannot escape them. Another problem with local reviewers is that they reflect Northern Ireland's artistic inferiority complex in refusing to believe that a local play can be as brilliant as one first mounted in London or Dublin. I know that some people in theatre claim as a self-protective mechanism that reviews don't matter; well, they do, vitally.

The Irish Times noted that the second act of *Here Comes the Night* is unusually lighter than the first: 'History, everybody knows, happens twice: the first time as tragedy, the second time as farce.' The caveat was that 'the play loses amperage,' but it was a conscious decision of mine not to end in tragic violence as I wanted it to reflect truthfully the more peaceful political times that we live in. I can always spot when a writer has run out of ideas and resorts to killing his or her characters off in a purging, redemptive bloodbath. When you have done that ending once, it is just boring to repeat it, but it tends to be a staple in contemporary Irish plays.

Most of the reviews were excellent. *The Stage* called it 'an intriguing new play that needs a little more development,' but I find with comedy in particular that overdevelopment can kill the pace stone dead.

The one thing that surprised me from all the reviews was that everyone assumed, because the play was a comedy, that Vincent Gallagher was a terrible writer. I may have overegged his prose, but I thought he was pretty good myself and he wrote the truth as he saw it (definitely deserving of a blue plaque!). It just goes to show that every view of theatre is subjective and, above all, that literary success is as fragile as the peace that we live in.

The Trouble with the Arts in Northern Ireland

The hijacking in *Here Comes the Night* of Vincent Gallagher's writing for political purposes is chiefly perpetrated by the Minister of Culture, Arts and Leisure. At the time of writing, the Minister was Carál Ní Chuilín and I did borrow a few elements of her public speeches, notably her Bobby Sands quote: 'The Men of Art have lost their heart ...' and her hilarious attribution of *Antigone* to Socrates rather than Sophocles. She rarely attended any arts events and, as it says in her entry in Wikipedia: 'In 1989, she was arrested after trying to place a booby-trap bomb under the gates of Crumlin Royal Ulster Constabulary station,' which could be interpreted as an early interest in performance art, but I somehow doubt it.

Joking aside, the main political point I was trying to make in *Here Comes the Night* was that cultural appreciation in this state often comes through a sectarian perspective. Sinn Féin will support

Catholic writers; the Democratic Unionist Party (DUP) will champion Protestant ones. Having said that, support for the arts in general in Northern Ireland is woeful. I may have lampooned our Culture Minister but now we have even been denied one as she has been replaced by the Minister for Communities.

The members of the Northern Ireland Assembly only seem to regard the arts in the light of tourism revenue; hence the new builds like the impressive Seamus Heaney HomePlace in Bellaghy and the C. S. Lewis Square in east Belfast. It is surely only a matter of time before Central Station is renamed as the C. S. Lewis Station and sells 'Narnia' discounts. It is ironic that Stormont lavishes funds on dead writers while increasingly impoverishing the lot of living writers. We also should blame the rulers at Westminster who feel that, since they don't have to pacify us warring natives any longer, they can palm us off with a risibly low budget.

The brilliant thing about being a playwright is that you can voice these opinions in your art. My tendency to be completely inappropriate has always been a bit of a drawback in terms of a conventional career, but that satirical impulse is a strength in a playwright. Laughter is gratifying; laughter with a sharp intake of breath is doubly gratifying. One of the targets in *Here Comes the Night* is the cultural branding of everything and the marketing slogans behind many new arts initiatives like the 'Unheard Voices' project. They sound so pompous; you barely have to use comic exaggeration.

Artistic Silencing in Northern Ireland

Over the past ten years, there has been a degree of suppression of plays connected to the Troubles and its aftermath. I find it ironic that there has been an appetite for screenplays about the Troubles – *'71* and *Hunger* – and, yet, even allowing for a certain war-weariness, Northern Ireland does not tune in to the potential for exporting Troubles drama. The real difficulty is an insistence on the prevailing narrative of the peace process. A lot of theatre companies believe we should be looking outwards, not inwards, and writing about concerns broader than our own and that is fine. But surely as playwrights we should question what is happening around us. In *Here Comes the Night* there is a reference to the arson attack by paramilitaries on Asta's Glam Factory, a Lithuanian-run nail salon, in 2015. While I was writing the play, I could even see the graffiti, 'Locals Only', from my front door. Also, in the lead up to the Easter Rising centenary, dissidents murdered a prison officer in a street near me.

We should be able to talk about topics like paramilitary activity freely. A previous play of mine, *A Midsummer Night's Riot*, was produced in Washington D.C. in 2014. My American director asked the Northern Ireland Bureau in D.C. if they would kindly promote our play, but the response was that it is not like that in Belfast anymore and they would prefer to endorse a more positive image. It was a maddening reply because I had witnessed at least eight riots for research. In December 2012, Belfast City Council's vote to limit the flying of the Union Flag from the City Hall sparked off frequent loyalist riots in my area over the following three months. I do not think there is anything worse for a writer than to be told that your subject matter does not exist!

January 2017
Looking back on *Here Comes the Night*, its success means that I have begun a new commission with the Lyric and I am also writing for the new era of the Abbey. For a long time I was writer-in-residence in my own bedroom. This year, I am writer-in-residence at the Lyric, which is a great boost. There are more political centenaries coming up and I would love to write about them, not just to celebrate Irish history but to try to gain a better understanding of our current society.

PHOTOGRAPHS

Preface to 'When They Put Their Hands Out Like Scales: Journeys', Photographs by Emma Campbell

Photographer, writer, and feminist activist Emma Campbell's cross-disciplinary project 'When They Put Their Hands Out Like Scales' (2013) includes a book, an exhibition of fine art documentary photography, and a short film, all of which examine the experiences of Northern Irish abortion seekers. As the title suggests, Campbell explores the issue of justice (traditionally personified as Lady Justice, a blindfolded woman holding scales, as well as a sword) with regard to women's reproductive rights. The photographs in 'Journeys' document Northern Irish women's journeys across the Irish Sea to abortion clinics in England. These are photographic travel narratives of the abortion seeker, and the pictures convey a sense of her life as it is glimpsed through multiple barriers. The images are shot so that the viewer experiences this crossing from the abortion seeker's perspective. Rather than making the woman into an object of the photographic gaze, Campbell subverts the documentary style by inviting the viewer to share her viewpoint. She notes, 'As a visual device, the subjectivity of an abortion seeker becomes embodied by the audience. It simply and powerfully presents an opportunity for empathy with a subject who is otherwise made invisible in society.' Campbell's artistic dialogue with abortion seekers and activists demonstrates the transformative potential for both the photographed subject and the viewer as witnesses. Women are not 'othered' or depicted as victims in Campbell's work; rather, they are represented in a way which visualises their hidden experiences and histories. The selected photographs featured here are black and white versions of the original colour images.

POETRY

Coastal Cumulus

Scooped from the ocean
they loom against degrees of blue.
We, running low on metaphors,
have drifted off from the urge

to abstract—in rapt moments,
in company—a likeness;
to wrest significance.
Mostly, they evade our notice

though when they intervene
we can't but take as a slight
the shade, the chill they cast.
Alone and shivering at the strand's

end, we gaze across the bay
at glinting cliffs and vivid greens
at a loss, abandoned somehow;
unsettled by longing until

turning for home we see
sweeping towards us,
at right angles to the waves,
a tidal bore of sunlight.

In the moments before it strikes,
we stand there, bowled over
by certainty; absolutists
awaiting absolution (and warmth).

Would that all erasures, all
endings, were like this.

Jean Bleakney

Bear in Mind

When you find a helium balloon
on the path after overnight rain,
do not go to the cutlery drawer
for scissors or a pointy knife.
Do not go straight to the bin.
Shake it. You will get wet,
but keep shaking. Enter a room.
Let go. See it settle at table height
and then (this is the magic bit)
run your gripped finger and thumb
the length of the ribbon. Let go
and watch the slow, ceiling-ward
resurrection. Let draughts, heaters
and open doors choreograph the
weeks' long denouement. Learn
about physics, second chances.
In recounting your experience
don't forget to emphasize
that such events need rain.

Jean Bleakney

After the Event

The Royal Ulster Agricultural Society (RUAS) says agreement has finally been given to purchase a 65-acre site at the former Maze Prison near Lisburn. The society said it means the largest agricultural show in Northern Ireland, the Balmoral Show, will be relocated from the King's Hall, where it has been held since 1895. (BBC News NI, 20 Mar 2012)

Now that the Balmoral Agricultural Show
has decided to up sticks and go;
has decamped, headed west,
we of Balmoral and environs confess:
Despite the traffic and how they hogged
our pavements and owned the roads they crossed,
we miss the wind-borne tannoy's
encouragement to showjumpers. The applause.
We kept a tight rein on our Shogun
envy, were alert to towbars and brogues
(Tyrone or Fermanagh?), saw some sights;
a family-packed saloon stalled at the lights
on Stockman's Lane, the felt-hatted grandfather
tapping his pipe on the passenger wing mirror.
On reflection maybe it's time to admit
we actually thought we were the better for it;
hoped something might have rubbed off on us.
Had we reached out, it could have been infectious,
that rootedness, their healthy glow, their unflappable

swagger, their capable hands, their chutzpah with cattle.
But we try not to take their flight too personally.
We do not dwell on what they thought of us. Not especially.
Though what has come to pass
feels like somewhere between being jilted and put out to grass.

Jean Bleakney

Stranger on the Shore

Dear '60s child who grimaced
at the bowler hat, the goatee,
your parents' swaying reverie …
A whole half century has passed

and beached you here, alert
to life's bass lines, key changes.
Braced. Inured to all save this
familiarly unspooling clarinet

and for the first few bars, it's as if
you've forgotten how to breathe;
forgotten that sough to sough reprise
supplanted now by Bilk's vibrato riff.

You're freefalling through memory
to linoleum, bakelite, tray cloths,
the wireless's Home Service, and loss.
For which there is no remedy.

Jean Bleakney

Bypass

1
The call comes at half past six on a raw March day.
The equinox has passed but spring is still
sour and rough and new.
My husband's father has died –
they have wakened us from our sleep to say –
and he goes to him alone, I back to sleep but
to a waking dream, the first of my life.

In the dream, I am on the threshold of my childhood home
and my father's garden is in ruins – his shelved lawns,
supported by brick walls he built himself,
are black and blasted – and just as I step out into it
the door becomes our door, in our hall
and my husband is back from the death of his father,
walking into the presentiment of mine.

2
In the middle of that winter, we fly together
for the first time: my mother, you and I,
the three of us retracing your honeymoon journey.
Then, you had just left your wedding breakfast
in the Windmill Café in Strabane and she would tease you
for years about how, all the way to London,
you discussed hens – the best layers and eaters –

with a man selling them in the North, a sign,
she said, of your lack of romance or perhaps just
a need to be distracted from what lay ahead.

Now we use the little bottles of Bloody Mary
and crackers as distraction from what you face –
having your heart taken out – as we will ours,
our hearts going out to you.

3
The waiting is erotic – the young doctor
full of sex as he checks you in and tells you
there is *a mortal risk of death.* We hear this from his lips
but my mother says it is no odds, you have no choice
and I am party to what have been intimate and private talks.
We leave you in your room knowing you must deal with the night,
worrying that you should have your milk, that the ordinary rituals
    be preserved.
We sleep in the nurses' quarters facing the gaol, beside a family
from Cyprus whose father is also on the ward.
They have no English, we no Greek, but we find
comfort in each other all the same.

4
In the morning we return as they prep you
and a bitter Sister from Sligo jokes
at the question that asks
if you have any tattoos.
I want to hit her.

5

That afternoon, as we leave you, the young Caribbean orderly
who takes you to theatre is the first to be gentle,
telling us and you, you'll be okay.

We walk back along a corridor of blue dolphins
incongruously gay but the paint is faded
and lends a dragging weight
to our sense of wading, dazed and weary
through a dark subterranean world.
We are told to go and pass the time
somehow. The Belfast sisters of another man
like the joke that they will go to the theatre
while he is *in theatre* – we silently applaud them
even if we're not ready to laugh yet.

6

We take the bus into the city – it is full of prisoners' wives
back from visiting the Scrubs.
We think of my grandmother who worked for the Post Office
in London during the war and visited IRA men
imprisoned there and now you,
the son who will come
in the next chapter of her life,
lie in the shadow of its dark walls.

7

Away from the hospital, we feel our senses heightened –
the petrol smells of traffic; the primary colours of the buses
and the Café Rouge; early Christmas lights and music;
the shunting of trains and sirens; the chatter of children.
It is Friday, we see men gathered outside mosques,

a Somali mother holds her child in a window;
an older Greek woman incenses her door.

I bring my mother to St Charles in the little Vatican
to pray in its quiet shell-pink chapel, the college in St Charles
    Square
where I learned to be a teacher. They say you meet your other
    selves
when you return to a place like this and I think of all the Fridays
and the good tiredness that came with the ending of a week with
    students
and how that younger self could not have imagined this.

Then to Westminster and more prayers.
From the window of Pizza Express we watch
the Christmas shoppers, envying them
the ordinariness of their day,
read of the sinking of Venice, remember
it is the one place my mother would like to see,
stare intently into the red carnations on our table
till we can put off returning no longer.

When we come back you are out of theatre
raised high on an IC bed, a ventilator breathing for you.
Your doctor tells us they have taken three ways past your heart
but some is so diseased – you will not live a long time
but maybe better.

8
On the day you should be going home:
infection, temperature, a return to theatre
and the beginning of a nightmare.

9

Her name is Pearl – she is from St Lucia.
She is maybe the hundredth nurse you've seen.
She is efficient and kind.
She calls you Mr Boyle.

Pearl is to remove a line from your neck –
you are so pierced that there is danger.
I take your hand and wonder how many years
since we held hands and how the last ever day of childhood
goes unremarked, unnoticed. There must have been a day
when you held my hand for the last time.
Now I hold yours and Pearl says,
'Just look at your daughter's face.'

10

On a very bad day we are sitting with my aunts in the canteen –
they have flown over and I am flying home.
We are all feeling lost.
My youngest brother looks at them and says,
'If Granny had stayed here, we might all be English!'

11

When I return, I leave my red leather gloves on the grey seat
of a black cab. My mother meets me and says,
'Your father is just trying to live.'
She keeps vigil, bringing you porridge
that the Caribbean women sprinkle
with cinnamon for a little spice.
The nurses teach her to disinfect the lines
with antiseptic to keep the infection at bay

and sometimes it seems you are being crucified
there in the bed before us and we are praying
just that it should be over.

12
But this is not the time to die
and just before Christmas
we bring you home
like a fragile parcel,
wondering how it will be possible
for you to travel but it is done
somehow and you are so pleased
to be alive, to have a cup of tea,
to sleep again in your own bed.

13
Earlier – between trips to London –
one Sunday there was nowhere else to go
and I walked out into the garden in the rain.
It was wrecked by winter - black and rotting,
wind-blown and freezing in the cutting wet
and it was the garden of my dream
but it was my garden and this
was the bleakness I had dreamed about.

Maureen Boyle

My Criterion

She writes *New Englandly*.

How do I?

Derrily? Verily.

Irelandly? 'Northernly.'

Emigrantly, evidently.

Colette Bryce

In the time-lapse/footage

In the time-lapse
footage of the
decomposition
of a pear,
a light lace crust
appears
and devours
the fruit
which collapses
in on itself
like a beast
brought down
by a pack.

Always, fungi
is feasting,
working
its quick
saprotrophic
magic on all
matter, even
this seasonal
litter I've just
finished clearing
from your grave,
your shelf

of the earth,
          yes you,
who don't
even realise
you're dead.

Colette Bryce

The White Horse

after Adomnán

When the saint's old bones wouldn't journey
any further, he paused for a breather,
sat down by a verge
that was humming with the unfinished business of spring
and there, the old workhorse approached him.

The animal nuzzled its long white skull
to Columba's chest
and wept, softly,
tears from its pale-fringed eye blotting
the shirt of its master, weary by the roadside.

Diarmait, embarrassed, tugged it by the rope
instructing the animal back to its duty,
but the saint shook his head
and mouthed 'Let it be'
allowing the white horse to pour out its grief,

stroking the salt-soaked bristles of its muzzle,
the two of them kindred
in the knowledge of his death.
Blossom in the hawthorn, tiny lights;
a halo of flies around both of their heads.

Colette Bryce

Fathom

... the furthest distances I've travelled
have been those between people

— Leontia Flynn

1. Father
(at the Forty-foot Gentlemen's Bathing Place)

Seven thirty a.m.
and I love that men
are different
when wet.

We're sea-changed,
leagues of seals,
rasping, clapping,
rapturing the air.

I'm glad the water's cold.
And though my father
taught me everything

I know about salt water,
for fifty weeks per annum
he remained arms' length inland.

2. Farther

Not necessarily needing to know
I launch into these buoyant
introductions: 'Hey Dad, it's Paula,
your favourite daughter your

beautiful blow-in from Belfast,'
my mother priming him well
in advance, so that I'm a little
deflated but hardly surprised

when he risks 'Are you married
to one of my sons?' 'Father'
I breeze 'Bishop Hegarty'd

never agree.' And his smile as he
fathoms the quip soon sinks, repeating
how terribly terribly sorry he is.

3. Further

Close to the close of your life, you wash up
in a strange house with a woman old enough
to be your mother insisting she is your wife.
Despite your rebuttals she's wedded to her lies.

You try the doors, her ladyship has them locked.
You spot your father's shooting-stick,
you've really got to fly, you say, and put
a window in. Next thing you la- la- la-

land in some class of hotel where the women
are very much younger with lovely hands;
the exits here, you swiftly establish, are shut

with a hush-hush code. You've stashed the stick
and smash a panel in. They belt you in a comfy chair,
to anchor you, they say, and call you 'pet'.

4. Faster

I don't think I ever married, did I? This
at the buzz-locked doors as I'm heading, the same day
he's quizzed me how long this interment (sic) will last.
You did Dad, the Star of the County you claimed.

He grins. And I've more to report. Go on.
She bore you six children. Away. It's true.
Would you like me to introduce you to one?
I would. God. That would be great.

Well Father. We shake.
It's a pleasure to meet you.
He beams.

When I leave I am borne
on the keen conviction
he liked me.

5. Falter

Our father one ankle in Heaven
trouser-leg rolled to the knee –
your time not come – the other one
stuck as it is and swollen.

There is yet time in this dry hotel,
as your wide straddle falters the tide recedes
til your greeting's a watery smile you float
for the baffling hosts of the faces you meet,

above whose static you tune to the sirens –
song with your name on –
well within reach;

though embracing's beyond us
I'd sing to deliver you
home for the last how long

Paula Cunningham

From 'In Response to Rilke:
I bhFreagairt ar Rilke'[1]

The Wind

But the night murmurs: the wind –
and I weep in my bed: I know it.

It is easy to blame
the wind even as
as you stand up to it

The petals of the daisies whisper its secret
and the rain sprays my coat
in refrain

You call to me across the void
but I cannot hear you –
the wind lifts your words

curving them to a question mark
that asks:
why are you standing there?

Celia de Fréine

---

1. These poems are from a work-in-progress in which de Fréine responds to
    Rilke's *Migration des Forces* (1984) from which the epigraphs preceding her
    own original poems are taken.

An Ghaoth

Mais la nuit murmure: le vent –
et je pleure dans mon lit: je le sais.

Is éasca an locht a leagan
ar an ngaoth
fiú agus an fód á sheasamh agat

Sioscann piotail na nóiníní a rún
is spraeálann an bháisteach mo chóta
lena athrá

Glaonn tú orm thar an bhfolúntas
ach níl mé in ann tú a chloisteáil –
scuabann an ghaoth do bhriathra

á lúbadh ina comhartha ceiste
a fhiafraíonn:
tuige a bhfuil tú id' sheasamh ansin?

Celia de Fréine

Tune

Take me by the hand,
for you it's so easy...

Angel, you are the road
even as you stand still

you summon me and I don't know
whether to run or stay as I am

You must be lonely
standing there on your own –

perhaps I should light a candle
fill the room with carnations

invite you in
over the threshold

At times I feel lonely too –
abandoned here

not because I didn't use to advantage
what was bestowed on me

but because I did
the very best on its behalf

There was a time we could have scattered
our tune to the four corners

but life's libretto hoisted its sail
and I was drowned by its chord

Celia de Fréine

Port

Prends-moi par la main,
c'est pour toi si facile...

A aingeal, is tú an ród
fiú agus tú id' lánstad

glaonn tú orm is níl a fhios agam
ar chóir rith nó fanacht socair

Caithfidh go bhfuil tú uaigneach
id' sheasamh ansin id' aonar –

seans gur chóir coinneal a lasadh
an seomra a líonadh le coróineacha

cuireadh a thabhairt duit
thar an tairscach isteach

Scaití, braithim féin uaigneach –
gur tréigeadh anseo mé

ní mar nár chuir mé chun tairbhe
ar bronnadh orm

ach mar go ndearna mé
mo sheacht ndícheall ar a shon

Tráth, d'fhéadfaimis ár bport
a scaipeadh chuig na ceithre hairde

ach chroch leabhróg an tsaoil a seol
is bádh ag a corda mé

Celia de Fréine

The Future

Future, who won't wait for you?
Everyone is headed there.

Why frighten us when you know
we'll arrive on your shore –
some washed quietly up
others flung there on foot of a tempest?

Future – we know
you are in store for us:
we've seen puppets onstage –
their limbs manipulated by a master such as you

But when the safety curtain is dropped
at the end of the show
we imagine those same puppets
pull against the strings of time

It is this thought – simple though it is –
that gives us hope

Celia de Fréine

An Todhchaí

Qui t'aura jamais attendu, avenir?
Tout le monde s'en va.

Tuige a gcuireann tú faitíos orainn
nuair is eol dúinn go mbainfimid do thrá amach –
cuid againn curtha i dtír go suaimhneach
cuid eile caite uirthi de bharr stoirme éicint

A thodhchaí – tuigtear dúinn
go bhfuil tú i ndán do chách
Tá na puipéid feicthe ar an stáitse againn –
a ngéaga á n-ionramháil ag do leithéid de mháistir

ach nuair a thagann an brat slándála anuas
ag deireadh an tseó
samhlaímid na puipéid chéanna
ag tarraingt i gcoinne shreanganna an ama

Is é an smaoineamh seo – ainneoin cé chomh simplí is atá –
a thugann dóchas dúinn

Celia de Fréine

The Fire's Reflection

Perhaps it's only the fire's reflection
on a shiny piece of furniture
that the child remembers much later
like a confession.

I was so looking forward
to seeing the fire lit in the parlour
meeting my mother's friend for the first time

I had heard so much about her
how they had journeyed to work together
during the war

how the war had created work for them
how rations had informed
the rest of their lives

And the soldiers – I wanted to hear
about the men in the photographs –
Americans guarding the coast

But the parlour filled up with heat
the flames licked the coal scuttle
lighting my small anxious face

devouring my expectation
until my eyes closed
and I reached that other world

where I could conjure
as many stories as I liked
to match those composed by the women

Celia de Fréine

Frithchaitheamh na Tine

Peut-être n'était-ce qu'un reflet du feu
sur quelque meuble luisant
que beaucoup plus tard l'enfant
se rappelle comme un aveu.

Bhí mé ag tnúth chomh mór sin leis
an tine a fheiceáil ar lasadh sa bparlús
castáil le cara mo mháthar den chéad uair

Bhí an oiread sin cloiste agam fúithi
faoi mar ar thaistil siad in éindí
chuig an obair le linn an chogaidh

faoi mar ar chruthaigh an cogadh
obair dóibh is ar ghlac na ciondálacha
seilbh ar a saol uaidh sin amach

Agus na saighdiúirí – theastaigh uaim a chloisteáil
faoi na fir sna grianghraif –
Meiriceánaigh a bhíodh ag cosaint an chósta

Ach líon an parlús le teas
is ligh na lasracha an sciathóg guail
ag lasadh m'aghaidh bheag mhíshuaimhneach

ag alpadh mo thnúthánachta
gur dúnadh mo shúile
is gur bhain mé an domhan úd amach

ina bhféadfainn a shamhlú
an oiread scéalta gur mhian liom –
iad inchurtha leo siúd a bhí á gcumadh ag na mná

Celia de Fréine

The Sixtieth Year of Horror Stories

When I was young I loved to scare myself
with stories read beneath the blankets
late at night by the light of a torch:
curse of the monkey's paw,
the haunted doll's house,
weight of a cat on the end of the bed
when you know there's no cat there.

Now all the what ifs follow me about,
sit on my chest, restrict my breath:
the late night phone call; blue lights;
the knock at the door; the cocked gun
of my children's lives pressed to my temple
day in day out; the diagnosis; the unlatched
gate – horses escaping into the night;
the hooked beak of grief: now it's real.

Moyra Donaldson

Stone

His companions, a little cast iron flying pig
with stumpy wings and a brass dragonfly,
for ten years Buddha has sat, eyes closed,
legs crossed, hands held cup shape in his lap.

I have watched him through this time, most patient
and unperturbed of creatures in this stone incarnation,
a perfect spring-perch for the crows, who carry twigs
and horsehair in their beaks, rest on him a moment
before their onward lift to build their chimney nests.
He doesn't mind the white shit crown that runs down
his face, across his eyelids; rain will wash it off again.
Winter snowfalls cap his head and cape his shoulders,
gather on his thighs, he does not shiver-shift beneath.
Summer sweet-peas curl their tendrils round his feet,
mossy autumn furs him green among the fallen leaves
and he is neither disturbed nor pleased, seated outside
my kitchen window, whilst inside, I grow less steady.

Moyra Donaldson

Will for Flight

When the owl came through the night
and landed on the ladder of my ribs,
I felt her heart beat hard into the hollow,
felt the strength it takes to hold to air

and my heart rose through the darkness,
joining its musculature with its desire.

Moyra Donaldson

Mare

I am not an obedient or dutiful woman
I never come when I'm called
when I'm hungry I eat
when I'm thirsty I drink

but I'm thinking of the herd of horses
kept from water for three days
then released; the stampede
to the river to be slaked at last.

I'm thinking of those five mares
who when The Prophet sounded
the battle horn, the call to war,
turned back despite their thirst.

These are the Foundation mares
the daughters of the wind
that bred the twelve Royal mares
that bred the winners, their genes

splicing with the three stallions –
faithfulness mingling with pride
duty with self-determination, perfect
combination for passing the post first.

*

I have dwelt in the small universe
of the womb before the world,

felt the power of the womb to expel
into the first sorrow and the first joy,

the abandonment of being: being.
I have been the universe for you.

The circle of the belly, the world,
the life, the mystery of love.

Have you ever heard the soft sound
of a mare whickering to her foal?

What whip will be laid to its back,
what race will it win or lose?

*

Scanned in foal, month after month
her belly became heavier, swollen
until her teats began to fill
and drip with milk; but as more time
went by and no foal came, we saw it was
a phantom that she'd grown, replacing
the clustered beginnings she'd lost long ago.

When most afraid for you, daughter, I think
of her lost embryo. I'd take you back into myself,
every cell, each chromosome. I'd have you back,
before birth, before conception, all your future
still ahead. I'd hold you as an imagined thing, safe.

Moyra Donaldson

The Radio

The radio hoots and mutters, hoots and mutters
out of the dark, each morning of my childhood.
A kind of plaintive, reedy, oboe note –
Deadlock … it mutters, *firearms* … *Sunningdale;*
Just before two this morning … *talks between.…*

and through its aperture, the outside world
comes streaming, like a magic lantern show,
into our bewildered solitude.
Unrest … it hoots now, *both sides* … *sources say* …
My mother stands, like a sentinel, by the sink.

*

I should probably tell you more about my mother:
Sixth child of twelve surviving – 'escapee'
from the half-ignited *powder keg* of Belfast;
from its *escalation*, its *tensions ratcheting*
its *fear of reprisals*, and its *tit-for-tat*.

She is small, freaked out, pragmatic, vigilant;
she's high-pitched and steely – like, in human form,
The RKO transmitter tower, glimpsed
just before films on Sunday afternoons,
where we loaf on poufs – or wet bank holidays.

Or perhaps a strangely tiny lightning rod
snatching the high and wild and worrying words
out of the air, then running them to ground.
My mother sighs and glances briefly round
at her five small children. *How* does she have five kids?

*

Since my mother fell on the Wheel of Motherhood
– that drags her, gasping, out of bed each dawn
bound to its form – she's had to rally back.
She wrangles her youngsters into one bright room
and tries to resist their centrifugal force

as she tries to resist the harrowing radio,
its *Diplock* ... and *burned out* .... and *Disappeared.*
So high, obscure and far from neighbouring farms
is the marvellous bungalow my father built,
birdsong and dog-barks ricochet for miles;

and wasn't my mother wise to stay put here
soothed by the rhythms of a *culchie* life
– birdsong in chimneys, the Shhhh of coal-truck brakes –
when women at home are queuing round the block
for their '*Valium, thank you doctor, and Librium*'?

*

So daily the radio drops its explosive news
and daily my mother turns to field the blow.
The words fall down, a little neutral now,
onto the stone-cold, cold, stone kitchen floor.
Our boiler slowly digests its anthracite

and somewhere outside, in the navy dark,
my father tends to his herd of unlikely cows.
A *Charolais*, the colour of cement,
thought to be lost for days has just turned up
simply standing – *ta da!* – in front of a concrete wall.

My mother, I think, is like that *Charolais* cow
in the Ulster of 1970 … 80 …what?
with its *tensions* … and its *local sympathies*.
She gets her head down, hidden in plain view,
and keeps us close. *'Look: Nothing to see here – right?'*

*

But when the night has rolled round again,
my mother will lie unsleeping in her bed;
she'll lie unsleeping in that bungalow bed
and if a car slows on the bend behind the house,
she's up, alert – fearing the worst, which is:

that a child of hers might die – or lose an eye;
or a child *anywhere* die or lose an eye …
That the car which slows on the bend behind the house
– *Midnight* … she thinks now … *random* … *father of five* –
is the agent of vile sectarian attack.

By the top field's wall, our unfenced slurry pit,
(villain of Public Information Films)
widens and gulps beneath the brittle stars.
My mother too thinks the worst, then gulps it back,
and in this way discovers equilibrium.

*

Death in the slurry pit, death beside the curb.
Death on the doorstep, bright-eyed, breathing hard.
My mother folds the tender, wobbling limbs
and outsized heads of her infants into herself;
she curls up, foetal, over our foetal forms.

Since my mother sailed down the Mekong river at nightfall
to the Heart of Darkness that is motherhood,
her mind's been an assemblage of wounds.
She thinks about Gerard McKinney, Jean McConville
– later the eyes of Madeline McCann

will level their gaze from every pleading poster
and pierce her heart like a rapier – needle-thin
as the high, wild, hardly audible cries of children.
Men of Violence ... says the radio.
My mother nods, then finally falls asleep.

*

And what if after my mother falls asleep
the hoots, half-words, and notes of high alarm
get loose from her head on little soot-soft wings?
Say they flap like bats. They fuck with the carriage clock.
They settle on her Hummel figurines.

Till the whole contraption of that home-made house
creaks, roars and bulges with the soundless strain
of my mother trying not to be afraid ...
Forgive me, this is all hypothesis.
It's conjecture, Doctor, of the crudest sort ...

Its gist being: beneath our bonhomie
and tight commercial smiles, this tone or timbre

flows on, like a circuit thrown into reverse –
and at the centre of concentric circles
that this is what plays behind an unmarked door.

*

Sometimes, rather, lying in my bed
I seem to hear the sound of the radio
issuing from a room, deep in the house;
it tells, in mournful tones, how two young men
were *taken from their car beside the road* ...

and afterwards ... nothing. All the stars come out
like sparkling glitter in a magic globe
that ends beyond the dunes fringing the fields –
and because I'm still a child and understand
nothing at all, I simply fall asleep.

Leontia Flynn

Bow and Arrow

for my father

You hold the arrow in your hand like time
as your elder brother saunters up the road.
As you flex the gut of the string,
savour its alluring elasticity, there stands,
lined up behind you, a frothing cavalry
of years: with iron on their feet, sour
steel against their tongues they are straining
for the order; should the arrow hit the air
they will shoot forth violently and in the time-
honoured fashion as a body.
You do not know them, but the year
a dapple-grey vision sends your brother
out loose among the traffic stands
sweating on the pavement at your rear,
and one is rattling great smooth
arcs of motorway on its flanks like scythes.
Of course you cannot hear
as you eye up gleefully the pointed metal tip
their frenzied neighing, nor feel the white
come spattering through your hair,
the ground beneath your small feet slip.
You are a boy of seven, larking about.
All you feel is a flood of whimsy.
You draw the arrow back like it's a dare.

Miriam Gamble

Gutties

On this shoe you have centred all your hopes
of becoming a finished person: you tie it onto you and wait
for the magic to occur.
You've perceived how, in the playground lines,
it heat-seals the tips of other children, the exclamatory stroke
that signals an artwork; how it holds them like a cup holds juice.
And now you tie it onto you, you admire
the clean white leather with the emerald flashes,
imitation Adidas out of Dunnes but
its credentials are neither here nor there;
it is the only hope for you
and you tie it on tightly though, admittedly, even in the shop,
the alchemy drains out of it inverse to your clammy presence –
with which desire and gain have nothing to do.

Miriam Gamble

Abandoned Asylum

Walking here is like walking the vacated spaces
of your own life: someone should be flitting
in a white gown through the corridors, someone
should be picking the depleted paintwork.

In each glass-fronted private room ought to be a mind
hard-clothed in exile, in exile and resistance;
against the starched garb and the rubber squeak
of the matron, pinked lips ought to be set.

In the woods, somebody, walking alone,
should depict with deliberate, futile steps
their hatred of the calm to be offered up boldly
to the broken – this greenery-slap of health –

and the gleam of the delicate golden plait
washed freshly and affixed with a ribbon
mirror life running through itself like rope
through the hands of a whaler. Against the birds,

pit-a-pat, should echo warm hands knitting
and unknitting horrors, palms pressed
to an upper window, somebody mouthing Help.
And, keeping himself to himself, the gardener

who each night exits with the sun pinned to his chest.

Miriam Gamble

Poem on the Landscape behind the Mona Lisa

A halt of her husband ahead,
useless legs, one so oddly protruding.
Why was she on her knees, crouching
instead of lying flat on her stomach?

With a slight drag of one foot,
Woman, what have I to do with thee?
That a person should have to lock themselves
into their clothes in a trusting mood after sex.

Her gratitude to God whom she did not
believe in, like a T-shirt with no message on it.
Her eyebrows now very scanty,
the cheapest box, into the ground immediately.

One longs to go to a hospital and have something
cut out; the whole church is lined with heartbeats.
It isn't cathedral enough. We seem to be
driving through the landscape of a missal

or a when-valley-was-in-flower book.
Lawns as brown as doormats, burning
and being burnt, other semi-tender
shrubs, perfume of hemlock woods.

Rooms and their reasons, in an honest
house, as sad a room as the shut-up best
parlour. The lamps have found
a clever way of coming together,

peach-bloom porcelain, directly in front
of you, the heart-shaped hooks,
the willow armchair, mother-of-pearl
buttons for the servants' bells.

Medbh McGuckian

Playing Ghost with Julie

As long as heads stay bowed
it was he had a life
the way the dark changes
you as you always were.

He thinks he will never want
that time back, slips somehow
into the locked church, the first
frosty flowerbed, first woods

and second woods. His voice
touches the soft summeriness
to go into the bone. The light
goes off on his voice, since all voice

comes from the end. But as long
as the words go on in the present,
as were we still, we are enfolded
in someone else's voice, in the brighter

darkness. The past often regards itself
as poetry, the heart racing faster
through the afternoon, like charity
in summer, the white feeling

of glimpses of the moon. Am I
as much as being seen, as big
as a minute, watched by still
deeper eyes or the futile harbours

of what is not yet? There are
deepenings, satiny movement
and depth, some sea-state
a reminder of desiccated gardens.

The earth has buried his arms
as rings turn pale when a beloved
is in trouble. A song has stopped
things in their course

and the warm dream is cut through;
all gone from mind, or what she calls
her mind, slight though it is.
There was no dream to blame

for needing to wake up so often
and drift into dreams so many times.
What has thought to do
with time and space; does water

dissolve thoughts, do thoughts drown
in this immensity of strangely
mental water? With a last flutter
thought settles on its perch

and goes quiet, as it sounded
in the moment. I removed the not
from the never-not-there breath
like comforting butterflies arising

naturally – like blue eyes, or
cells when stained by the inspired air,
the wintry air after a heavy dinner,
the flower hospital where all is prayer.

Medbh McGuckian

The Seed Mantra:
A Gift Poem

Sweeping up a leaf
that blew in last November,
I thought there would be no more
autumns; I shall have no winter
this year. I thought it best
to omit the season.

Flowers – well – if anybody,
under less than complete darkness,
the never quite safe blowing
curtain of a flower, the blowing
clover. The sky without colour
marrying bright colours,

tired and self-deceived.
My writing so very needless,
my tied-together poems.
An air might be just a look,
a moon might be a world,
a system seen from nowhere.

Violently breaking a cloud,
to shape itself a moment
to a star. A ship might break

its back like a holed stone,
though she might think herself
far from the sea, a forever thought.

I went out in a fiery field
to find a propitious name
for a child in the four
afterlife realms, and something
was bestowed, a plaited blonde
wave-shape in faded yellow.

Yet everything was white,
the textile handles with ribbons.
The double line of gold
around the dust of some,
the scythes cutting through the pearl
of this year's sequence of wet and fine.

Medbh McGuckian

Whitelessness

1
The Geologist

The rocks on Greenland are the oldest on Earth.
This one's a fossilised algal mat; this one
contains the ridges of human teeth:
some early Palaeolithic adolescent caught
grinning at the moment of death
in a stone photograph. We manoeuvre
them down to the beach on a stretcher.
Ochres and greys and blacks
ricochet back and forth across the massif,
as denuded of white as the West of Ireland,
while the shed ice bobs in the bay
begging smaller and smaller comparisons –
lozenges dissolving visibly on the tongue;
droplets of fat on broth. *If it's life
that controls the geological machinery
of the planet, rather than the other way round,
we are neither new, nor tragic.* This came
to me one morning as I sorted out my cabin
and the hundreds of marathon runners
in my brain stopped and changed direction.

2
The Photographer

The world speaks to me through signs.
Tiny signs. Missable signs. The stones
in the river are speaking to me.
How many decades has this ox skull lain here?
It looks like a crime scene. A waterfall
rises as mist off the face of the rock,
missing its ending. The red earth holds up
a rainbow on its outstretched hands.
We sailed right to the edge of a glacier
in a dinghy yesterday, pushed
against it, hard, but it didn't budge,
or squeal. It was the colour
of desert turquoise and implacable.
When we got back, I made a map
of my life, with holes for hideouts
between birth and death, and showed it
to my friend. In the beginning,
God put a rainbow in the sky
as a promise
that He'd never let the ocean rise again.

3
The Geographer

IKKE OPMÅLT says the map: unexplored.
– *What's this valley called?*
– *What would you like to call it?*
For the first few days, we practise
with rifles on the pebbly beach
though it's hardly dangerous –

polar bears are visible for miles
against the darker hillsides. Bog cotton
nods in swathes above the permafrost.
Lars and Simon buzz about the sky
in their flying dinghy, taking aerial
photographs, while we concentrate
on drilling up the planet's large intestine
and seeing what it's eaten. Ridiculously
overdressed, two musk ox trundle past.
We must sound enormous –
where before there were only kittiwakes,
the occasional seaward explosion
of an iceberg disintegrating –
but they blank us nevertheless.

4
The Artist

I packed Anthrax,
Megadeth, Metallica. I packed
two dozen sketchpads and sixteen
boxes of pencils. Shell's Arctic exploratory
outriders in their magenta lifejackets
can kiss my shiny metal ass.
I did not pack colours. Our foremast
resembles a crucifix. I stuck my boot
on the skull of an ox as though I'd shot it
and smiled at the camera. *Running / On our way
hiding / You will pay dying / One thousand deaths* –
I straddle the prow of the ship to sketch
whatever it is I'm looking at
and the daylight lasts and lasts.
For all the white animals – the hares,

the foxes, the wolves – I just leave
spaces on the paper where their bodies were
last time I glanced up. The rest
I filibuster in in grey or black
to stop the quiet.

5
The Marine Biologist

FUCK EVERYTHING BECOME A PIRATE
declares my T-shirt, but I don't mean it.
Ocean invertebrates are inconceivably lovely.
Each morning, I lower a bucket over
the side of the ship, clank it back up
on deck, then stick my hand
inside the sea's feely bag. In countless
numbers, the fjord system's summer whales
perform their languid acrobatics
within metres of the bowsprit.
Transfer even a soupçon of meltwater
to a Petri dish and, hush, the world's
most previously inaccessible ballet-
dancers are practising arabesques.
Such secretly parted curtains!
Last Friday I identified
an entirely new species of Annelid,
a male and a female, framed
and translucid under the microscope's hood:
they appeared to be having sex.

6
The Archaeologist

Uncover a single nick on a flint
made to sharpen it and you've nailed it:
the Paleo-Eskimo village –
which must have existed
here, where this gneiss is –
hoves into view: their Big Tent
(open to the sea); their Stone-Age
playground. Laughter. Dogs. Fire.
Then nothing for three hundred
thousand years and now me, in my Ushanka.
The fact was he'd gone looking for his father.
Lower down the coast, we stood
on the deck of the ship
and watched a polar bear
attacking an outpost. Then
we went to look. It had shredded
the pages of a *Reader's Digest.*
Before we got there, its long body had lolloped
away over the rocks and, even from a distance,
had kept on flashing back at us, like Morse.

Sinéad Morrissey

How Can I Forget John Donne

His voice in St Paul's Cathedral
a sonorous noose of poetry circling the congregation,
those queuing outside, envious.
No man is an island.

But earlier he had written
love poems to God,
had stretched out in his shroud,
kept his lungs tight in his chest,
had ordered for himself a death mask,
lay while white gypsum was smeared
on his face – over his eyes.
Smoothed, smoothed by his nostrils, his lips.
Did he lie like a corpse until it dried?
Ask not for whom the bell tolls.
It tolls for thee.

Did these rehearsals help
when the bell tolled?
Was he already ready to leave –
his shallow breathing –
his costume – his mask –
did he don it like a darkness?

His three-line regret
after his marriage:
Ann Donne
John Donne
Undone
Was that when he sought
the services of a seamstress
celebrated for making superior shrouds?

Joan Newmann

Samuel, Samuel

I hope you hadn't told Mrs Thrale
in the bluntest manner,
that *I'm Dr Johnson and I know almost everything* tone,
of your ailment. I hope
you didn't mention how you had rigorously
to gauge every ounce of fluid
that entered your body
and every ounce of fluid
that you expelled. That often
the quantity expelled
was a mere trickle
of what you had drunk.

Of course you told Mrs Thrale.
Mrs Thrale, you knew, would sympathise.
And you had added,
Perhaps the mercury,
the potion given by the apothecary,
the mercury is bound to be the cure.

Mrs Thrale did feel for you
but decided she needed love,
that she needed love now.
Mrs Thrale measured
all she had
against all she had not

and, I believe, married an Italian
and went with him
to Europe.

Joan Newmann

Speaking Privately with Emily

for Kathleen Galloway

Dear, dear Emily,
was it a fly, or maybe a wasp
or one of those variety of bees?

You knew that the sense
of hearing was the last to leave,
and a fly always
sounds like a fly.

I heard a fly buzz
when I died, you said
with certainty. But
Emily, no flies were permitted
to your final room.

You had only
the inconsistent suppressed gloat
of the yet-alive.

No leave-taking,
no trading the sense of hearing
for a buzz,
no allowing the flora and fauna
to express their little busynesses.

Joan Newmann

The Wounded Heron

for Niall Vallely

A heron's legs are so still
standing; so still
flowing behind it in flight.

Returning from Niall's funeral
a dead heron on the roadside,
its legs still still.

The wingspan of sorrow wider than us.
Six-foot-wide, the wingspan
of a grey heron.

Once, when my car screamed across
an ice-road, yet I lived,
shaken into my skin with the nearness

of leaving, skidding
back into my own life,
I saw a heron,

larger than life.
Larger than my life.
Standing by me.

When he took flight, startled
from his spilling, sloping perpendicular self,
his back all curl and curve,

I became a witness
to the ease of how to lift
into a whole spontaneous grace.

It is less like bird-song, more
like anti-song, the bony noise raucous-retching
from the heron's throat

after all that silent watching,
that immense light flight
across our cloudy eyes.

The heron's wings pulse through twilight
as an uilleann piper
kneads the bellows with his elbow

mysterious rhythm feeding the chanter and the drones,
controlling the breath. Your brother at your graveside, Niall,
as the day darkened – not able to stop playing his pipes

– wanting
the skirl to go down into the earth with you
so it wouldn't be so cold so heavy

so finite the finite clay
whatever the flight you'd take
away from our clumsy dusk

startling you from your rapport with grey, with rock,
to be glimpsed against the aching sky clinging
to its hold on light, before you merge with everything

we can't quite make out by sight, and straining
for the heron cry – its jagged unsingable angulars of loss –
unsure if that was what we heard.

Kate Newmann

The Leviathan of Parsonstown

You barely needed to look down
to see the leaves blackening
as if from drought in field
after sodden field

and then the stench
fogging up the senses
of townland
after townland

and they knew – they who
slept nights under rooves of nightshade
where there were no rushes
to thatch mud walls.

They were told to try
to eat the rotten potatoes
in a jelly mixed with sugar.
The famished

were told they should have planted
Egyptian beans,
Jerusalem artichokes.
Told to make potato flour.

In the castle, talk was of the telescope –
the largest in the world;
its length hungry
for the heavens' light.

Talk of tarnish.
Huge peat fires blazed to cook
the alloy for the speculum mirror
threatening to deform under its own weight.

Lord Rosse brought Mr Lyle
from Scotland, and Mr Lyle
slaked blighted potatoes
with lime; pitted

blighted potatoes with sand; left
blighted potatoes out in the open. He
immersed blighted potatoes
in boiling water

for twenty seconds; blighted potatoes
in boiling water for forty seconds;
blighted potatoes in boiling water
for sixty seconds. Frantic,

Mr Lyle soaked blighted potatoes
in acid; he soaked blighted potatoes
in alkali; he soaked
blighted potatoes in chlorine;

he buried
blighted potatoes
in a bog-hole
for forty-eight hours.

Like an instrument of war, the telescope
with its universal joint,
its winches and chains,
its racks and pinions,

its azimuth and altitude,
its counterweights.
A man could stand upright
in its six-foot aperture.

Lord Rosse spent nights frozen,
staring, craving some pattern,
sketching the wisps of light,
the mysterious meaning of space.

The pulpy crop clustered in the clay,
like dead stars in the night-black earth,
the spirits of the starved
spiralling like nebulae

out of the field of vision.
No pity
in the eyes
of a rotting potato.

Kate Newmann

Blackbird and Crow

The blackbird sang in my garden.
I began to sing with it in the last heat of summer;
the rosemary in blossom, the hydrangea. I sang of loss
until I was one with the smoky purple mountain,
the blackbird.

Every afternoon for a week I sang to the blackbird.
I had sold my home.

The crow waited a few days before it joined in,
Its clicks and calls were the undersound of omen,
future coming toward me, messages from earth gods
who had after all not withdrawn. Crow called
and clicked meaning, deepened harmonies, counterpoint.

Two birds and a woman making music in a back garden,
my head a rush of childhood drawings as I sang:
a house on a green hill, its large windows facing a lake,
a long pathway up from the gate. The future uncertain
but holding there.

Janice Fitzpatrick Simmons

View from Black
Pig's Dyke

From the heart of winter days that draw down to twilight,
mists from Loughs Allen, Mahanagh, rise
along valleys. Dark comes early with its voices,
its warriors and magic; comes with foreboding.

The Morrigan feasts on human flesh. Rulers of kingdoms
call dying glory, take lives not theirs to take. I hear the voices
in the wind that disperses cloud, nothing changed. There is a
    keening
in it; in the voices of lost children, faces down on the sand, but
    it is now.

The archaeologist was tortured and hanged for guarding treasures;
spoils of kingdoms that would teach that our enemy is war,
that there are no heroes. When Cuchulain carried Ferdia's broken
    body
from the ford, he carried his brother. Where was Conor, where
    was Fergus,

devious and dangerous? And Medbh, looking over her herds,
    counting up
her silver, counting up her gold? Here we are in another year that
    gathers

toward the darkest day. There is no magic that will save us but
    one:

the human kind of perceiving clearly; to see
in the artefacts of war, portents of the fall.

Janice Fitzpatrick Simmons

Shackleton Barracks, Ballykelly

It was a main thoroughfare
though the quietness of the mountain
said otherwise

Douglas firs
on either side
hid the airfield

The road had an air of definition
hard to define
a speed limit of thirty

an armed gate
and a council estate
that wasn't

Its name was valiant
Its mission: the extremes
Its purpose was to leave no mark.

*

There was no music
in the music room
There were no toilets

in the boiler-suits
They took day out
and made a man a lightless star

made the wall make him stand
made thirst a Kenyan of him
made hunger a South Pole of him

hung the black lampshade
of him from the ceiling
shattered sleep from his future

made the wall a Kenyan
made the north a hunger
hung thirst from the ceiling

lightless day in boiler-suits
toilets in the music room
crying through the toes

Some voices tumbled out
of the helicopter
and hid in the wardrobe

Some voices came out of the walls
and hung sightless
on the front grass

Some voices met other voices
travelling in Farsi
dressed as a brother

Words translated
meant the same
It must be so described.

Cherry Smyth

Note:
'What was done to Daddy was torture. It must be so described,'
Mary McKenna, daughter of Séan, one of fourteen men 'deeply
interrogated' by British intelligence in 1971, at Shackleton
Barracks.

Cold Spring in Lisbon

I

Black and white pavements, smoothed
to old ice, teach unremembering, how to stay
soft with each hard step. The marble cake
walls are stale but butter-gold shines
from every *pastelaria. Campo de Ourique*
at the top, the market spruced up,
palm trees shading British graves.
The Gulbenkian skulks in moss
and lichen, split-levelling the trees,
the lakes, the sunlight, still vital in its
concrete line. 'Who am I?' chases down
the half-night passageways. Her likeness
detonates a stranger in Estrela Park.

II

With and without words there was a clean calm
in his face I took as Franciscan. 'When is going
against your grain delusion,' I asked,
'or the healthy plane of a new pattern?'
He smiled his monkish smile.

I slept with a false truth, then woke.
The violent klaxon rang me out of the flowers
and that drowsy half-life. My bit of kingdom
quaked.

There is torment in cut flowers.
She took care to renew them
in the yellow, the orange vases.
I forgot soil, forgot wither.
I meditated on love being short,
colour being long.

A sign in English reads:
'We regret
NO
artificial flowers
in the cemetery.'

Attachment is not love.
Buddhists call it a plastic flower.

III
I speak to the ghost.
She speaks back.
I kill her again.

This is its own darkness:
I am far from all I knew myself by.
No skin for crowds, for noise,
for maps, the miradors.
I need to lie on unmown grass
in space and stillness,
what feeds a flower,
to suffer well.

High white waves carry the tail
of the storm in the dusk
and my arms open to the breath

of the *bacalhau*, turn away to return
to the empty city, the higher self
muttering: 'Stop longing for a dead thing.'

Memory gives off heat.
The touch of two index fingers
when we had no time to fuck,
God to mortal, clothed,
the naked, laughing rush.

Chew some ash to be real.

IV
From purpose, a world can grow:
write outwards from this seldom scratch.
It must be full of faith,
not feigned. That's how we begin
to live inwards, lie by lie.

Shirts blow in the wind
like everywhere else.
Love passes between people.
The young rise for the old
in the trolley cars,
impervious to faultlines.
Wisdom is always accompanied
by a new challenge
in which to live it.

She wouldn't open so I couldn't stay.
She wouldn't stay so I couldn't open.

V

The evergreens at Sintra
are mighty in depth and height.
I chose my own dead end in a fever of aging,
'where the light pains me like a lost garden'.[1]

Pessoa lived in this street, polished
the paving stones like the sun as it sets
at the top of the west in such a March.
His dogged joy in uselessness
takes off with the sparrows.
There's nothing for it but to keep
walking *Rua Coelho Da Rocha*
or fall empty to weather
and the routine of bells.

VI

A tree must know
when spring has passed
and no blossom has come.
We thought the air, the rain,
the sun, the earth enough, and our
touch, which made bloom.
Love was a decision we tried to take.

Birdsong fills the morning,
the passing whistle of the knife-grinder,
my face in sunlight and the near death of friends.

---

1.   From Sophia de Melo Breyner, *The Perfect Hour*, trans. by Colin Rorrison &
     Margaret Jull Costa (Lyttelton: Cold Hub Press, 2015)

The decorator has left shades of pink try-outs
on the walls. A baying makes whimper,
falling like rain, flecks on the pane, no crisp apples,
or the sound of guitar. Threadbare
clouds divide loss into portions.

I wake before dawn confused by the taste
of dissection, the disproportionate.
I've made three cardboard boats
and one seaplane in four months.
The scissors were wonderful to work.
I could invite a line: bend, form, glue.
Separate the rice from the lentils.
It doesn't matter what you count as long
as it's something: buttons, coins, seedlings.
Net worth. O flesh commodity. Ticker abundance.
Thank you, dear heart, for bearing up.

VII
For months, poems are depressing.
Like high gloss.
An arrow to the *padrão*:
I gave up my creed.

Light has to pour out or in to sustain love.
The passage of insight as light. The passion
of passage. There was once a good mirror
between us. It cracked under heavy skies.
It's called bad luck: the accident
of falling out of love.

VIII
How to surrender:
make every third thought about death.
Hold your breath, keep thin past the sensors.

You can't count in this language.
You empty your pockets, withered ears
that stopped listening to the white nights' siren.

Among pink buildings, the hung laundry.
I watch for the launderers. I count the church
bells. Someone is chipping at tired cement. Men
throw words I can't catch. Kids shout and scatter
a ball round a yard. The planes roar to the north.
I experience stillness. I go nowhere.

IX
All love is a copy
searching for the original.
I did everything to be moral.
Except speak, except leave.

There are exceptions
but there are no substitutes.
We acted as if there were.
We hurt as if there weren't.

Cherry Smyth

Where Were You in 1916?

Where were you in 1916? I wasn't born. Excuses, always excuses!

– Brendan Behan

Of course I wasn't born, but I was included
with a quarter of the country's population
at the Eucharistic Congress of 1932,
latent in a pair of ten-year-olds who were yet to meet.

An ovum in her reserves, *the boast of Catholic Ireland*,
I hid inside my mother, who wore her good coat
on the excursion train from Portarlington
in fine weather, said to be God's answer
to thirty-seven thousand spiritual acts of self-denial
undertaken by the new and ancient nation
and placed on record in the archbishop's office.

The child who grew up to be my father
wore the lanyard and badges of a Limerick troop
of the Catholic Boy Scouts of Ireland,
one of fourteen hundred *plucky little fellows*
encamped with trench latrines on a boarding-school lawn
and tireless in fifteen acres of the Phoenix Park,
directing a million pilgrims, holding lines and fetching water.

Where are their two faces in the crowd
that knelt with its shriven leaders in the grass?
The hungry streets, *a supernatural toyshop*
of angelic toy theatres, as by night
the Post Office roof beamed sky-writing,
GLORIFICAMUS. And I hear the last
of the ornate urinals made for the Congress
was bought in the seventies, in homage
to Marcel Duchamp, by a student of art.

Gráinne Tobin

Passing Number Twenty

Ballynahinch

Among fake frontages on derelict shops, someone
with money and sense has handed us a share
in this defiance - granite doorstep, polished brass -
has hung curtains of fine lace to shade an aspidistra
which may not exist beyond the long front windows.
Is it a folly, to put hope in good repair?

Two tall storeys, glossy with sage-green paint,
though grass sprouts in nearby gutters, and wages
have drained away. The courtyard's double doors
are latched wide open, now there are no more horses
to be stabled in these streets, no servant girls,
the spit of me at fourteen, kennelled in the attics.

It's more than the pleasure of a well-kept façade,
seen for years from a moving car on a stale main street -
this archway to a paved close, with lighted trees in pots,
like something glimpsed in an old town in Spain,
where houses turn inwards to stone courtyards
left by the Romans or the Caliphate.

Gráinne Tobin

Note

for Lila Stuart

Everything with me is on the back boiler,
and the arse is out of every saucepan in the house.

A magic stockpot full of onion, carrot peelings,
herb stalks and the dodgy bits of leeks,
the skin and bone of passing days, topped up
as and when, detritus not to be discarded –
gathering strength on the back of the hob,
while ordinary hours shout for attention
and the elixir concentrates to danger point.

If you don't do something soon, you'll find
the kitchen filled with fumes that sting your eyes,
stop up your mouth and catch at the back of your throat,
the delicious makings boiled to toxic varnish,
your heaviest pan a crucible of loss.

Gráinne Tobin

Conversation over a
farm gate

Five-barred,
like the one I sat on top of
to spot cars with out-of-county licence plates.

Whenever
he was sent away up to fetch the cows for milking
he'd pretend his donkey was a horse and him a cowboy.

Now he has a pinto mare, a black pony, and a black
donkey in foal
kept for the look of them, entirely.

In dusty Idaho
we made do with the chestnut workhorse
so slow you could fall asleep on her back

cowboy hats and red bandannas

and for a few months until the money got low
a palomino filly my father took a notion to.

I want to climb up
and sit on top of the gate.

Instead

I compliment him
on his green land and well-kept animals
as if I still know about such things

and he wishes me safe home.

Ann Zell

First reading of the beach in autumn

Where there was a slope there's now a sandbar
and rocks half-buried in spring
stand proud along the margin
        each in its wave-contoured hollow.

The sand is a needle worker's sampler,
a geography of mountain ranges and river systems,
a twice-daily visitors' log.

Bird arrows
pointing back the way they came

meandering dog trails,
the miniature bicycle tracks of sand crabs,
the bunched dents of the hare.

Stepping into my five-toed prints
        for a second lap of the beach

triggers
decades of déjà vu.

Ann Zell

In retrospect

With my eyesight and the failing light
it might have been a mink
spied from the corner of my eye

on the long granite slope when the tide was out
and no other mammals were about.

At the end of a day with no surprises
I wasn't expecting
any.

Faces on full alert
we stood on our hind legs
pointing noses at each other

until
it collapsed into a brown fur piece
and flicked away.

It might have been a mink –

but there on the edge of the known world
I thought I saw an otter.

Ann Zell

Leaving

While the others pack up
and the sea havers at high tide

I sit on the chalet stoop
watching a little brown mouse of a bird on springs

open its beak and shake the air
with its territorial imperative.

Planning ahead
I might come back as a bird:

never a morbid thought
never a maudlin thought

never an evil thought
never a thought.

I might come back as a ring of orange lichen
feeding on air and rock

or a patented puncture-proof
bicycle tire.

Ann Zell

ESSAYS

Rewriting History

Julieann Campbell

Due to my involvement with people affected by the Troubles, I've been fortunate to engage in some of the most fulfilling work I've ever done – helping others to tell their stories. As Heritage & Programmes Coordinator with the Museum of Free Derry, I'm currently helping to build up a new oral history archive – it's a role I relish, contacting old community leaders, politicians, activists and ordinary citizens who took to the streets to demand equality and civil rights. Before taking up the museum role, I facilitated the oral history strand of Derry's 'Unheard Voices' programme – an intensive, challenging project and one that made a huge impression on me. It became much more than just a project. It consumed me for months at a time.

The programme, developed by Creggan Enterprises and funded by the International Fund for Ireland, focused solely on the experiences of women who have remained largely silent about any grief, persecution or trauma they have suffered during Northern Ireland's recent conflict. We often had no idea what we would hear. Our aims were simple – to ask and to listen – a challenge which immediately drew me in as facilitator and editor of the resulting book. In all, twenty-eight women from diverse backgrounds shared their deeply personal stories with myself and Carol Cunningham, the coordinator of 'Unheard Voices'.

Having provided women with a safe space in which to share their experiences and examine the recent history of which many of them were a part, we were shocked to realise just how powerful their collective words could be. Published in 2016 as *Beyond the Silence: Women's Unheard Voices from the Troubles*, the collection provides a stark reflection of women's lives in Northern Ireland as we settle into the twenty-first century.

It is a powerful experience to witness these women – each with different experiences and backgrounds, and with different perspectives on the same period – all sharing and taking part in the storytelling process. Friendships have been forged and barriers broken down. Participants challenged their own belief systems in order to fully engage and learn from their respective experiences. The process has been a healing, restorative one.

I felt an instant sense of responsibility towards these women. Realising the task required sensitivity, patience, research and accuracy, my years of training as a writer and journalist were put to good use. It helped that every person we met was so genuinely warm and welcoming, even those terrified at the prospect of speaking to us. 'Unheard Voices' challenged me in a way I hadn't prepared for – both emotionally and creatively. It gave me a new appreciation for storytelling and the role I could play in bringing people's stories to life. I now see the immense potential of oral history in helping to heal and restore one's soul. Indeed, I can think of few more meaningful careers for me as a writer and a history enthusiast.

It was by no means easy to find women willing to share their life experiences with us. We sought the assistance of trusted women who play huge roles within their communities, which allowed quicker access to finding women willing to speak out. Building trust was all-important as we knew that without the assistance of these key figures, many interviews could not have happened. Most interviews took place in the home, others wherever women felt most comfortable. Each testimony depended on the full approval of participants, which was obviously vital to the storytelling process and ensured that women retained ownership of their stories. Others spoke anonymously.

One thing that struck me was just how many of these women presumed that their story was unimportant, and how they found it cathartic to speak out at last. On the whole, women expressed gratitude that someone had asked about their experiences and cared enough to listen. It's hard to remain professional in situations like these. We often abandoned formal questioning to just let the women talk – and by God, talk they did. On many occasions, we shared tears and held hands as women wept while recounting their life experiences. It was an arduous task at times, and I frequently felt overwhelmed by the grief and candour of participants.

One particular moment stands out as I write this – something the daughter of an IRA political prisoner once said about her father: 'Sometimes I used to wish he *had* died in the Troubles, because then at least I'd have a grave to visit. To me, it feels like I mourn something that's not dead.' I thought about that statement every night for weeks afterwards, and how she cried her way through the interview. Some stories had been buried so deeply they had yet to be shared with other family members, and these accounts were possibly the most difficult to procure and conduct. It was a surreal feeling, being privy to someone's deepest, most painful secrets, and it was not something I took lightly.

It is not surprising that wounds run so deep. The civil unrest in Northern Ireland between 1969 and 1994 resulted in over 3,600 deaths and over 50,000 people were injured. Of the 3,600 people who lost their lives, about one-tenth of these were women, but it was mainly the mothers, wives, sisters, daughters or grandmothers who were left to pick up the pieces and rebuild families. According to the Northern Ireland Statistical Research Agency (NISRA) it's estimated that over 500,000 people suffered directly from the conflict, through personal experience, the loss of someone in their lives, physical injury or trauma. The 1999 *Cost of the Troubles Study* indicated that civilians accounted for more than half of the fatalities. Given the North's population at the turn of the century – one and a half million people – the number of people closely associated to those killed or injured was therefore estimated to be about half the population.[1]

Northern Ireland's conflict came at a psychological cost, too. A 2009 study by the Psychology Institute at Ulster University and the Northern Ireland Centre for Trauma and Transformation found that two-thirds of Northern Ireland's adult population have suffered one or more serious traumatic experiences – half of which were 'Troubles'-related. The same study found high levels of post-traumatic stress disorder, with one in one hundred adults affected by post-traumatic stress disorder and an estimated 40,000 adults experiencing mental health problems related to the past.[2]

Findings from a 2014 study also suggest that despite the formal end to the conflict, significant numbers continue to be affected by adverse mental health related to trauma exposure.[3] Furthermore, several studies into suicidal behaviour across the North also indicate associations with conflict-related trauma. These stark figures lead me on to another vital requirement of oral history work – ensuring participants have access to counselling or support services, should the need arise. While women are often remarkably resilient, they may also acknowledge a sense of shared fragility, with some seeking further referrals to manage trauma and stress. The same process applied during my time as Press Officer for the Bloody Sunday Trust – another undertaking that had a huge impact on me, both as a person and as a writer. Ahead of the publication of the *Report of the Bloody Sunday Inquiry* in 2010, relatives of those killed and those who survived were encouraged to recount their experiences and urged to seek support. We

1.   INCORE, University of Ulster & The United Nations University, 1999.
2.   Initiative for Conflict-Related Trauma, 2009.
3.   Finola Ferry, Brendan Bunting, Samuel Murphy, Siobhan O'Neill, Dan Stein and Karestan Koenen, 'Traumatic events and their relative PTSD burden in Northern Ireland: a consideration of the impact of the "Troubles,"' *Social Psychiatry and Psychiatric Epidemiology* 49 (2014), pp. 435-436; p. 435.

assessed the risks of re-traumatising participants, particularly with the bereaved or those sharing traumatic experiences for the first time.

One of the surviving wounded whom I interviewed during my Bloody Sunday work was Alana Burke, a wonderfully warm and determined campaigner. Alana was eighteen years old in 1972 and she remembers enjoying the chance to show off her new corduroy coat at that Sunday's civil rights march. Crushed by an armoured Saracen as she and hundreds of others fled the advancing British paratroopers in the Bogside, Alana sustained serious, life-changing injuries. 'The worst part of it all was the ambulance,' Alana told me. 'I was semi-conscious on the floor and there were bodies on either side of me. It's hazy, but I just remember thinking: are these people dead? Am I dead? I thought maybe I was dead and looking down on the bodies in the ambulance.' Alana slowly learnt to walk again, but suffered long-term physical damage to her pelvis and reproductive organs. 'It was a terrible, terrible time. No matter how many times you tell the story or how much therapy you have, it makes no difference – Bloody Sunday changed everything. It's something that will never, ever go away. You live with it every day and, the longer it goes on, the angrier you get,' she said. We were aware of how precious those interviews were, and how they might conceivably be the last time some of them spoke about the events of Bloody Sunday. Work like this takes time, but it offers an important glimpse into the scars and resilience of people in the North, as well as the inadequacies still surrounding the current effects of the peace process.

One theme recurring in my work in recent years is the lack of aftercare or statutory support offered to bereaved or traumatised families. For example, in 1974, Sharon Austin's teenage brother, Winston, was abducted and murdered by the IRA, and it ripped their family apart. Sharon told me, 'My parents got no support when he died. My father became an abusive alcoholic … my mother became totally dependent on drugs and tried to commit suicide. She must have tried at least twenty or thirty times. We didn't matter anymore … my childhood was horrific. I could have disappeared off to anywhere and nobody would have noticed me gone. Nobody gave a damn.'

Marie Newton lost her first love and father of her seven young children in 1976, when the Ulster Freedom Fighters (UFF) gunned down John Toland in his pub, the Happy Landing in Eglinton, Co. Derry. Marie welcomed the opportunity to talk about John and the life they shared together. She said, 'It's sad that it took us so long to talk about it. We were never offered counsellors at the time. We felt like the only people in the world who had lost someone. When John died, no one wanted to listen to us or cared what we had to say. Our own community and neighbours were the only ones to help us.' She went on, 'We were only beginning our lives. If only they'd phoned and threatened him, that would have been enough – we would have given up everything and left. They didn't need to kill him.'

Life was tough for many and this hardship has left a painful legacy. Lorraine Murray, a survivor of the Greysteel massacre in Co. Derry, broke her twenty-year silence during the 'Unheard Voices' project. On Hallowe'en night in 1993, Ulster Defence Association (UDA) gunmen opened fire on customers in a sleepy village pub – shouting 'Trick or Treat' and leaving seven people dead and twelve more injured. Lorraine's harrowing account describes how she and her mother felt abandoned and forgotten in the wake of Greysteel – an admission that made front-page news upon the collection's release. She stated, 'It feels like my mother and I weren't even there. When they talk about Greysteel, we're not included … they offered us nothing but a counsellor when it happened and then they forgot about us. It feels like I should be talking about it now, however hard it might be.'

In 1982, Donna Porter witnessed a Royal Ulster Constabulary (RUC) officer shot and killed before she ran to the aid of his badly wounded partner. The experience left an indelible impression on the young woman. She stated, 'People weren't offered counselling or anything in those days, they just got on with it. But for years, I haven't been able to touch a piece of meat to cook it, because of the blood. I still can't eat red meat to this day, either. My daughter puts the meat in the pot because I can't even look at it.'

Noticeable trends emerge from the storytelling process, too, like the prevalence of prescription drugs or alcohol as a means of coping with traumatic memory. 'Maybe it would have helped to talk to someone about it,' said one participant in the programme, 'but in this country, you aren't offered counselling, you get offered a tablet and told to go on home.' 'I worried I wouldn't be able to manage,' said another participant, 'because I'd been on medication for years – the same stuff they give prisoners to calm them down.' Statistics back this up. Research conducted by University of Ulster, *Troubled Consequences: A Report on the Mental Health Impact of the Civil Conflict in Northern Ireland,* found that, by 2011, antidepressant use had trebled in Northern Ireland.[4]

'It made me an alcoholic,' admitted Sylvia, whose husband was shot dead by paramilitaries through the living room window of their family home. 'My nerves were terrible, and I began having a drink to help me sleep and that escalated … it was just an easy way to deal with things at the time. It's a daily struggle to control the alcoholism. If I get upset, the slightest wee thing can trigger me off and I'll go missing for days. I can never hold down a job either, because drink gets the better of me in the end and I get sacked.' The danger is that these underlying problems will remain unchecked, occurring as they do within the confines of the home. We must reach out to the marginalised within our communities and continue to demand that governments implement acceptable and effective mechanisms for dealing with the past.

---

4. *Troubled Consequences: A Report on the Mental Health Impact of the Civil Conflict in Northern Ireland,* University of Ulster & The Commission for Victims and Survivors, 2011.

The work took its toll on me personally. At times, it was a very isolating experience, sitting up late and transcribing every word of somebody else's tragedy. I felt weighed down by the task before me, and by the importance of getting it right. Sometimes, it felt all too real. I remember once working on an account of a woman whose sister, Ethel, who had joined the IRA, was preparing a bomb that exploded accidentally. It was around 3 a.m., and I was busy transcribing the raw interview when suddenly Philomena mentioned how her sister always stayed at a certain friend's house – a few doors from mine. I can't explain the impact of suddenly feeling so close to history, so immersed in the words I was typing that it sent chills up my spine. In a way, I felt that Ethel's spirit had been doing the typing. Another time, I became so caught up and emotional at the story of the woman whose husband was shot dead through their living room window, I'm not ashamed to say I sought solace in a bottle of Shiraz and a bout of Cartoon Network at 2 a.m. I felt that I would do anything to rid my mind of those images.

There seems to be a prevalent idea that women played mostly domestic roles during the conflict, a fallacy often reinforced by historians and researchers. In reality, women were the backbone of society, and besides the so-called duties expected of them, many pursued careers and became police officers, entered politics or became combatants or reporters caught up in atrocities – a fact rarely acknowledged in accounts of the conflict or proposals on how to deal with it.

The fact that so many women still feel ignored or marginalised in today's post-conflict Northern Ireland is indicative of a wider discontent. If we can address even a fraction of this discontent through storytelling, then similar projects should continue to be implemented and nurtured. 'It's good that women are beginning to talk now – we have a lot to say,' agrees Jane McMorris, a grandmother in her late seventies who lived on the front line of the conflict in one of Derry's interface areas, the heavily barricaded Irish Street in the Waterside. I'm not suggesting that women here have historically been weak or silent – but somewhere along the line, many women felt left behind and never caught up, and these are the women I want to listen to. These are the stories I want to play a part in telling – words with a purpose.

Importantly, several accounts for 'Unheard Voices' are from those affected by state violence, highlighting the continuing failure of the British state in dealing with historical cases. These include daughters of Sammy Devenny, the first person to die in the Troubles after a savage RUC beating. Colette O'Connor (née Devenny) said the family have never been able to grieve properly, having never been told the truth about Sammy's death. She affirms, 'It's still too painful; because nothing has ever been explained. It annoys me that people – politicians – think you can brush things under the carpet. You can't. Too many people here need answers, and that should be made a priority.'

This frustration is visible elsewhere too. When hired to organise the island-wide 'In Their Footsteps' campaign on behalf of the Bloody Sunday Trust and the Pat Finucane Centre for Human Rights in 2014, I met scores of families who shared similar feelings of hurt and abandonment – by history, by their community, and by the British government. The campaign invited bereaved and affected families from across Ireland to contribute a pair of shoes representing their loved one, creating a sea of shoes in cities like Derry, Dublin, Belfast and London. The most powerful thing about the campaign was the collective remembering that took place between strangers. Hundreds of families got involved, and many I spoke to throughout the day spoke of their comfort in talking to others and realising they weren't alone. It gave families a rare opportunity to tell their stories to passers-by, press and other campaigners. This campaign continues today, and invites all families and individuals to contribute to its growing, incredibly moving exhibition.

Clearly, individual families want different things. Of primary importance is the need for an independent mechanism for dealing with the past, something that addresses the needs of families first and foremost. Many cases in the North have never been properly investigated, or had any official investigation whatsoever. An impartial, thorough investigation to establish facts is long overdue, particularly for family members and victims who are not getting any younger. I include my own family in this category, having watched my aunts and uncles campaign tirelessly to clear the name of my seventeen-year-old uncle, Jackie Duddy – the first person to die on Bloody Sunday. Those same campaigning aunts and uncles are now greying pensioners, and it is only now – forty-five years later – that the police are conducting the first murder investigation into Bloody Sunday. My family was fortunate in that we had an inquiry and we received some semblance of truth – many more need answers. There is a great need for transparency. People need clarification and the truth about their own injuries or the deaths of loved ones – much of which could be contained in classified Ministry of Defence files. So much information has emerged from these files in recent years: in an ideal world, every relevant document relating to the conflict would be made available in pursuit of truth.

Many remain uneasy about the fragile peace process and unsure of their role within it. Eileen is one of many people disillusioned by the peace process: 'I was delighted with the peace process, but it hasn't worked,' she told me. 'Nothing has really changed for me, or my friends or the communities we live in. We're actually worse off now, because nobody will speak out about the things that continue to happen nowadays. Is it any wonder we've lost faith in the peace process?'

'There are houses and families still being raided in Creggan to this day – but it's never reported or talked about. Nobody wants to know. People are afraid to speak out because they'll be labelled a dissident – I'm not a dissident, I just stopped supporting the process and I was honest about that. Now I've been labelled ... it's no wonder so many people are screwed up; no wonder so many are on tablets or benefits. If we lived in England, we would be getting counselling today for trauma, but here nobody cares. We're just forgotten about.'

Life is no easier today for women with military or security force backgrounds, either. Recent incidences of bombs under police officers' cars remind us that tensions persist, and peace can never be guaranteed. While I honestly believe that we have become a much more progressive, peaceful society, I also can't ignore the sad fact that serving or former police officers are forced to maintain secrecy.

'Elizabeth' served as a reservist for seventeen years and witnessed the horror of the Troubles first-hand. She explained, 'I never felt safe in the RUC, and I felt I had to keep my job a secret a lot of the time ... there was no support for us ... After I left the RUC, I think I had a nervous breakdown. I wasn't coping anymore. I was always nervous and I didn't want to go out anywhere or involve myself with anyone.' It was only when invited to take part in oral history that Elizabeth felt ready to speak with a modicum of ease about the things she saw and experienced. 'I haven't ever really talked about any of this before. It's only now, when I think about some of the things we experienced, that it really hits me,' she told me. 'I can understand why so many ex-RUC people are alcoholics today. The RUC hierarchy are fine – it was the ordinary police officers, men and women, sent out to do the dirty jobs who suffered most.'

Another woman described how the pressure of being an RUC wife permeated every aspect of her life and personality. She recalled, 'We never saw our men. They were working eighteen hours a day and we just had to get on with it ... Because I was an RUC man's wife, nobody spoke to me. Even Protestants – your own community – didn't want to know you because you were police. Nobody wanted to be your friend.' It is significant that all but one of the security force-related people we interviewed chose to speak anonymously. Clearly, perceived links to the RUC or the British military, however historic, continue to present problems despite the Good Friday Agreement. Even within my own circle, there is a young man who left town to join the Police Service of Northern Ireland (PSNI), keeping his profession a secret since then. While perhaps understandable in the context of these islands, it is unfortunate that we still tolerate such daily, normalised fear.

Now that I work for Northern Ireland's first dedicated civil rights museum – the Museum of Free Derry – visitors often share their own experiences with us. I'm continually struck by just how unrestrained they are in imparting such personal information to strangers, and how they seem glad of a chance to mention it. One grandmother from Belfast wept leaving our exhibition room, telling us how 'it brings it all flooding back'. She went on to explain that her family were persecuted and burned out of their home in the early 1970s. She lost brothers and many friends to the conflict, and admitted that she has lived with acute depression and anxiety since then.

Oral history projects are growing in popularity because they offer participants a long-overdue opportunity to talk about difficult, painful issues. 'I never thought I would speak about these experiences, but maybe the time is right,' one RUC reservist told us. 'I know too many people who now see psychiatrists because of the things they've seen in the past.' Decades after her husband's murder, Sylvia still refuses to discuss the incident with her two now-adult children. 'We still don't talk about the past at all. Now that I have talked about it here, I won't mention it again, or read it back. I might let my children read this story someday. To help them understand more about me, and about what happened that night.'

Today's post-conflict society is also a traumatised society, one which is still hurting from the damage inflicted by the Troubles but which all too often lacks the means to express it. While much has been achieved in the past two decades there is clearly much still to do if people continue to suffer in silence – and, as I have witnessed, feeling able to speak about the past can play a crucial first step towards finding the acknowledgement, acceptance and healing that our society so badly needs.

In this context, the absence of any institutional commitment to dealing with the past is nothing short of negligent. It is no coincidence that one of the sticking points in negotiations aimed at reinstating Stormont's power-sharing government is so-called 'legacy issues' – and it is the one that is the most politically sensitive, and therefore the most intractable. Attempts have been made. In 2009, the Consultative Group on the Past – an independent body commissioned by the Secretary of State and co-chaired by Robin Eames and Denis Bradley – recommended the establishment of an independent Legacy Commission, recognition and support to those who have suffered, and a Reconciliation Forum. Their proposals were not implemented.

In 2013, talks chaired by US Senator Richard Haass and Dr Meghan O'Sullivan resulted in proposals which included an information retrieval process, but their plans were not supported by all political parties and again were not implemented. The Stormont House Agreement of 2014 again attempted to address the legacy of the past, and while measures for its implementation were included in the 2015 Fresh Start Agreement, that agreement itself foundered amid a political crisis at Stormont, which has, at the time of writing, seen Northern Ireland in limbo and without a government since January 2017.

In this vacuum, it has been left to the community and arts sectors to lead the way. The Museum of Free Derry exists today because of the determination of Bloody Sunday campaigners to tell their story and educate others. Likewise, the 'Unheard Voices' programme gave voice to women from both communities who have suffered silently for decades, and I have seen first-hand how the relationships formed and bridges built within the group have rippled out to influence families, friends, and communities. The play *Green and Blue* (2016) by former hunger striker Laurence McKeown, was based on first-hand testimony from former RUC and Garda Síochána officers who served on the border during the Troubles and highlighted yet again what has become a familiar theme – the fact that this was the first time many of those involved had ever spoken about their experiences.

A few years ago, I heard a radio interview that stayed with me. Two women, both of whom had lost brothers in the Troubles, spoke about the pain of their loss and the hole their brothers' deaths had left in their own lives and that of their families. They spoke of empty chairs at Christmas, of nieces and nephews growing up without an uncle, of the wives and children their brothers might have had. Only afterwards did the interviewer identify the women – one a Protestant whose brother had been in the Ulster Defence Regiment (UDR) and was shot by an IRA sniper, the other a Catholic whose brother was shot by the Special Air Service (SAS). Much has been said about the disturbing concept of a 'hierarchy of victims', but grief and trauma know no hierarchy. Grief and trauma are human emotions, human hurts, and until those in power accept this, I doubt there will be any agreement on the past, nor any collective way of moving forward – even though it is the very least our people deserve.

In the meantime, we must do what we can to continue to address the divisions that still exist by encouraging discussion, reconciliation and education at a community level, and supporting the campaigns of so many bereaved families who still await inquests, action or accountability for the loss of their loved ones. Trauma support should become a priority. Ultimately, my faith is in the people of Northern Ireland, and it is based on the strength of all those who have shared their stories with me and who still have a story to tell. As Colette O'Connor, still determined to uncover the truth about her father's death, says, 'People need to know the real history – from those who lived it, and we shouldn't be afraid to talk.'

Sisters Are Doin' It for Themselves: The Practice and Ethos of Word of Mouth Poetry Collective, 1991–2016[1]

Ruth Carr

The publication of *The Female Line* in November 1985 came as a welcome revelation for a number of women.[2] They discovered, to their astonishment, that there was a readership for what they wrote. They also learned that they were not writing in isolation, that there were other women like themselves privately nurturing their 'two inches of ivory' all across Northern Ireland.[3] The series of readings that followed in venues in Belfast, Derry-Londonderry, Dublin, and beyond, gave their writing a profile and allowed them to share their work. It also enabled writers to meet, exchange information, forge friendships, find critical support and form informal writing groups. One such group found space in the Linen Hall Library, a place that first opened its doors to female members in the 1790s and, in this case, offered very supportive terms to Writing Women.

Writing Women met monthly and was open to any woman who wrote creatively and wished to come along, exchange news and discuss

---

1. *Sisters Are Doin' It for Themselves* is the title of a song by Annie Lennox and David A. Stewart, famously sung by Annie Lennox and Aretha Franklin.
2. *The Female Line, Northern Irish Women Writers*, edited by Ruth Hooley [Carr] (Belfast: Northern Ireland Women's Rights Movement, 1985).
3. From a letter by Jane Austen to her nephew, Edward; taken as a metaphor for her writing.

her work and that of others. As the organiser of this open group, during 1987-88, I arranged occasional workshops and readings by authors such as Frances Molloy, Jennifer Johnston and Nuala Ní Dhomhnaill. It was at Nuala's workshop that I first heard Ann Zell share a poem in public.[4] At this point in her life Ann was experiencing a seismic creative surge into writing, with poetry emerging as her true vocation. Shortly after she returned from a residential writing course at The Poets' House at Islandmagee in 1991, she rang me up and declared that if she couldn't join a support group solely devoted to poetry, then she would surely die. In response to this, recognising that I too felt some merit in that sentiment, I contacted those women whose poetry I had come across and been impressed by in *The Female Line*, *The Honest Ulsterman* (which I then co-edited with Robert Johnstone), Writing Women and other groups. Needless to say, none of them had published collections; but I do recall coming across a pamphlet by Joan Newmann entitled *Suffer Little Children* (1991) and being stunned by her poems.[5]

So, on a Saturday morning in the autumn of 1991, the Word of Mouth Poetry Collective met for the first time in the Linen Hall Library. Those attending included Joan Newmann, Margaret Curran, Sally Wheeler, Mary Twomey, Gráinne Tobin, Pia Gore, Ann Zell, of course, and myself.[6] Sally Wheeler recalls:

> I was rather surprised when Ann Zell approached me about a new group, saying 'You are a poet'. I thought I was but I kept it a secret. We met … once a month … Some had published poems, others had not, but there was a great solidarity between us.

---

4. The poem was 'Herself,' which later appeared in Ann Zell, *Weathering* (Cliffs of Moher: Salmon, 1998).

5. Joan Newmann, *Suffer Little Children* (Diamond Poets, University of Ulster, 1991).

6. In the months following the start of Word of Mouth, a few more women joined: Kate Newmann and Elaine Gaston first; then Eilish Martin and Ann McKay. Others later to join for the duration or some period of time included Pamela Greene (Acheson), Natasha Cuddington, Olive Broderick, Sonia Abercrombie and Judith Thurley.

I had not met all of these women face to face, but I had met their work and knew that they were all serious about their writing. We sat round the square mahogany table in the Governors' Room, where I put forward a proposal of how we might proceed. Our aim was clear: to hear and respond to one another's poems, both supportively and critically, in a non-hierarchical environment. Things soon fell into place. I remember how remarkably in tune we were on these matters. It was as if we had been waiting individually for a group like this to offer us creative space in our lives. Joan Newmann recollects:

> I was living in Ballycastle, and though I had belonged to the Philip Hobsbaum Group in the early sixties, I had not been part of a poetry group since then. It was with surprise that I received Ruth's telephone call, with an invitation to take part in a group that she and other women were founding. I was worried about whether journeying for 120 miles was going to be a disappointment, but in fact it was a highly organised, very well-structured meeting, with very powerful intellectual responses to the work, and a deal of enthusiasm. It certainly prompted me to take stock of what I had written, and what I might write, and there is no greater impetus than that.[7]

What each person at that table shared was a desire to have her work and herself taken seriously. We wanted to create an environment in which our poetry would thrive, uninhibited and uncensored (at least by others if not entirely by ourselves). We were looking for something more egalitarian in structure – where 'Each of us is writer, reader and facilitator in turn at our sessions, each with an equal say in, and responsibility for, all that the group does.' (So I

---

7. Personal communication, Joan Newmann. Sincere thanks to those members of the Collective who kindly offered their comments and reflections on Word of Mouth to add to this record: Joan Newmann, Sally Wheeler, Gráinne Tobin, Eilis Martin, Natasha Cuddington and Kate Newmann. This correspondence took place between January and March 2017.

declared in the introduction to our anthology, *Word of Mouth*.)[8] We rotated the role of facilitator at each session. Everyone did their stint, whether they were accustomed to the role or not, freeing the rest to give their full concentration to the work at hand.

In workshopping poems, we held to the practice which we found most effective. Each brought copies of a poem that was a work in progress. We would hear it read twice, once in the voice of the poet and then read by another. The author was not allowed to say anything until everyone had responded to the poem, respecting the author's autonomy but reading closely to convey its full import from a reader's point of view. Gráinne Tobin's comment on this process reflects the experience for many of us:

> It astonished me that the simple act of hearing the poem in another's voice could reveal blockages in the meaning conveyed, unintended sounds or associations, details such as line breaks that might mislead or confuse a reader.

In this practice it is essential to bear in mind that the poem offered is not yours to 'fix', but yours to respond to as language, form, sound, rhythm, ideas; drawing on a range of associations and cultural ties – with all the subtleties that consciously and sub-consciously fuel its poetry. This approach frees the reader to convey what the poem carries. And the effect is cumulative, with the next response often building on the one before. In a workshop the group had with poet Paula Meehan, she recommended beginning each critical response with, 'If this was my poem …' This care of approach helps to ensure that feedback does not become reductive. Gráinne Tobin continues:

> This regular scrutiny of each other's poems made me realise that there is a place for many kinds of poetry and that one reader's orthodoxy will be another's irritant, but that the poet

---

8.   Word of Mouth Poetry Collective, Introduction to *Word of Mouth: Poems* (Belfast: Blackstaff Press, 1996).

herself has to be able to stand by her choices. We had different origins, backgrounds and education, so each member brought particular expertise into the discussion, and the occasional dissonance was stimulating. It was useful that we could allow each other to unlock ourselves from the tradition of the Ulster well-made poem and look more to international examples. It led several of us to be more adventurous in style and form.

I remember moments of illumination. It might be a question, a comment, an inflexion of the voice in reading a line, that magically opens the poem up to reveal itself to you in a new light and you can see what way to go with it. Or those rare occasions when a poem elicits the kind of response that you were hoping it might and you feel communication is near complete. It is also rewarding to be able to do this, collectively, for others.

Of course it was not all epiphanies. There were some disagreements and clashes of personality. One early incident almost upended the group before it had got underway. But we found ways of overcoming differences. We all needed and valued the group too much to allow it to fail. Our primary concern was ever with poetic practice. This objective remained at the core of Word of Mouth throughout its twenty-five years. Had the focus been on competition and 'success', I doubt if the Collective would have survived. One thing that helped to preserve this focus was having a neutral and appropriate venue for our meetings. Members lived as far apart as Co. Derry, Newcastle, Downpatrick and Donegal. Although it meant that some members had very far to travel to Belfast each month, the Linen Hall Library provided a suitably focussed and literary atmosphere for our workshops, without which the group might have foundered.

The workshop process can bring about much creative development. Gradually, one accrues skills of the ear, of the eye, of judgement, but above all one begins to acquire self-belief, as Gráinne affirms:

Word of Mouth gave me confidence through regular, rigorous criticism from knowledgeable and attentive readers of poetry. It made me pay more heed to technical issues in every line I wrote. The respect I felt for other members' work grew to include my own, and the practice of paying close attention to others' poems kept my head in the poetry zone during periods when I could not write. The group sustained me.

Eilish Martin goes one step further:

> Engaged in the serious intent of poetry, I was encouraged to value the rigour of poetic practice and I was ambitious to take my work forward testing out the tensions inherent in poetic expression. I felt it possible to call myself a poet.

The women-only nature of the collective and our practical approach had a positive impact, as Gráinne notes:

> As women writing and reading in the context of our time and society, no effort needed to be wasted on explaining female experience to a mixed-sex or mixed-genre group: we could just concentrate on the work.

While we were seeking to foster a 'safe' environment, bringing any creative work to the table involves risk. If it did not involve risk it would be less worthwhile. To trust one's personal creation to a first audience is to leave oneself vulnerable and easily hurt. But with practice the risk can become less than the gain. Natasha Cuddington describes something of this process:

> With what seems to me – a prescient admix of delight and trepidation – a poet attaches herself to the poetry workshop. Notionally, the workshop is never a place of danger, but a location wherein a collectivity bangs against the sharp edge of poetics, hones a poem in the service of craft.

As a younger and a Canadian poet whose work is concerned with the deconstruction of traditional form, Natasha experienced that sense of risk or danger in – if anything – more accentuated form:

> What is hotly discovered, out on a limb, is that when a poet proffers poetry that falls short of expectation – when a poem's formal tone asserts itself away from collectively held convention, say, away from legible narrative or that manifest locomotion of rhetoric – tentative contingents jostle to endanger a poem's innovation … [T]he workshop is never a site for declarations or affiliation. It is space wherein the endangered poem – and I use endangered here to not only inflect the making of poetry that is formally radical, but also and often, the making of poetry by women or other marginal constituencies – can work itself into being.

Reading and listening to her work came as a wake-up call to reappraise notional concepts of poetic form and broaden our horizons. As a result, we all became more aware of form and Ann Zell and, in particular, Eilish Martin experimented with form in their later poetry. As Eilish puts it:

> For me, the demands of poetic form became a discipline to embrace and then a constraint to subvert or overthrow as discourse and suggested reading both widened and deepened my understanding of poetic possibility... Wanting more from my work, wanting something other I felt a growing need to risk my own practice – though most tentatively – against experimental forms of poetic expression.

The collectivism of the group became absorbing, as did its Saturday morning colloquiums. As the introduction to *Word of Mouth* puts it: 'You could not pay for the quality of critical attention involved in this process. Essentially we [were] listening to each other as poets.'[9] This had its dangers, as Gráinne notes:

> The availability of expert first readers at our monthly meetings made it easier not to seek a wider audience by submitting poems to magazines or competitions. There was a danger of being satisfied to use each other as our only readers – though I think not all of us would consider this a danger.

But the group looked outwards as well as inwards. The paucity of opportunities for women writers twenty-five years ago, particularly opportunities for those not taken up by academia, cannot be overstated. Only those who lived through this period can really know what it was like.

Acutely conscious of this lack of visibility and opportunity, Word of Mouth made a commitment to a second line of action: to run reading events and workshops that would give the writers a platform and, where possible, would be free and accessible. These included a Poetry Festival in Ballycastle, 'Knocking on Heaven's Door', which was inspired by a similar event held in Killybegs, Donegal by the late Noelle Vial and sister poets. We ran events from time to time in the Linen Hall Library and the Ulster Hall and undertook a regular series of incredibly well attended open platform readings at St Patrick's Church hall in Belfast, at which, after a couple of scheduled readings (mostly by women), the platform was turned over to all comers, female or male, with each reading a poem of their own and one by a poet they admired.

We exchanged visits with women poets in Sligo and hosted an Irish reading tour for Russian poet Alla Mikhalevich. We met Alla through Joan and Kate Newmann who knew her through their association with the Pushkin Prize. We worked on translations of

---

9.   See note 7.

her poetry[10] and that of other women poets from St Petersburg. These Russian poets and translators went on to produce a book of Russian translations of *Word of Mouth*.[11] Eilish Martin, Ann Zell, Elaine Gaston and Gráinne Tobin secured a travel grant from the Arts Council of Northern Ireland to attend the launch and give joint readings in St Petersburg. Word of Mouth eventually reciprocated this wonderful tribute with the publication of a bilingual anthology of five St Petersburg poets in 2013: *When the Neva Rushes Backwards.*[12]

The *Word of Mouth* anthology, from which so many good things flowed, had its origins in the spring of 1995 when Ann and I overlapped at Annaghmakerrig (she was leaving when I arrived). I remember there had been a 'Night of the big Wind' grade storm and we were out in the grounds, clambering over fallen trees, trying to figure out who might publish an anthology of Word of Mouth, when it occurred that really we could simply publish ourselves. It was such a liberating idea that we put together a manuscript of all twelve members' poems in no time. It was almost as an afterthought that we sent it in to Blackstaff Press, making it clear in the accompanying letter that we were simply sending it to them in case they might be interested, but that in any event we would be bringing the work out ourselves. It came as a welcome surprise when they promptly offered to publish it.

Publication showed that the old shibboleths remained firmly in place. Gráinne reflects:

When our Blackstaff anthology was published, one influ-ential reviewer's comments sneered at the idea of us as a

---

10. With the expert assistance of Professor Marcus Wheeler, Word of Mouth produced a poster featuring a Russian poem by Alla Mikhalevich and mul-tiple English versions in translation, 1999.

11. СЛОВО ИЗ УСТ, Стихи современ нрландскиих (Санкт-Петероург, 2003), St Petersburg.

12. *When the Neva Rushes Backwards, Five St Petersburg Poets,* A bilingual anthology compiled and translated by Word of Mouth Poetry Collective (Belfast: Lagan Press, 2014).

collective, and even suggested that we did not have individual authorship of the poems. I got the impression from
several sources that as a women writers' group we were
accorded amateur status.

Now that we were collectively published, it was a matter for each
of us to produce a collection if we so wished and the Newmanns'
role in this was critical. They make a remarkable team. They were
constantly on the road, travelling from workshop to reading, to
class, inspiring adults and children alike. Many budding writers flowered under their encouragement. Word of Mouth was
supposed to be about focussing on one's own work. But for the
Newmanns, with their tremendous vision, it led to an even greater
commitment to the work of others. As Joan Newmann states:

> I am grateful to all the voices [in Word of Mouth]...The stan-
> dard of the work was so high that it was crucial that it be
> published, and that was the catalyst for the establishment of
> the Summer Palace Press, which has published forty-six books.

I had the tremendous honour and pleasure to be the first poet published by Summer Palace. It was like entering a new era. Collections
by Eilish Martin and Ann McKay followed – a great tribute to Word
of Mouth, and several more Word of Mouth poets joined the ever-
growing roster of Summer Palace poets over the next six years.[13]
Gráinne reflects the feelings of many:

> Without Word of Mouth, and especially Joan and Kate
> Newmann who set up Summer Palace Press, I don't think I

---

13. Summer Palace titles by members of Word of Mouth: Ruth Carr, *There is
   a House* (1999); *The Airing Cupboard* (2008); Eilish Martin, *Slitting the
   Tongues of Jackdaws*, (1999); *Ups Bounce Dash* (2008); Ann McKay, *Giving
   Shine*, (2000); Kate Newmann, *The Blind Woman in the Blue House* (2001);
   Pamela Greene, *Tattoo Me* (2002); Gráinne Tobin, *Banjaxed* (2002) ; *The
   Nervous Flyer's Companion* (2010) ; Sally Wheeler, *Mosaic* (2004); Ann
   Zell, *Between Me and All Harm* (2005); Joan Newmann, *Prone* (2007).

would have managed to publish much poetry. (I am now on my third collection.) I'd avoided submitting enough poems to magazines. I was far too afraid of seeming pushy, and unable to face much rejection. Joan and Kate, who already knew the poems well, made a beautiful book of them with such gentle efficiency that I got quite the wrong impression of the world of poetry publishing. After that, I was braver.

Summer Palace made a crucial difference to Northern literary publishing. Because most of its authors were women, it went a significant way towards redressing the customary gender imbalance in Northern Ireland. This in itself increased the chances of women poets being included in anthologies, as the criteria for selection usually ruled out those without a collection. The Newmanns' approach to publishing was exhilarating, exacting high standards yet including authors in the decision-making process. As Joan told *Poetry Ireland* in 2010: 'Rather than moan about the ageism and sexism of the poetry scene, we decided to pool our joint expertise.'[14] Both the Word of Mouth Poetry Collective and Summer Palace Press were part of the larger movement to which Eavan Boland refers in *Object Lessons*:

> ... over a relatively short time – certainly no more than a generation or so – women have moved from being the objects of Irish poems to being the authors of them. It is a momentous transit. It is also a disruptive one.[15]

The publication of a substantial body of work changed the way the group and its members were seen. Gráinne observes that:

---

14. Joan Newmann. Mary Turley-McGrath, *Poetry Ireland*, News, March/April, 2010.
15. *Object Lessons*, Eavan Boland (Manchester: Carcanet, 1995). Regarded by the editors of *A History of Twentieth Century British Women's Poetry* to be 'of the same calibre as *A Room of One's Own*' by Virginia Woolf.

In the last few years of Word of Mouth's existence the Collective gained a new respect, based on longevity, publication record, and the public events we ran, notably the Of Mouth reading series.[16] This is what happens to lowly DIY organisations that start by being dismissed, lacking the official imprimatur, but last long enough to look solidly established.

It is difficult to assess the group's legacy. For members it was our shared and ongoing journey into words. It tempted each of us to venture further (for ourselves) than we might have ventured on our own. For Kate Newmann, it was the quality of engagement:

> It was unlike anything else that was happening in Belfast at that time. It was the seriousness with which women treated their own and each other's work, and the intellectual integrity, which has remained with me.

Eilish Martin sums up the winding down of Word of Mouth:

> Time shifts, circumstances change and as with most long-standing groups the originating dynamic that served so well for so long begins to lose momentum, becomes less energised. The drawback of being a self-sustaining group, enough of a stimulus in itself and offering the satisfaction of peer appreciation and validation – always inherent in such a body – begins to define it. Over-reliant on a core group of poets whose work is equally sustained within and without

---

16. The Of Mouth Reading Series was set up in 2013 and organised by Word of Mouth in partnership with the Linen Hall Library to principally offer a platform for new work by local and guest poets. It continues to be run by Natasha Cuddington and Ruth Carr and occasionally publishes poetry. The first title was Ann Zell's posthumous collection, *Donegal is a red door* (Belfast: Of Mouth, 2016).

Word of Mouth, the ethos of a body alive to itself because it is quickened by its individual parts, becomes less vibrant. Always alive to these drawbacks it is to its great credit that Word of Mouth served well so many poets from its beginning in 1991 until its ending in 2016.

Has Word of Mouth a legacy beyond itself? Did it help quash the notion of women's writing as being merely domestic, amateur, marginal or self-concerned? To the extent that these notions have gone, their disappearance is probably a function of the broader social, cultural and legislative impetus towards gender equality. But all such movements need their innovators, their landmark judgements, their creative agitators. They need things happening not just at a national level but at the end of the street and in the local arts centre or library (if it is still open). Each generation of writers, each community, each group, marginalised or not, must find its own way of supporting its own work and cultivating its own voices. Our experience is that a concentrated, collective workshop, with all its inevitable foibles, is not a bad place to begin.

> Past and future are
> present in me.
> I see before and after,
> rimmed lozenges for eyes,
> cryptic as tombs.
> You cannot tell what
> I am thinking.
> I am the open-ended solution.[17]

---

17. From 'Caldragh Idol' by Mary Twomey, a founding member of Word of Mouth Poetry Collective, who died in 2006. Published in the *Word of Mouth* anthology. See note 7.

Thatcher on the radio. Blue lights flashing up the road

Susan McKay

My teenage years in Derry coincided with the eruption of the northern conflict. It was also the era of creeps like Jimmy Savile on TV. (We knew he was a creep, by the way. We just didn't know how right we were.) My Granda, an Orangeman, shouted at civil rights marchers on the television. Summers in Donegal, Seamus Heaney and Leonard Cohen, a boy in a Moroccan djellaba. All led me down a path to elsewhere.

I had, as I blithely thought, escaped across the border to Dublin after I left school in 1975. Some troubling imperative had, however, driven me north again – a confused need, I suppose, to find out who I was and where I stood in the mayhem of sectarianism and war in the north and Catholic theocracy in the south. To learn my place and play my part. In 1981 I got accepted into Queen's University Belfast to write an MA, and arrived into Belfast Central Station and the bitter exhaustion of the end of the IRA hunger strikes. The broken sign on the platform said 'Fast Central'.

My diaries thereafter are full of the violence, the bombs and the shootings, the belligerent political pronouncements. *Funerals on the news. Faces torn with grief.* I had been working as a volunteer in the Dublin Rape Crisis Centre and so I was also attuned from the start to intimations of aggression towards women. Belfast was,

I quickly realised, harsher than Derry, and one hell of a macho city. Waiting for a train I noted: *Uncouth youth at Botanic Station demands at the ticket booth, 'Give us two barmaids by the nipple, would ye?'* At that time, when you bought a packet of peanuts in a bar they were taken from a poster-type card and each packet removed revealed a bit more of a pouting model with big breasts wearing a miniscule bikini, in what was known as a provocative pose. Cans of lager also featured such images. The models had names, too, like Helga and Candy.

My sister lived beside the women's refuge. She told me that furious men came and roared outside at night. One evening at her house I heard a woman screaming: *'I just want to die.'* Another day *a child was standing behind an upstairs window, between the curtain and the glass, tapping with a gun on the pane. Skinheads bearing Union Jacks heading up the Lisburn Road to a football match.* I lived in a rambling old flat on Cromwell Road, off Botanic Avenue, where the lime trees cast their sweet scent on the air. The poet Padraic Fiacc lived a few doors away and wrote of the area: 'our Paris part of Belfast / has decapitated lampposts now.' Ours was the only garden on the street so all the local dogs frequented it, but there was lily of the valley hidden away under the hedge and a flamboyant laburnum tree that flounced its yellow tassels under the streetlights. Our rooms had tall windows and fireplaces. Mary Wall wore gold-coloured ankle boots and played the guitar and sang.

One night as Mary and I came out of the York Hotel we saw a couple arguing outside the bookshop, and suddenly he was hitting her and she cried out, stumbled and fell. We ran to help, asked her was she all right. 'She's fine,' he said. 'Physically, anyway.' She didn't say anything. She looked at the ground, accepted his arm when he offered it. Another night we rescued a sobbing woman running from a man outside our flat. We took her in while he prowled up and down the street looking for her. We persuaded her to let us call the police and she said only if they could come in an unmarked car. She said her husband would kill her if he knew she'd sent for them. When three Land Rovers screeched to a stop at our gate she cursed us. *The sky is the colour of an RUC Land Rover. A helicopter whines like a trapped bluebottle.*[1] I spent a long time one day studying a print in the Ulster Museum. It was called 'Lovers with helicopter' but I could not find the lovers.

There was always some wildness going on in the flat. Mary favoured sad, lovely ballads but would do Leon Rosselson's 'Don't Get Married Girls' ('Don't get married, girls; you'll sign away your life / You may start off as a woman but you'll end up as the wife') on request. Monica Coll did a version of 'Are You Lonesome Tonight' in which a woman poisons a violent husband ('Does your tea taste all right?'). Marie Mulholland belted out Holly Near's 'Mountain Song': 'you can't just take my dreams away – not with me watching …' Much Three Princes 'wine from more than one country of the EU' was consumed and we talked into the early hours.

The living room turned into a factory for torches for Belfast's first Reclaim the Night march – sawing wood, hammering on empty cans, inserting firelighters. I was in the English Society at Queen's and got to invite the glorious Angela Carter to come and do a reading. One of my male friends, a poet, marvelled at her gentle demeanour. 'I expected a Saracen tank,' he said. I invited her to meet some of the feminists the next day. Our big living room still reeked of petrol from the firelighters. In the cloud of her silvery hair she sat cross-legged with us, warzone women avid for glimpses of another world. She spoke about violence in the romantic literary tradition, and of Emily Brontë's *Wuthering Heights* in particular: *'You spend the first sixteen years searching for Heathcliff and the next sixteen trying to avoid him,'* she warned, with her brilliant, enigmatic smile. Another poet initiated a conversation about *Wuthering Heights* one night. 'Jesus I wouldn't

---

1.   RUC stands for Royal Ulster Constabulary.

have minded being Heathcliff and getting off with Emily,' he said, transformed from a fine lyricist into a pantomime lecher. We read Shulamith Firestone's furious *The Dialectic of Sex* and debated whether or not women who washed the socks of men were colluding with the enemy. I read Adrienne Rich, underlining just about everything. Out on the street, *The ice cream van played 'Lili Marlene'.*

In 1983, a carload of us headed northwest across the border to Donegal to help the Anti-Amendment Campaign by handing out leaflets. The referendum was an attempt to use the Irish Constitution to ban all abortions in all circumstances in Ireland and to prevent women from attempting to leave the country to obtain abortions elsewhere. In one small town a teenage boy turned on one of our group, shouting into her face: 'Youse should all be put up against a wall and raped and raped and made to get pregnant.' This was a time when the Catholic church still held arrogant control over the public morals of the Republic. Feminism was denounced as a conspiracy against the family. A bishop stated that the most dangerous place for a baby to be was in its mother's womb. Anti-choice militants laid claim to the designation 'pro-life' and declared that the Dublin Rape Crisis Centre was just a front for pro-abortion baby killers. The referendum was passed. (To this day it continues to create misery.)

In the north, the national question was brutally, ruinously, all around. 'The Violence', as it was called. I found I could not live in Belfast, that belligerent city, without being politically engaged. I realised that some of my rage at the Catholic church, gained by feminist activism in the Republic, risked sounding like anti-Catholic sectarianism in the Protestant North. There were several priests who spoke out strongly against state oppression, but who were also vehemently anti-abortion. Women's Aid had set up refuges in Belfast and Derry but there was no Rape Crisis Centre in Northern Ireland, so, with my Dublin training behind me, it was the obvious place to start. A group of women formed a collective. After a stint above a deserted showroom on dark Great Victoria Street, we found tiny offices high up above Royal Avenue in the city centre. We chose them because the area was 'neutral' and accessible by buses, taxis and trains from all over the city.

In early summer, boys in Orange parades below twirled their batons high up in the air and I thought as they flew by the open window that I could reach out and catch one, like some sort of intervening divinity. On Cromwell Road in the hot summer of 1984, Stevie Wonder's 'I Just Called to Say I Love You' blared out and we sat out like all our neighbours on the doorsteps and fire escapes taking the sun.

One terrible night a bomb exploded around the corner and I woke to hear a man screaming a woman's name. We learned the next day he was a part-time Ulster Defence Regiment (UDR) soldier crying out to his girlfriend, whose flat he had just left. The IRA had put a bomb under his car. Later that year some neighbours organised a street party to try to get everyone over the lingering horror.

The Female Line features in my diary from 1985. I had been irked because a female magazine editor had chosen to give it to the man with whom I then lived for review rather than to me. He was a writer. I was still nominally writing a thesis about portrayals of the mother in Irish fiction, but after a few years during which I spent less and less time in the library, I had finally, without formally acknowledging it, abandoned my literary studies. I was, in fact, working full-time in the Rape Crisis Centre. When I told the professor who was my supervisor at Queen's that I was doing some work on rape, she said vaguely, 'Against, I suppose?'

Dregs of the Ulster Says No rally lurching down Great Victoria Street with their flags. 'Where's the fuckin Taigs? I'll take on any fuckin Taig.' I had moved with my lover to a flat on the poorer end of the Ravenhill Road. I had chosen it for its romantic view across the Ormeau Park to Divis Mountain, on top of which a British Army fortress glittered like a spaceship. I had put aside my misgivings about paramilitary flags and National Front graffiti. *The UFF says southerners are to be viewed as hostile. White scrawl on the pavement by the bus stop on the Ravenhill: 'Fuck off Taigs'. I walked down to the shops this afternoon. All closed for the demo. On my way a youth sneered out of a car: 'Multiple orgasms.' D. on the phone drunk in Dundalk.* The Female Line *book and notes for the review all lost and it expected in the morning. Ms L. the editor may regret not going for the feminist reviewer after all! Tomorrow Paisley is preaching up the road on 'the enemy's plan for Ulster's destruction – God's plan for Ulster's deliverance'.*[2]

In a café, I told a few of my colleagues at the Rape Crisis Centre about the 'multiple orgasms' shout. They found it hilarious. 'Oh! I think I had one of those once,' one of them said. She told us she'd gone to a performance of *Animal Farm* and enjoyed it except *she was annoyed that of course it had to be the female who gave in first, who was fickle and frivolous. She said the others she was with had thought she was silly and she wished I'd been there because I would have understood.* (Years later my enjoyment of Disney's *The Jungle Book* was marred because I hated the flirty squirming of the little girl for whom Mowgli abandons the wild fun of his animal pals. I didn't want my daughters to feel they had to identify with her. They had fun imitating her fluttering eyelashes, but still.)

For some, we undoubtedly epitomised the 'humourless feminist', one of the hostile designations of those days. Yet we laughed ourselves to helpless tears over stories that really were, looking back, anything but funny. How we'd had to conduct a discussion with lawyers, all men, about why the law on rape failed women, holding forth about the requirement to prove penetration of the vagina by the penis, while eating sausage rolls at a reception. Some women who came to the Rape Crisis Centre told their stories like comedies. One described how the man who had offered her a lift home had beaten her about the head with one of her stilettos,

---

2.   UFF stands for Ulster Freedom Fighters.

raped her and flung her out of the car. Hooting with laughter, she showed me how she'd walked along the mountain road with one high heel and one bare foot. I had to calm things down, to get her to talk about how she'd felt and how she felt now, which was hurt and scared then – hurt, scared and ashamed now.

We refused to accept a donation from the Rag Committee at Queen's because the Rag Mag contained rape jokes. A man in the York Hotel told a joke about rugby players raping a woman and I poured my pint over his head. One day a cartoon appeared in a political magazine, a joke at the expense of feminists. The grim-faced women depicted were all in dungarees and had hennaed hair that stood up on their heads as though a pony tail had been grabbed and sawn off with blunt scissors. We glared angrily at the image, muttering furiously about stereotypes. Several of us were wearing or at least owned dungarees and several had the hair. The woman in the drawing on the front of *The Female Line* has the hair, too. The drawing was done by Rose Ann McGreevy, one of our circle, and we were very proud of her.

We were warrior women really though our mission was anti-violence. There was urgent work to be done, and the feeling of solidarity was wonderful. However, then and now, the women's movement is notorious for its splits and for the way those who are deemed to have broken ranks are ostracised – the grown-up version of the worst sort of girl bullying. There were ideological battles from which we emerged wounded and distraught and hating each other – until we needed to unite again.

For some women, feminism had to shoulder its way in among their other allegiances. I remember a row after a British army foot patrol found a parcel bomb in a bin outside the Rape Crisis Centre. One of our republican friends said we had to accept that it wasn't meant for us and that anyway: 'All's fair in love and war.' Another declared at a conference that she did not know what feminists were complaining about: 'Sure, youse have had it all handed to you on a plate.' I went to speak at a feminist conference in Dublin and, feeling the hard eyes of a republican ex-prisoner on me, spoke far more about the scandal of strip-searching in Armagh prison than about rape in every other context.

Not all of the women in the Rape Crisis Centre were as reckless and consumed by the struggle to define their politics. Those who had children and proper homes tended to be calmer and more sensible. And to drink less. My diaries are soaked in gin, white wine, pints of lager and, briefly, a concoction known as a Red Witch which was a lethal mix of cider, Pernod and blackcurrant. Our fad for it was short-lived simply because it was guaranteed to result in a murderous hangover. I remember the brilliant academic feminist Eileen Evason, who called Northern Ireland an 'armed patriarchy', saying that Belfast was drowning in vodka.

Armed patriarchs abounded. Women who came to the Centre told us tales of horrific violence, sometimes involving men who had guns, or claimed to have guns, which were meant to be for the protection of their communities. Women were expected to remain loyal to men in jail and faced punishment if there was any suspicion that they had strayed. I learned about tarring and feathering; about the history of Noreen Winchester, who was convicted of murdering her father, and whose early release from jail was secured by a feminist campaign which demanded that attention be paid to the fact that he had been violent and sexually abusive to his family for many years; about Ann Ogilby, beaten to death by a paramilitary gang of women and girls loyal to the wife of a UDA man, then in jail, with whom she was having a relationship. I did not know about Jean McConville, disappeared and murdered by the IRA, until years later. When I researched her life for an essay I found out she had also been the victim of familial and domestic violence and had been driven from her home by loyalist intimidation.[3]

We saw women of all ages, and girls, too, because there was nowhere else for them to go. Rape was not much spoken about

---

3.   Susan McKay, 'Diary', *London Review of Books*, 19 December 2013.

in the public domain, but when it was, one of the things that was said was that it was 'a crime second only to murder'. This was not, in reality, how it was regarded by the police or in the courts. Most women did not report rape, for a range of very significant reasons. But rape was still linked to the idea of ruin, of the fallen woman. One mother who brought her daughter to the Rape Crisis Centre said of the silently weeping teenager: 'She'd have been better off to have died.'

We acted as if we were fearless and invincible. We wrote articles challenging the IRA and the Ulster Defence Association (UDA), the police and the patriarchal family. We took off in taxis in the middle of the night to meet women who rang us from phone boxes in deserted streets in parts of the city usually described as dangerous. We accompanied women to heavily fortified police stations. Once I was with a woman and her little boy, who had been abused by a journalist, and who marched along doing a very good imitation of a soldier in a foot patrol, occasionally aiming his imaginary gun at real targets. I gave him my old portable typewriter.

A radio journalist asked if a woman wasn't partly responsible for rape if she wore provocative clothes. You might as well tell a woman not to get married, by that logic, we countered, since a husband has a legal right to rape his wife. A judge we criticised sent for us and received us, all decked out in his wig and gown, in his chambers. We discussed women's experience of the courts *until the usher, the only female one in Northern Ireland, came and said, 'Your honour, the women want to know if they can go ahead and clean the courtrooms.' Women in the legal system!*

The personal is political. It was our mantra in the face of a society in which some of the men who presented themselves in public as heroes, privately beat up and abused their wives and children, or had sex with teenagers. My own personal life sometimes sat uneasily within the certainties of my political life. Early in our relationship I was shocked when a woman who had known him a long time warned me about my partner: 'Just make sure you don't get pregnant. He's the sort likes his women on their backs or cleaning the kitchen.' But in time I saw that he did indeed have the gender politics of the classic sixties lefty male. He had left a string of disappointed lovers behind him and he was at once unfaithful and possessive. I returned into a shop we had just left one day and heard the shopkeeper say to another man: 'Women? Sure he throws them away like lollipops.'

He was a reckless man, and a drinker. He would come home late with wild stories about encounters in bars he should not have gone into, of men with guns, and scarcely veiled threats. We got warnings about 'bad boys'. One day we clutched each other, rigid with terror, as someone blattered on the door and shouted my name. My fear for my lover's safety made me careless of my own fears about rape. Once, after midnight, when he'd stood me up, I walked home alone along the Ormeau Embankment, the Lagan to my left, the park to my right, ... *imagining my cross-examination in the rape trial. Why did I walk that dark and lonely road? For the daffodils, the Lagan, the trees and the swans. Two swans together, one of them sleeping. I leaned down and said, 'Hello swan' to the other.*

My job was poorly paid through a government community employment scheme, and I would hitch to visit my man when he was away, setting off from Belfast in the dusk of a Friday evening. Once I arrived at a pub in a border village near the artists' retreat where he was staying. *The barman said what a fine-looking woman I was and he was sure I had made plenty of money on the way down. He insisted on leaving me out to the house. As we left the bar someone said to him, 'Do you want a pack of Durex?' A paper open at Page 3 was spread out in the car. On the way he touched my breasts. I was scared.* I told the writer and asked him what he felt about this encounter. *He said it turned him on. He blushed.* I laughed.

Why did I stay with such a man? When I heard women describe in counselling relationships with men whose behaviour was comparable, I wondered why they tolerated such a low level of respect. But most men I met were probably terrified of me, a fierce feminist given to swift denunciatory polemics regardless of the social situation. A woman who preferred the company of women to that of men. He looked me in the eye. We taught each other a private language laced with outrageous humour and a sweet, occasional tenderness. Behind all the bluster and strut and sometimes boorishness, I came to know a fine soul. I loved his writing, and he encouraged me to write too. He told me *I was a born writer and I would never be happy 'til I realised it.* Sometimes we were giddy with happiness.

I loved him, and in his way, I believe that he loved me. But I am forced to admit that he was casually cruel more than he was kind. My granny said it would end in tears, and it did. In the years since we parted I sometimes dream of him in the way I also still sometimes dream that I am smoking. In the dream I realise I am succumbing again to an addiction it took me years to break, and I wish I could stop but I don't. I wake up and Linda Thompson's song is in my head: 'I cover my ears I close my eyes/ Still hear your voice, telling me lies".

I wrote an article about pornography, forcing myself into Belfast's first 'sex shop' to buy magazines from which huge busts and buttocks loomed out of black leather and chains and the women's faces were masks with wet swollen red lips pouting. We supported the campaign by British Labour MP Clare Short against Page 3 spreads featuring what the tabloids called 'lovelies'. I remember a bus full of these models was sent around to Short's house. Much was made of the fact that she did not look like them. Feminists were 'uglies'.

One night I was sitting in a bar with a friend, leaning close into each other, talking, when a man who had been staring at us from his stool at the counter stomped over. He had a copy of *The Sun* which he slammed down in front of us, open at Page 3: 'Are they your sisters? Are they your fucking sisters?' he demanded. Another man, in another bar (yes, I know, a lot of bars) turned round and called me a 'stupid cunt'. But at least we had the witty and wonderful Jane Posner fighting back with her graffiti. She had famously defaced a 1979 billboard ad which had the slogan: 'If this car was a lady it would have its bottom pinched' so that it read 'If this car was a lady she'd run you down'.

We were learning the terrifying language of misogyny, getting to know the common practices of abuse. The prevalence of marital rape, and of incest. The co-existence of child abuse with violence against mothers. The abuse of children by men who take up with single mothers to gain access to them. Abuse by priests, ministers, scoutmasters. How children and young women were groomed until they colluded in their own exploitation. How a woman's confidence could be destroyed so that she came to despise herself and feel that she deserved to be abused. It sometimes seemed that there was more compassion for sexually violent men than for their victims. It was common for men to claim in their defence that they had been driven to violence by a woman's unreasonable behaviour. A friend of my lover's family was murdered by her husband. One of his relatives told me about the husband's distress: *'You wouldn't wish what he's going through on anybody.'*

Double standards prevailed at every level. Women who did not consent to sex were 'frigid'. Those who did were 'slags'. What was known as 'soft porn' was mainstream but women who looked like its models were 'asking for it'. One Belfast defence lawyer relentlessly cross-examined a young woman and got her to 'admit' that she had a sexual relationship with her boyfriend and also that when the accused had tried to remove her T-shirt she had told him to 'fuck off'. She broke down. The barrister was satisfied: 'Those tears are just a front to hide the kind of person you really are.' The following day the woman told the court she couldn't go on with her evidence and the case was dismissed.

Andrea Dworkin, the great campaigner against pornography, came to Belfast, and, after her public event, came to meet some feminists. Some of the separatists in our circle pressed her to agree that it was anti-feminist to be heterosexual. She declined to pass judgement. Her writing supported separatism, but her life did not. I had been on the local BBC news talking about some sentencing outrage, and I kept my television makeup on to meet her. I doubt if the makeup impressed her but she praised our work in the Rape Crisis Centre and I was proud. I felt she was weighed down, damaged, by the horrors of what she had forced herself to investigate.

Thatcher on the radio. Blue lights flashing up the road. I was convinced of the need to stay in Belfast. My lover and I sat by the fire in our flat and read each other Russian poems. He loved me to say the Marina Tsvetaeva line to him: 'your lashes are longer than anyone's.' He'd flutter his and swoon. I knew some of these poems by heart and wrote them into my diary. In one of Anna Akhmatova's poems, the poet scorns those who leave the place of conflagration: *I am not one of those who left the land... /... We the survivors do not flinch / from anything, not from a single blow..*

I loved the Rape Crisis work, and knew what we were doing was good, important and necessary. We had got past the in-feuding stage, and were making gains in terms of public support and acceptance of our ideas. But in truth I was getting weary. We had no concept of vicarious traumatisation, no strategies for self-care. I began to feel I could not listen to another woman wrestling with her pain and shame to tell me about the rape she had endured, the rapes that she was enduring in an abusive relationship, the helplessness she felt at the rape of her child. We were not professionals. What we offered women was support and solidarity. We helped them to explore their often contradictory feelings. We listened to women who had not been listened to. We believed women who had not been believed. One of my diary entries describes how I held a sobbing woman: *her tears ran down my neck.*

Joseph Brodsky came to Belfast. After his reading, I showed him a photograph in the *Irish News* of an elderly woman whose house had been smashed up in some sectarian incident. I said the people who needed to hear his poetry would never come over to the university, that most people stayed in their own areas out of fear. Years later, my by then ex-lover sent me via a poet messenger a photocopied page from a book. The poem was called 'Belfast Tune' and Brodsky had written by hand below the title that it was for us:

Here's a girl from a dangerous town…

I dream of her either loved or killed

I took to walking for miles around the city. One day I passed the blackened ruins of a house on the gable wall of which had been painted: 'Get out or burn out.' I took it as a personal sign. Soon afterwards I found another job, far from Belfast, in a place where, the writer said, 'You can still see trout in pools.' He would come with me. My going away party was in a pub on the docks. I walked arm in arm through the dark streets with my colleagues through a biblical downpour, laughing. I bought boots and a camera with my last wages, and left, as I thought, forever.

Reflections on Commemorating 1916

Margaret Ward

In September 2015, it was announced that the role of women in the foundation of the Irish state would be a key strand in the commemorations of the Easter Rising. This decision to include women in the historical narrative was a response to the insistence by significant sections of civil society that women's participation had to be one of the themes if Irish public history was to be fully representative and inclusive. Civil servants from the Republic have told me of their experience of consultations across the country during the lead-up to 2016, with many people expressing strong views on the importance of gender equality rather than tokenistic acknowledgement of women's contribution to the whole revolutionary era. Decades of scholarly work on women's history, a gradual inclusion of gendered perspectives by some prominent historians and a feminist activism that includes academics, journalists, writers and actors has provided the foundation for this public interest in women's history and support for female-led projects. As a result, events highlighting the contributions made by women from nationalist, suffrage and labour organisations have been held on both sides of the Irish border.

What happened in Ireland in 2016 is even more significant when compared with past commemorative periods. In 1966, during the 50th anniversary, the specific contribution of women was rarely mentioned. Women as significant as Nora Connolly and Kathleen Clarke were interviewed – but their importance was in relation to what they said about their dead male relatives, as father or husband, not what they did themselves. Their role was to bear witness to the last words and legacy of their menfolk. This silence mirrors the struggle of Irish women for recognition and equality. Irish women were not vocal in the mid-1960s. It would take the re-emergence of feminism in the 1970s to change that situation.

Commemoration and feminism made for an uneasy combination during the decades of conflict in the north. Forcible removal by the Royal Ulster Constabulary (RUC) of the banned tricolour from the Falls Road in 1966 led to renewed resistance by the nationalist minority. In those circumstances, public commemoration was impossible. A few years later, the stark reality of the 'Troubles' engendered nervousness on the part of the Irish state regarding republican commemorations by anyone, male or female. In 1976, on the 60th anniversary of the Easter Rising, former Cumann na mBan activist Maire Comerford, at the age of eighty-three, was fined £10 for taking part in a Sinn Féin commemoration in Dublin. As the hardy revolutionary she was, she offered to go to jail instead. That seems extraordinary today, but it was hardly remarked upon at the time. Twenty-five years later, on the 75th anniversary, it was radicals from civil society, inspired by the artist Robert Ballagh, who organised events around the theme of the Spirit of 1916. I was honoured to have been part of a large meeting in Dublin's Mansion House that focused on women, with myself speaking on Cumann na mBan, author Diana Norman on Constance Markievicz and trade unionist Avila Kilmurray on women in the labour movement. Times have now – thankfully – changed. For the centenary year of 2016 it was possible to hold commemorative events focused on women, even in formerly unionist-controlled venues like Belfast City Hall.

During the past four decades, historians of women have been researching and writing about women's position in Irish society, including their role within Irish nationalist movements. This scholarship has undeniably helped to ensure that there would be some focus on women. Indeed, an early key event, a two-day conference in April 2014 organised by the Women's History Association of Ireland to commemorate the centenary of the foundation of the republican women's organisation Cumann na mBan, was opened by the Minister for Arts, Heritage and the Gaeltacht and a special commemorative stamp was issued by government. It was an important marker that women were part of the Decade of Centenaries and were fully expecting acknowledgement from officialdom.

However, the inclusion of female historians and recognition of their expertise could not be taken for granted; having a focus on women's participation did not mean necessarily that women historians themselves would be contributing to events, apart from those they organised themselves. One particularly egregious example occurred in London in the summer of 2015. This was an event billed as a 'discussion on women in Ireland with the most important Irish historians from Ireland'. The organiser was quite happy to have a theme on women and could not see anything wrong in having an all-male panel. When queried via Twitter he replied that the historians were there 'on merit', oblivious to the fact that many women could have been there 'on merit' also. Only when some of us began a concerted hashtag campaign against what has been coined as 'manels' did we finally get one woman added to that panel. It was an important alert, prompting feminist academics to begin a systematic campaign against the existence of commemorative 'manels'. The ubiquity of the same small cohort of male speakers is being challenged by Twitter account Academic Manel Watch (on Twitter @manelwatchIre), campaigning for gender parity in Irish academia, culture, politics and within the media.

A key factor contributing to the momentum building up to 2016 was the emergence of what has become an important pressure group: Waking the Feminists. In November 2015, the Abbey Theatre announced the list of plays making up their centenary celebration, entitled 'Waking the Nation'. Nine out of the ten plays were written by men. It emerged that from 1995–2014, of 320 plays, only thirty-six written by women had been produced. Yet women were crucial in the early years of the Abbey: it was funded by Annie Horniman and partly managed by Lady Gregory, who was so highly regarded that plays by herself and W.B. Yeats premiered on its opening night in 1904. Now, one hundred years later, Ireland's national theatre was writing women like Lady Gregory out of its history while also ignoring contemporary women playwrights. This provoked an explosion of outrage in the press and social media. Una Mullally articulated this anger and suggested it might be time for another Abbey riot[1] and the set designer Lian Bell rose to the challenge and coordinated that anger under the hashtag #wakingthefeminists. Five hundred tickets sold in ten minutes for a meeting in the Abbey to confront Fiach MacConall, the Abbey director. His very unwise initial reaction had been to send out a tweet declaring 'them's the breaks.' Now, on the Abbey stage, he had to, as he put it, echoing the words of Panti Bliss, 'check his privilege'. As Emer O'Toole wrote afterwards, there was a 'new feminist energy now powerfully present in public life. We won't be erased again. We won't be dismissed again. We won't be silenced again. This is our republic too.'[2] 'Waking the Feminists' has become a pressure group to be reckoned with. Their research on the gender imbalance in Irish state support of theatres will certainly, over time, result in substantial changes. The Abbey example also had a significance that went beyond theatrical circles by helping to develop a greater

---

1. Una Mullally, 'Abbey Theatre celebrates 1916 centenary with only one woman playwright', *Irish Times*, 2 November 2015. http://www.irishtimes. com/opinion/una-mullally-abbey-theatre-celebrates-1916-centenary-with-only-one-woman-playwright-1.2413277
2. Emer O'Toole, 'Irish women will not put up with being written out of history any longer', *The Guardian*, 13 November 2015. https://www. theguardian.com/commentisfree/2015/nov/13/irish-women-abbey-the-atre-centenery-feminist

sense of gender sensitivity – or at least nervousness – on the part of organisers of events. Many events around the country, north and south, were organised with a far greater degree of inclusion than might otherwise have been the case.

This growing critical mass became evident in the variety of events and speakers during 2016. A women's history project based in Richmond Barracks – where seventy-seven of the women were detained following their involvement in the Rising – saw women who had been entirely hidden from history resurrected from the archives and brought into public focus. Alongside the work of historians Mary McAuliffe and Liz Gillis in researching the biographies of the women and compiling a narrative of the period,[3] an innovative 'Quilt Project' saw women participants each allocated one of the women to research further so that they could come up with a concept for a panel that would honour her particular woman. This facilitated a creative process that enabled participants to create links between women's experiences in the past and in the present. In conceptualising their subject, those who had little familiarity with the history of 1916 not only discovered a great deal about women's agency at that period, but related this information to their experience of women in present-day Ireland. The book was launched on International Women's Day 2016 at an event addressed by the Irish President and attended by many dignitaries. While this was official Ireland's recognition of women's involvement in the Easter Rising, the commemorative project also enabled Irish feminism to ask uncomfortable questions, subverting what might have been an unquestioning acceptance of the status quo. Women not only understood much more about the ideals for which women fought one hundred years ago, but they then related the promises of equality contained in the Proclamation to the reality of an Ireland in which women remain

---

3.   Mary McAuliffe and Liz Gillis, Richmond Barracks 1916, We were there: 77 Women of the Easter Rising (Dublin: Dublin City Council, 2016).

greatly under-represented in public and political life, without full reproductive rights and still disadvantaged in terms of equal pay and access to affordable childcare.[4]

The RTÉ programme 'Reflecting the Rising' was an inspirational event that took over large parts of Dublin city centre on Easter Monday. It appeared as if every historian in Ireland was engaged in giving talks, to audiences totally engaged in learning more about the events of one hundred years previously. The contribution made by women to the Rising – in Stephen's Green, the City Hall, Jacob's factory and many other locations – was well represented in numerous talks, with women historians fully involved, often speaking at more than one event. Another highlight of the year was an all-women event in May, organised in Lissadell (home of the Gore-Booths, ancestral home of Constance Markievicz) by the Sligo Field Club. Entitled 'Ireland's Women – revolution and remembrance', six women from different disciplines talked about aspects of women's contribution to revolution. The journalist Olivia O'Leary, chairing the event, later talked about it on Irish radio, stating how much she learned, and how the experience was for her like 'listening to history with the gaps filled in.' Her response was a welcome recognition that mainstream history has largely omitted the experiences and contributions of women. The challenge posed by feminist historians is not only to write from a feminist perspective, conscious of the structural obstacles facing the female subject, but to challenge historians in general to 'fill in the gaps' while also understanding why male and female experiences are often very different.

Important archival developments have also contributed to a greater awareness of women's role in the national liberation

---

4. *Mary McAuliffe, Liz Gillis, Éadaoin Ní Chléirigh, Marja Almqvist,* 'Forgetting and Remembering – Uncovering Women's Histories at Richmond Barracks: A Public History Project', *Studies in Arts and Humanities,* Vol 2/1. 2016.

movement, particularly the release, in 2003, of documents from the Bureau of Military History in Dublin, followed by the ongoing release of applications for pensions from veterans of the War of Independence. The eventual release of the archival documents (even if comparatively few women – 146 – were interviewed for the Military Archives) followed by the constantly unfolding riches of the pension applications, have provided opportunities for reassessment of women's roles, the environment in which they lived and obstacles they encountered. It is quite extraordinary, for example, to read Winifred Carney's application for a pension based on her service in the General Post Office (GPO), in which she stayed for the entire duration of the Rising, and her plea to be awarded a pension from Grade D rather than Grade E (the only two grades open to women) given the importance of the role she played. The powers that be eventually decided that as aide-de-camp to James Connolly and utterly in his confidence, she could be considered to have had officer status and she was awarded a Grade D pension.[5] However, the release of documents alone is not enough – there has to be an understanding of the importance of the documents, a commitment to ensure that they are understood within the historiography of Irish women's history.

In comparing the situation in academia in the 1970s to that of today, it is evident that considerable progress has been made. As a young postgraduate student in Queen's University, Belfast, wanting to research the role of women within nationalist movements, I struggled to counter the reaction of a senior academic who asserted that women had not done anything, which was why nothing had been written about them. Of course, once I began researching, I discovered that there was a substantial body of work in existence and that women of a previous generation who had been revolutionaries in the early decades of the twentieth century were still concerned to make sure their contribution would be recorded. Maire Comerford

---

5.   Winifred Carney, MSP34REF56077, Military Service Pension Application.

had written a fascinating autobiography, detailing her upbringing and role in the revolutionary movement, now lodged in UCD Archives but unpublished. When I interviewed Eithne Coyle, Cumann na mBan President 1926–41 (notorious in the War of Independence for holding up trains with a revolver and removing goods destined for Belfast, in support of the Dáil 'Belfast Boycott'), she lamented the fact that the Bureau of Military History archives would not be opened until she and her comrades were all dead. At the same time, she gave me a copy of her own personal testimony and of questionnaires that she and others had compiled when they tried to collate material for a history of Cumann na mBan that remained unwritten at the time. Now, forty years later, the centenary year had become a people's commemoration, as local communities came together to celebrate and commemorate their local heroes and heroines. People raided attics, delved into their family history and figures scarcely known were brought into the light. This happened throughout Ireland. I give some examples from Belfast, which is particularly rewarding, given our difficult history.

In the Lower Ormeau Road, a small working-class, nationalist community, the history of the Corr family was excavated. This was backed by the Heritage Lottery Fund, in part because some family members fought in the First World War (one brother dying at the Somme) while other family members were part of the Irish Volunteers and Cumann na mBan. Elizabeth and Nell Corr were early members of the Belfast branch of Cumann na mBan and were mobilised in 1916 – accompanying the northern Volunteers to their rendezvous point in Coalisland and then with Nora and Ina Connolly, Eilis Allen and Kathleen Murphy, catching the midnight train from Portadown to Dublin to warn the leadership that the north was in disarray because of MacNeill's countermanding orders. As a result, they were amongst the first to see the Proclamation, memorising it so that they would be able to tell people in the north what was happening. The women then returned north, travelling in horse and cart and other transport to search for leaders then in hiding. Elizabeth Corr, a typist in Belfast's Central Library, wrote to the Chief Librarian to explain her absence from work. She only gave him a small part of her story, excluding her midnight trip to Dublin. She was dismissed with one month's wages in lieu of notice, but in her own words, 'each year as Easter comes round I recall vividly the most thrilling moment of my life.'[6]

The Lower Ormeau Road community was able to erect commemorative banners and to commission a large-scale wall mural (with substantial financial support from the Housing Executive) to remember the contribution of the Corr family, but most particularly of Elizabeth and Nell Corr. Family members unearthed all the material that Elizabeth had kept, including her diaries, newspaper articles and correspondence with Terence McSwiney when he was imprisoned in Crumlin Road jail. An exhibition was mounted in the Linen Hall Library and transferred later to the Ulster Museum, formerly a pillar of the Ulster establishment. While a small example, it is one that has considerable significance. Since the Peace Process, the nationalist community in the north has been able to acknowledge its aspirations for a united Ireland, and to be public about its role in historical events. Ulster Museum, Queen's University, Libraries NI, the Public Record Office, Belfast City Council and all the other council areas in the north have staged commemorative events where there has been scholarly debate and discussion on key figures from the north's nationalist tradition, and on the role of women, not only republican women, but their involvement with other movements, particularly the suffrage and trade union movements. At the Easter Rising commemorative dinner in Belfast City Hall (unfortunately not attended by unionist parties), the dramatic readings focused primarily on the role played by women, from the Protestant nationalist poet Alice Milligan (born in Omagh but brought up in Belfast) to the

---

6. Elizabeth Corr, Witness Statement 179, Bureau of Military History, Dublin.

formation of Inghinidhe na hÉireann and Cumann na mBan. What was previously a hidden history has now been disseminated widely.

Belfast Central Library has an exhibition case devoted to Elizabeth Corr, including her letter of explanation for her absence and the minutes of the Library and Technical Instruction Committee for 4 May, deciding her explanation was unsatisfactory. In an adjoining display case and in a larger exhibition, now digitised by the Central Library, is a very different experience of the period – letters written by the 'Library Men' – the thirteen men of the library staff who volunteered to fight for the British forces in the war, and who were given half pay by the library on condition they wrote back regularly to Mr Elliott, the chief librarian. They were Catholic and Protestant. Two died and the rest returned from war to continue their work for the library services. If it were not for the evidence of the Library men, which adds political 'balance' when one sees the two display cases side by side, one wonders if Elizabeth Corr could be displayed in this way, even in post-peace agreement Belfast?

Another woman from Belfast is Winifred Carney, who marched into the GPO with James Connolly, armed with her typewriter and a Webley. However, so little known was she that it was only in 1985 that a headstone was finally erected over her grave in Millfield cemetery in Belfast (and that was after a campaign by some Belfast socialists). She has been named the 'silent radical' because she appeared to write very little about her experiences, despite also being the only woman, apart from Constance Markievicz, to stand for Sinn Féin in the 1918 election. Long hidden has been a thirteen-page memoir of her time in the GPO, in which, touchingly, she regrets not telling her mother the truth about her proposed Easter in Dublin. She states, 'I had no responsibilities in those days and so a rebellion was but an exciting interlude.' This new material from Carney is a significant addition to 1916 historiography. It gives us vivid impressions of the excitement of the first minutes of the Rising as well as her bravery; the first woman to enter the headquarters of the revolutionaries, marching together with her comrades. The brief memoirs reveal her to have been a very different woman from the 'quiet radical' she is so often termed. She is perceptive, notices everything, understands the different political views of participants, and never seems to feel fear as the buildings surrounding the GPO gradually become a blazing mass, 'with the whole block an inferno with the noise of burning and falling masonry' until the GPO too begins to burn. Carney writes, 'Pearse asks me if I insist on remaining and I reply I do'.[7]

To read her account is to understand that Carney was a revolutionary woman, fearless and dedicated to the socialist policies articulated by her comrade Connolly. BBC NI has made much of Winnie Carney's life, with a short news feature and her incorporation into their 1916 website. But would they have done so if it were not for her later marriage to former Ulster Volunteer Force member and Somme veteran – and dedicated socialist activist – the Protestant George McBride? It meant that they were then able to 'balance' their coverage with a story of love across the divide, which was in fact the major focus of the piece. I pose the question – could the roles of Elizabeth Corr and Winifred Carney have been highlighted without their family history, which enabled 'inclusive commemoration', a key characteristic of the northern method of commemoration?

There is still much to do in relation to the participation of northern women. For example, Margaret Dobbs in the Glens of Antrim, from a Protestant Ascendancy background, rejected the beliefs of her childhood to the extent that she became an executive member of Cumann na mBan, taught Irish and funded scholarships to the Gaeltacht, her home in the Glens an important meeting place for kindred souls. She is known primarily for the fact that she was a friend of Roger Casement, but she deserves reclamation for her own contribution to Irish political life.

---

7. With thanks to Professor Bill Rolston for showing me the unpublished memoirs of Winifred Carney, in private hands.

In 1983, when I published *Unmanageable Revolutionaries: women and Irish nationalism*, I began with a challenge, using a quotation from Adrienne Rich's *Lies, Secrets and Silence* (1979) to illuminate the fact that Irish women had a proud, if hidden history of activism:

> The entire history of women's struggle for self-determination has been muffled in silence over and over. One serious cultural obstacle encountered by any feminist writer is that each feminist work has tended to be received as if it emerged from nowhere ... this is one of the ways in which women's work and thinking has been made to seem sporadic, errant, orphaned of any tradition of its own.[8]

There is now a considerable body of scholarship on Irish women's history, one that has built on the discoveries and conclusions of previous works. There is much more evidence of the numerous roles performed by women. They repeatedly risked their lives, braving military checkpoints and sniper fire to maintain rebel communications. They carried weapons, ammunitions, and other supplies hidden in the hems and folds of their clothes. Talking their way through the cordons that began tightening around the rebel positions by midweek, they scouted the streets to facilitate the movement of Volunteers. In *Unmanageable Revolutionaries* I included, for example, the women from Marrowbone Lane, and their insistence on surrendering alongside the men they had fought with, aided by the information that Eithne Coyle had collected from Cumann na mBan members, but I didn't have the additional memoir of Rose McNamara of that garrison, who provided a real sense of the daily reality when she recollected the difficulties of getting food for the outpost, how they had to resort

---

8. Margaret Ward, *Unmanageable Revolutionaries: women and Irish nationalism* (London: Pluto Press, 1983).

to hijacking, commandeering milk, bread, three cows and at least twenty-eight chickens, improvising by 'taking the chickens out of the pots with bayonets, not having any forks or utensils for cooking.'[9] The Military Archive statements add much colour and detail to what was previously known.

The experience of women as couriers was one of the most vital during the Rising. It was, testified Leslie Price, who volunteered in the GPO, a 'most miserable job' carrying dispatches from HQ to other outposts. She gives a terrifying account of being requested by Tom Clarke to bring a priest from Marlborough Street Presbytery to the GPO on the Thursday evening and having to dart from doorways, crawling along by walls with people shouting to her from windows to come in as it wasn't safe, seeing barricades and dead bodies in the streets.[10]

In retrieving women's voices from the newly available archival material, new histories have emerged, exploring the varied and unequal terms by which women participated in working for Irish national freedom. Lucy McDiarmid[11] focuses on what she terms 'small acts' and domestic space to illuminate her contention that the sites of the Rising replicated in gender hierarchies the practices of the Irish home. While the women were out in the revolution they were not as far 'out' as the men; instead, women existed in a 'borderland', positioned between the house and the front line – cooking, distributing food, dressing wounds – in a territory where women were using domestic skills to serve the military purposes of men. Their actual involvement in the Rising was characterised by what McDiarmid calls a 'slight gender-driven delay', mainly because of all the confusion after the countermanding orders. Women did not receive mobilisation orders at the same time as men (apart from Irish Citizen Army women, where, as we see from the Carney memoirs,

9. Rose McNamara, Witness Statement 482, Bureau of Military History.
10. Leslie Price Barry, Witness Statement 1,754, Bureau of Military History.
11. Lucy McDiarmid, *At Home in the Revolution: what women said and did in 1916* (Dublin: Royal Irish Academy, 2015).

men and women under Connolly marched out together to their outposts.) Catherine Byrne, refused entry into the GPO in the early minutes of the Rising, persuaded a Volunteer friend to lift her up to a side window, where she kicked in the glass, in order to be able to jump into the building, landing on top of a very surprised Volunteer. This was what McDiarmid terms a 'dramatic entry into revolutionary space', one of the 'small acts' performed by women, symbolic of their position in Irish society, highlighting the male dominance of that society at the time and the strategies women had to pursue in order to participate on anything like equal terms with the men.

We have the painstaking research of Sinéad McCoole's *Easter Widows*[12] in demonstrating the variety of work, despite the enormity of their grief, that the widows of Easter Week engaged in and the important contribution they made to the political movement. Even in times of revolutionary ferment, households had to be looked after and the women found they now had to be sole carers and providers for their children. It is sobering to realise that the wives of some of those who were executed immediately after the Rising – Grace Gifford, Agnes Mallin and Kathleen Clarke – were pregnant. Two had miscarriages and Agnes Mallin's daughter, born in August, named Maura Constance Connolly Mallin, had the imprisoned Markievciz as godmother with Lillie Connolly standing in as proxy godparent. A new sisterhood, borne of sorrow and near destitution, was forged as many of the bereaved women threw their energies into working for the continuation of a revolution that had only just begun.

There has never been simply one narrative on women's roles in 1916, but now we recognise a greater complexity, understand the class dimensions, the concept of intersectionality, the existence of a number of lesbian women in prominent roles, and see that there were Protestant women not only in the élite, like Markievicz and Kathleen Lynn, but also amongst working-class Dubliners who joined the Irish

---

12. Sinéad McCoole, *Easter Widows* (Dublin: Doubleday, 2014).

Citizen Army and took part in the Rising. For example, Annie and Emily Norgrove were young working-class Protestants who served with the City Hall garrison. They had lost their jobs after the Lockout. Their father was a gas fitter, a trade unionist and a Lieutenant in the Citizen Army. He and his wife also fought in the Rising. Maria Norgrove was in the Jacob's factory garrison, one of the many women who slipped away before the surrender. The Proclamation of Easter Week, with its promise of equal rights and equal opportunities and a government elected by a suffrage of all the people, inspired them and gave them a sense of entitlement.

The revival of northern feminism has, since 2011, included efforts to promote the historical contribution made by women. A collective of women based in Belfast, calling themselves 'Reclaim the Agenda', has assumed responsibility for the International Women's Day events. International Women's Day (IWD) has become a vehicle for a number of innovative ventures: lectures in the Ulster Hall; a booklet *Celebrating Belfast Women: a city guide through women's eyes*,[13] women trained as guides to deliver feminist bus tours of Belfast; yearly IWD marches through Belfast's city centre, attended by every women's group and women's centre in the city, as well as assorted activists, trade unionists and students. The different themes chosen for International Women's Day reflect the circumstances of women living in the north, where the nationalist narrative remains highly contested and where considerable sensitivity to differing viewpoints is required. IWD 2013 had a focus on the suffrage movement while IWD 2015 'No Peace Without Women' referenced feminist opposition to war. For IWD 2016 the theme was an uncompromising 'Women Reclaim 1916 Agenda'. The organisers declared that the true spirit of 1916 was the fight for suffrage, the Easter Rising, the Battle of the Somme, women's opposition to World War One and the fight for worker's rights. The programme of events was therefore intended

---

13. Funded by the Heritage Lottery Fund, available on line www.wrda.net/resources/researchreports

to reflect 'the diversity and bravery of women'.[14] That year also Belfast City Council, following up a pledge made in response to a motion initiated by feminists in 2011, unveiled a women's window in City Hall dedicated to the women of Belfast, depicting linen workers and including suffrage and feminist symbolism. For IWD 2017 there was a deliberate move away from historical themes with 'Peace, Solidarity and Sustenance – keeping body and soul together'.

On International Women's Day 2016 President Higgins spoke eloquently at the state event to honour the participation of the women of Easter Week. In his summary of what happened then and what needs still to happen, he made clear the importance of recent scholarship and the connection between scholarship and political activism:

> All this new knowledge has thoroughly reshaped our grasp of the period, giving it more texture, accuracy and complexity … Recent scholarship has also widened the lens of our understanding to include the vibrancy of the pre-revolutionary period – the new ideas, intellectual debates, cultural movements and political struggles with which the women engaged – as well as the often disappointing realities of independent Ireland.
>
> Taking stock of what we have achieved, we must relentlessly seek to complete our collective journey towards the full enjoyment of women's rights, in Ireland and beyond. Indeed the rights of women run to the heart of the political, socio-economic and cultural challenges of our contemporary world, none of which can be understood without recognising the gendered nature of inequality and injustice. [15]

---

14. International Women's Day 2016 Programme, available online www.wrda. net/IWD
15. http://www.president.ie/en/media-library/Speeches/speech-by-president-michael-d.-higgins-to-commemorate-the-role-of-women-in-1916

As the Decade of Centenaries continues, so too must the pressure to maintain a focus on women. There were some mutterings in 2016 that there had been too great a representation of women and Irish history is full of examples of backlash against women and the subsequent impact this has had on their status in public life and in the workplace. Commemorations of key events like the Sinn Féin Convention of 1917 and the 1918 election will focus on the theme of representation, providing important opportunities for reflection and action. We also must remember the harsh years when northern nationalists found themselves in a partitioned Ireland, unwilling inhabitants of a northern entity that discriminated against Catholics and imprisoned those who tried to resist. In 1922 Elizabeth Corr watched from the gallery as Cumann na mBan voted upon the Treaty, all the northern delegates mandated to oppose a solution that would leave them marooned in a six-county statelet:

> The counties were taken alphabetically, beginning with Antrim and our delegate's name was called first. Her 'NI toil' was flung into the assembly in a voice that could have been heard at the Cave Hill. 'Up Belfast!' said my neighbour on the gallery. The other Belfast and County Antrim delegates were as emphatic. [16]

Hanna Sheehy Skeffington, a suffrage militant in the early years of the twentieth century, was one figure who later found herself barred from the north, serving a prison sentence in Armagh Jail in 1933 for daring to cross the border to speak on behalf of imprisoned republican women.

One hundred years ago the lives of women in Ireland, north and south, were intertwined. Movements for the vote, national

---

16. Elizabeth Corr papers, in the possession of the May family. 'Ni toil' was the Irish way of expressing 'Against' or 'Not willing'. Corr said that nearly all delegates used the Irish expression.

freedom and trade union rights were all-Ireland and activists travelled around the country, organising events and sharing experiences. One hundred years ago women were on the cusp of winning the vote and were flocking to join the nationalist movement, albeit with a substantial group of members in the Ulster Women's Unionist Council determined to resist any imposition of home rule. Has there been significant change? 2018 will see the centenary of that momentous occasion when some women in Ireland and Britain finally won the right to vote and to stand for election. Constance Markievicz became the first woman to be elected to the British House of Commons, even though, as an Irish republican, she did not take her seat. In Belfast Winifred Carney stood, bravely though unsuccessfully, on a Workers' Republic platform in a unionist-dominated constituency. That milestone deserves more than cursory attention or one-off ceremonial events in various parliament buildings.

The demands of the Reclaim the Agenda group, for women to live lives free from discrimination, domestic violence and abuse; with healthcare that meets the needs of women; with equal representation in decision-making and access to affordable childcare, are demands that have not yet been met north or south of the border. The issues facing women are the same, wherever they live. In this period of historical commemoration and reflection the challenge must be to attain gender parity in terms of panels and speakers, and by this to encourage and facilitate a process that can more accurately consider the lives of women as well as men. When this has happened, we will have history that is not only evidence-based and scholarly, but also transformative in its potential. My experience as a feminist historian in the past decades has demonstrated the importance of permanent vigilance, so that we do not return to a time when women were 'hidden from history'.

Notes on the Contributors

Jean Bleakney was born in 1956 in Newry, where her father worked as a border customs officer. She studied biochemistry at Queen's University Belfast and worked for eight years in medical research. Thereafter, motherhood and developing passions for plants and poetry prevailed. She studied horticulture and subsequently worked in a garden centre for over twenty years. She has published three poetry collections with Lagan Press: *The Ripple Tank Experiment* (1999), *The Poet's Ivy* (2003) and *ions* (2011). Her *Selected Poems* (2016) was published by Templar Poetry to coincide with the appearance of her work on the GCE Advanced Level syllabus in Northern Ireland. A fourth collection, *No Remedy*, is due from Templar Poetry in late 2017. She lives in Belfast.

Maureen Boyle began writing as a child in Sion Mills, Co. Tyrone, winning a UNESCO medal for a book of poems in 1979 at eighteen. She studied at Trinity College and did postgraduate study at the University of East Anglia and University of Ulster. In 2005 she was awarded the MA in Creative Writing at Queen's University, Belfast. She has won various awards including the Ireland Chair of Poetry Prize and the Strokestown International Poetry Prize, both in 2007. In 2013 she won the Fish Short Memoir Prize. She has received several individual awards from the Arts Council of Northern Ireland. In 2008 she was commissioned to write a poem on the Crown Bar in Belfast for a BBC documentary and some of her work has been translated into German. She has recently received the Ireland Chair of Poetry's Inaugural Travel Bursary for work on Anne More, the wife of John Donne, and her first poetry collection, *Incunabula* is due out from Arlen House in autumn 2017. She taught Creative Writing with the Open University for ten years and currently teaches English at St Dominic's Grammar School in Belfast.

Colette Bryce was born and brought up in Derry. After studying in England, she settled in London for some years while starting out as a writer. Since then she has lived in Madrid, Scotland, and currently Newcastle upon Tyne, where she works as a freelance poet and editor. Her collections with Picador include *The Heel of Bernadette* (2000), winner of the Aldeburgh Prize, *The Full Indian Rope Trick* (2004), shortlisted for the T.S. Eliot Prize, and *Self-Portrait in the Dark* (2008). She received the Cholmondeley Award for her poetry in 2010. *The Whole & Rain-domed Universe* (2014), which draws on her experience of growing up in Derry during the Troubles, was shortlisted for the Forward, Costa, and Roehampton poetry prizes, and won a special Ewart-Biggs Award in memory of Seamus Heaney. *Selected Poems*, drawing on all her books, is a Poetry Book Society Special Commendation 2017.

Lucy Caldwell, born in Belfast in 1981, is a multi-award-winning novelist, playwright, radio dramatist and short story writer. As a playwright, her works have been widely staged across the UK and Ireland, in New York, France, China, Singapore and Australia; awards for theatre include the PMA Award for Most Promising Playwright, the Imison Award, the BBC NI Stewart Parker Award, the George Devine Award for Most Promising Playwright, a Peggy Ramsay Award and the Susan Smith Blackburn Award. She has been playwright-in-residence at the National Theatre Studio in London and at the Eugene O'Neill Center in Connecticut. Her version of Anton Chekhov's masterpiece *Three Sisters*, about which she writes in this anthology, was staged at the Lyric, Belfast in the autumn of 2016 and is published by Faber. Her website is www.lucycaldwell.com.

Emma Campbell is an artist and activist whose practice and research over the last six years have aimed to normalise the experience of abortion and campaign for legal reform in Northern Ireland and Ireland. She is currently a PhD researcher at the University of Ulster, where she is completing her thesis on the history of feminist activist photography practice and how earlier models can be adapted for a contemporary feminist art practice such as her own. As current Co-Chair of Alliance for Choice Belfast, Emma helped lead the group's 'Trust Women' campaign which aims to remove criminal sanctions from abortion and provide safe and legal reproductive healthcare for all women in Northern Ireland. As a core administrative activist in the Belfast Feminist Network, Emma has been vocal on a range of issues affecting women, LGBTQ people, and workers since 2010. She also makes work relating to abortion stigma as part of the X-ile project and collaborates in artworks on bodily integrity as part of the home/work art collective, funded by Create, the National Development Agency for Collaborative Arts in 2015. Emma has shown her photographic work in Bangkok, Belfast, Berlin, Dublin, Donegal, London, Prince Edward Island and Stockholm.

Julieann Campbell, poet, author and former reporter for the *Derry Journal*, was born in Derry in 1976. A love of poetry led to her first solo poetry collection, *Milk Teeth* (Guildhall Press), in 2015. Julieann has worked alongside the Bloody Sunday Trust on various projects. In 2008, she and Dr Tom Herron co-edited *Harrowing of the Heart: The Poetry of Bloody Sunday* (Guildhall Press), which contained previously unseen local work alongside the likes of Seamus Heaney, Brian Friel and John Lennon. As Press Officer for the Trust during the 2010 *Report of the Bloody Sunday Inquiry*, Julieann liaised with bereaved families, survivors and the global press. Her first non-fiction book, *Setting the Truth Free: The Inside Story of the Bloody Sunday Justice Campaign* (Liberties Press), won the 2013 Christopher Ewart-Biggs Memorial Prize. As oral history facilitator with Creggan Enterprises' 'Unheard Voices' Programme, Julieann compiled and edited the 2016 book, *Beyond the Silence: Women's Unheard Voices from the Troubles* (Guildhall Press). Other publishing credits include chapters in *City of Music: Derry's Music Heritage* (Guildhall Press, 2009). Julieann is now Heritage and Programmes Coordinator with the Museum of Free Derry, helping to generate and preserve oral histories for its National Civil Rights Archive. She lives in Derry with her seven-year-old daughter Saffron.

Ruth Carr lives in Belfast where she has worked in adult education for over thirty years, firstly as an associate lecturer for the Belfast Institute of Further & Higher Education and currently as a freelance tutor and editor. She edited *The Female Line* in 1985 (under the name Hooley) for the Northern Ireland Women's Rights Movement (released as an ebook in 2016) and compiled the section on contemporary women's fiction in *The Field Day Anthology of Irish Writing (vols. IV/V)*. She was a co-editor of *The Honest Ulsterman (HU* poetry magazine) for about fifteen years and produced its final hard copy issue in 2003. She was a founder member of the Word of Mouth women's poetry collective whose *Word of Mouth* anthology (Blackstaff, 1998) has been translated into Russian and was launched in St Petersburg in November 2006. She is also involved in running Of Mouth, a reading series (and occasional publisher) based in the Linen Hall Library, Belfast. She is a poet, with two collections, *There is a House* and *The Airing Cupboard*, both published by Summer Palace Press. Her third collection is due in Autumn 2017 from Arlen House.

Jan Carson is a writer based in Belfast. Her first novel, *Malcolm Orange Disappears*, was published by Liberties Press in 2014, followed by a short story collection, *Children's Children* in 2016. Her short story 'Settling' was included in the anthology *The Glass Shore: Short Stories by Women Writers from the North of Ireland*, published by New Island in 2016 and winner of the Bord Gáis Energy Best Irish Published Book of the Year in 2016. She has had short stories broadcast on BBC Radio 3 and 4. Her flash fiction book, *Postcard Stories*, was published by The Emma Press in May 2017. Her stories have appeared in journals such as *Storm Cellar, Banshee, Harper's Bazaar* and *The Honest Ulsterman*. In 2014, she was a recipient of the Arts Council Northern Ireland Artist's Career Enhancement Bursary. She was longlisted for the Séan Ó Faoláin Short Story Prize in 2015 and shortlisted in 2016. Jan won the Harper's Bazaar Short Story Competition in 2016. She was shortlisted for the Doolin Short Story Prize in 2017 and for a Sabotage Award for best short story collection in 2015/16.

Paula Cunningham is from Omagh and lives and works in Belfast. Her chapbook 'A Dog called Chance' and her debut collection *Heimlich's Manoeuvre* (2013) are both from smith/doorstop. She has received awards from the Arts Council of Northern Ireland and her poems have won national and international prizes. *Heimlich's Manoeuvre* was shortlisted for the Seamus Heaney Centre, Fenton-Aldeburgh, and Shine/Strong first collection awards.

Celia de Fréine is a poet, playwright, screenwriter, translator and librettist who writes in Irish and English. Awards for her poetry include the Patrick Kavanagh Award (1994) and Gradam Litríochta Chló Iar-Chonnacht (2004). She has published eight collections of poetry to date, of which *cuir amach seo dom: riddle me this* (Arlen House, 2014), *Blood Debts* (Scotus Press, 2014) and *A Lesson in Can't* (Scotus Press, 2014) are her most recent. Her plays have won many Oireachtas awards. She is one of the co-founders of Umbrella Theatre Company, who regularly perform her plays. Celia is at present writing the biography of Louise Gavan Duffy. Her website is www.celiadefreine.com.

Anne Devlin is a playwright and short story author who has worked in theatre, film, TV and radio. Her plays include *Ourselves Alone* (Faber 1986), *After Easter* (1994) and for radio *The Long March* (Faber 1986) and *The Forgotten* (2009). She co-authored the Birmingham community play *Heartlanders* (Nick Hern Books 1989). After a residency in Sweden in 1990 she began to work for Paramount on the screenplay of *Wuthering Heights* (1993), followed by *Vigo* (1995), and later *Titanic Town* (Faber 1998). Her own original screenplays include *Naming the Names*, based on a story from her collection *The Way-Paver* (Faber 1986); and *The Venus de Milo Instead,* commissioned by Danny Boyle. She spent thirty years in England, a decade in each of three cities: Bristol, Birmingham and London, before returning to Belfast in 2007. Her most recently published stories are in *The Long Gaze Back* anthology (New Island 2015) and *The Glass Shore* anthology (New Island 2016). She is currently working on a collection of short stories. Her most recent essay on Seamus Heaney and *The Mantle of Aeschylus* was published in *The Irish Review* (Winter

2015). She was the recipient of a Major Individual Award from the Arts Council of Northern Ireland in October 2016.

Moyra Donaldson lives in Co. Down and is the author of seven collections of poetry: *Kissing Ghosts* (1996), Lapwing Publications; *Snakeskin Stilettos* (1998), *Beneath the Ice* (2001), *The Horse's Nest* (2006), and *Miracle Fruit* (2010), all from Lagan Press. An American edition of *Snakeskin Stilettos* from CavanKerry Press, New Jersey was shortlisted for a Foreword Book of the Year Award. Her *Selected Poems* was published in 2012 and a new collection, *The Goose Tree*, was published in 2014, both from Liberties Press. Her poetry has won a number of awards and her poems have been anthologised and have featured on UK and American radio and television. She has read at festivals in Europe, Canada and America. In 2015, *Disease* was a collaboration with photographic artist, Victoria J. Dean, culminating in an exhibition and publication. Moyra is a Creative Writing facilitator with twenty-five years' experience and an editor and mentor, both freelance and for literary organisations.

Wendy Erskine lives in Belfast. She has a forthcoming debut collection of stories with The Stinging Fly Press.

Leontia Flynn has published three collections of poetry and a book of criticism. Her poetry collections are *These Days* (Jonathan Cape 2004), *Drives* (Cape 2008) and *Profit and Loss* (Cape 2011). *Reading Medbh McGuckian,* a critical study of Medbh McGuckian's poetry, was published by Irish Academic Press in 2014. *These Days* won the Forward Prize for Best First Collection, and lead to her being selected one of twenty 'Next Generation' Poets by the Poetry Book Society; *Profit and Loss* was Poetry Book Society Recommendation, and it was nominated for the T.S. Eliot Prize. Leontia has also won the Rooney Prize for Irish Literature, a major Individual Artist Award from the Arts Council of Northern Ireland; the seventeenth Lawrence O'Shaughnessy Prize for Irish Poetry and the AWB Vincent American Ireland Literary Fund Award. She is a lecturer at the Seamus Heaney Centre for Poetry at Queen's University Belfast.

Miriam Gamble was born in Brussels in 1980, and grew up in Belfast. She studied at Oxford and at Queen's University, Belfast, where she attended the writers' group while completing her PhD. She moved to Scotland in 2010 and has been employed as a lecturer in creative writing at the University of Edinburgh since 2012. In 2007, Miriam won an Eric Gregory Award and published a pamphlet, *This Man's Town*, with tall-lighthouse press. A selection of her poems featured in the 2009 Bloodaxe anthology *Voice Recognition: 21 Poets for the 21st Century* and, in 2010, Bloodaxe published her first full collection, *The Squirrels Are Dead*, which won a Somerset Maugham Award in 2011. She has also won the Ireland Chair of Poetry Bursary Award and the Vincent Buckley Poetry Prize. Her second collection, *Pirate Music*, was published by Bloodaxe in 2014. She also writes essays, and has contributed recent work on the poetry of Janet Frame and on D.H. Lawrence's collection *Birds, Beasts and Flowers* to *The Dark Horse* magazine. She is currently working on her third collection.

Rosemary Jenkinson was born in Belfast in 1967. She studied Medieval Literature at Durham University and has had a variety of jobs including teaching English in Greece, France, Poland and the Czech Republic. A first collection of short stories, *Contemporary Problems Nos. 53 & 54*, was published by Lagan Press in 2004 and a second, *Aphrodite's Kiss*, by Whittrick Press in 2016. Other stories have appeared in the *Irish Times*, *Sunday Tribune*, *The Stinging Fly*, the *Fish* anthology, *Verbal Magazine* and in *The Glass Shore* anthology. She is also a playwright and her work has been performed in London, Dublin, Belfast, Edinburgh, Washington DC and New York. Plays include: *The Bonefire* (Rough Magic), *The Winners* (Ransom), *Johnny Meister + the Stitch* (Jigsaw, Solas Nua), *The Lemon Tree* (Origin), *Meeting Miss Ireland* (the Abbey), *Basra Boy* (Brassneck, the Keegan), *Come to Where I'm From* (Paines Plough), *Planet Belfast*, (Tinderbox), *Lives in Translation*, (Kabosh), *Stitched Up*, *Love or Money* (c21), *White Star of the North* and *Here Comes the Night* (the Lyric). Writing for radio includes *Castlereagh to Kandahar* (BBC Radio 3) and *The Blackthorn Tree* (BBC Radio 4). *The Bonefire* was winner of the Stewart Parker BBC Radio Award 2006. She has received Arts

Council, Peggy Ramsay and Oppenheim-John Downes Awards. She was writer-on-attachment at the National Theatre Studio in London 2010 and is currently artist-in-residence at the Lyric, Belfast.

Deirdre Madden has published eight novels, including *The Birds of the Innocent Wood, Authenticity, Molly Fox's Birthday* and, most recently, *Time Present and Time Past*. She has also published three novels for children and edited the anthology *All Over Ireland: New Irish Short Stories*. All of her work is published by Faber and Faber. She has won awards including the Rooney Prize, the Hennessy Award, the Somerset Maugham Award and the Kerry Book of the Year. She was twice shortlisted for the Orange Prize, and her first novel for children won the Eilis Dillon Award. Her novel *One by One in the Darkness* was selected by *The Irish Times* in 2000 as one of the 50 Best Novels of the Twentieth Century, and *Molly Fox's Birthday* was chosen by Fintan O'Toole for *Modern Ireland in 100 Artworks*. Her work has been widely anthologised and translated. She teaches Creative Writing at Trinity College Dublin to undergraduates and on the MPhil programme at Trinity's Oscar Wilde Centre. She is a member of Aosdána.

Bernie McGill is the author of *Sleepwalkers*, a collection of stories shortlisted in 2014 for the Edge Hill Short Story Prize, and of *The Butterfly Cabinet* (named in 2012 by *Downton Abbey* creator Julian Fellowes as his novel of the year). Her work has been placed in the Seán Ó Faoláin, Bridport, and Michael McLaverty Short Story Prizes and she won the *Zoetrope: All-Story* Award in the US in 2008. Her stories have been anthologised in both *The Long Gaze Back* and in *The Glass Shore*. She is the recipient of a number of Arts Council of Northern Ireland Awards and was granted a research bursary in 2013 from the Society of Authors. She is a creative writing facilitator in the community and with Poetry Ireland's Writers in Schools Programme and a Professional Mentor for the Irish Writers' Centre. Her second novel, *The Watch House*, set on Rathlin Island at the time of the Marconi wireless experiments of 1898, was published by Tinder Press in August 2017. Her website is www.berniemcgill.com.

Medbh McGuckian was born in 1950 in Belfast, where she continues to live. She studied English at Queen's University Belfast, where she was taught by Seamus Heaney. Friendships with Paul Muldoon and Ciaran Carson fuelled her early work. Her first three books of poetry were published by Oxford University Press, followed by numerous collections with Gallery Press and Wake Forest University Press. She was Writer-in-Residence at Trinity College Dublin and Queen's University Belfast, Visiting Fellow at the University of California, Berkeley, and Writer-Fellow at the University of Ulster, Coleraine. Among the prizes she has won are: the British National Poetry Competition, the Cheltenham Award, the Alice Hunt Bartlett prize, the Rooney Prize, and the American Ireland Fund Literary Award. Her latest collection, *Blaris Moor* (2015), was shortlisted for the *Irish Times* Poetry Now Award and she published her *New Selected Poems* in 2015.

Susan McKay is a writer from Derry, whose recent work has appeared in the *London Review of Books* and *The Irish Times*. She was one of the founders of the Belfast Rape Crisis Centre and later wrote extensively about Northern Ireland as a journalist. She was Northern Editor of the *Sunday Tribune* during the final years of the conflict and during the peace process. Her books include *Sophia's Story* (Gill and Macmillan, 1998), *Northern Protestants: An Unsettled People* (Blackstaff, 2000), *Without Fear: A History of the Dublin Rape Crisis Centre* (New Island, 2005) and *Bear in Mind These Dead* (Faber, 2007). She has won several awards for her work, including, twice, print journalist of the year. She was also named Woman of the Year in Public Life in 2010 by *Irish Tatler* for her 'contribution to justice, peace and reconciliation.' She ran the National Women's Council of Ireland from 2009–2012, during the economic crisis. She has also run a centre for young unemployed people, and worked with rural community groups along the border. She currently directs the Glens Centre, an arts centre in Co. Leitrim, and she is writing a new book. She is married to Mike Allen, and they have two daughters.

Sinéad Morrissey was born in 1972 and grew up in Belfast. Her awards include the Patrick Kavanagh Award, a Lannan Literary

Fellowship, first prize in the UK National Poetry Competition, the *Irish Times* Poetry Prize (2009, 2013), and the T.S. Eliot Prize (2013). *Parallax and Selected Poems* (Farrar, Straus & Giroux) was shortlisted for the National Book Critics' Circle Award for Poetry in 2015 and in 2016 she received the E.M. Forster Award from the American Academy of Arts and Letters. Morrissey has served as Belfast's inaugural Poet Laureate and is currently Professor of Creative Writing at Newcastle University.

Joan Newmann was a member of the Belfast Philip Hobsbaum Group in the 1960s, along with Seamus Heaney, Stewart Parker, James Simmons and Bernard MacLaverty. She is the recipient of the Craobh na hÉigse, an award marking her contribution to poetry in Co. Donegal. Her fourth collection of poetry, *Dead End*, will be published in 2017.

Kate Newmann has published four collections of poetry, and a fifth, *Ask Me Next Saturday*, is due out in 2017. She has worked as a writer with children and adults throughout Ireland and has compiled, edited and produced fourteen community books. With Joan Newmann, she is co-director of the Summer Palace Press. She has won the James Prize (King's College Cambridge), the Swansea Roundyhouse Prize, the Allingham and the Listowel poetry prizes, and was shortlisted for the UK National Poetry Competition (2008).

Roisín O'Donnell grew up in Sheffield but with family roots in Derry city. A graduate of Trinity College Dublin and the University of Ulster, her stories and poems have been published internationally, featuring in *The Stinging Fly*, *The Irish Times*, *Structo*, *Popshot Magazine*, *Unthology* and elsewhere. Her short stories appear in *Young Irelanders* (2015), and in the award-winning anthologies of Irish women's writing *The Long Gaze Back* (2015) and *The Glass Shore* (2016). Nominated for a Pushcart Prize and the Forward Prize, she has been shortlisted for many international awards, including the Cúirt New Writing Prize, the Brighton Prize, the *Wasafiri* New Writing Prize and the Hennessy New Irish Writing Award. Her story 'Under the Jasmine Tree' received an Honorary Mention in the Bath Short Story Award. Another story, 'Him', received an Honorary Mention in Fish Flash Fiction Prize. In 2015, Roisín was awarded a Literature Bursary from the Arts Council of Ireland. Her debut short story collection, *Wild Quiet* was published in 2016 by New Island Books. It was listed as one of *The Irish Times'* Favourite Books of 2016, shortlisted for the Kate O'Brien Award and longlisted for the Edge Hill Short Story Prize. Roisín lives in Dublin with her husband and her daughter.

Heather Richardson was born in Newtownards in 1964. She is one of three featured writers in *Short Story Introductions 1* (Lagan Press 2007), and had a story included in *Brace: A New Generation in Short Fiction* (Comma Press 2008). Her fiction, poetry and creative nonfiction have also been published in magazines in the UK, Ireland, Europe and Australia, including *The Stinging Fly, Meniscus, Incubator* and the *European Journal of Life Writing*. In 2000 she was winner of the Brian Moore Short Story Award. Her first novel, *Magdeburg* (Lagan Press 2010), is set in Germany during the Thirty Years War and her second novel, *Doubting Thomas*, is due from Vagabond Voices in late 2017. She is currently working on a multi-media creative nonfiction project, *A dress for Kathleen*, funded by the Arts Council of Northern Ireland. The project uses text and textiles to explore family, memory and storytelling.

Janice Fitzpatrick Simmons, poet and lifelong teacher of creative writing, has published five collections of poetry and her work has appeared in many journals and anthologies. With her late husband James Simmons, she founded The Poets' House and co-directed the first MA in Creative Writing in Ireland. She received The Patrick and Katherine Kavanagh Fellowship in 2009 and The Royal Literary Fund Bursary in 2010. Her most recent collection is *St. Michael and the Peril of the* Sea (Salmon Poetry).

Cherry Smyth is an Irish writer, born in Co. Antrim, living in London. Her first two poetry collections, *When the Lights Go Up* (2001) and *One Wanted Thing* (2006) were published by Lagan Press. *The Irish Times* wrote of the latter: 'Here is clarity and realism, couched in language that is accessible and inventive. The title poem carries all Smyth's hallmarks: precision, linguistic inventiveness and joy.' Her third collection, *Test, Orange,* 2012, was published by Pindrop Press and her debut novel, *Hold Still,* Holland Park Press, appeared in 2013. She also writes for visual art magazines including *Art Monthly.* She is currently working on a feminist punk libretto and has collaborated with the Dublin band, Roamer, on a forthcoming album. Her website is www.cherrysmyth.com.

Gráinne Tobin grew up in Armagh and lives in Newcastle, Co. Down. After a degree in England, a year in Dublin, teacher training and various jobs, she came back to Northern Ireland in 1975 with her English husband, Andy Carden – reversing the usual migration route – and their daughter and son were born and reared in Co. Down. She taught English in further and adult education and in Shimna Integrated College. Her books are *Banjaxed* and *The Nervous Flyer's Companion* (Summer Palace Press) and a third collection is to be published in Spring 2018 by Arlen House. She was a founder member of the Word of Mouth Poetry Collective, which met for twenty-five years in the Linen Hall Library in Belfast. She contributed to *Word of Mouth* (Blackstaff) which was translated into Russian, and to the anthology of members' translations from five St Petersburg women poets, *When the Neva Rushes Backwards* (Lagan Press). Her poems have appeared in anthologies and in literary magazines. She has given many poetry workshops and readings and has had Northern Ireland Arts Council support for developing her work. Some of her poems are available in the Arts Council's online Troubles Archive. She won the Segora Poetry competition in France, was longlisted for the UK's National Poetry Competition, shortlisted for the *Aesthetica, Mslexia, Wordpool,* Fish, Gregory O'Donoghue and North-West Words Donegal Creameries competitions, and commended in the Torbay/ Acumen competition. Her poem 'Learning to Whistle' was made into a sculpture and is on display in Down Arts Centre.

Margaret Ward is a graduate of Queen's University Belfast. She was Director of the Women's Resource and Development Agency, a regional organisation for women, based in Belfast, from 2005 until her retirement in December 2013. She has worked at Bath Spa University and the University of the West of England and in 2014 was awarded an honorary Doctor of Laws by Ulster University for her contribution to advancing women's equality. She is the author of a number of books, including *Unmanageable Revolutionaries: women and Irish nationalism* and biographies of Hanna Sheehy Skeffington and Maud Gonne. She has edited *Hanna Sheehy Skeffington: suffragette and Sinn Feiner, her memoirs and political writings*, UCD Press, due in autumn 2017. Margaret is currently Visiting Fellow in the School of History, Anthropology, Philosophy and Politics at Queen's University, Belfast.

Tara West had already made a career as an advertising copywriter when she wrote her first novel, *Fodder*, published by Blackstaff Press in 2002 and established her reputation as a fresh and original new Irish voice. Her second novel, *Poets Are Eaten as a Delicacy in Japan* was published by Liberties Press in 2013 and was described by Ian Sansom as 'the funniest book written by a Northern Irish author this century'. Her writing has also been published in *The Glass Shore,* the award-winning collection of short stories by Northern Irish women writers, and *Blackbird*, the inaugural anthology of writing from Queen's University Belfast's Seamus Heaney Centre alumni. Her most recent work includes a memoir about depression and recovery, *Happy Dark*. She lives in Co. Antrim with her husband and daughter.

Sheena Wilkinson has been described as 'one of our foremost writers for young people' (*The Irish Times*, March 2015). Since the publication of the multi-award-winning *Taking Flight* (Little Island) in 2010, she has published several acclaimed novels. *Grounded* won the overall CBI Book of the Year in 2013. Her first historical novel, *Name Upon Name*, set in 1916 Belfast, was chosen as Waterford's 'One Community, One Book' title. In 2012, Sheena was granted a Major Award from the Arts Council of Northern Ireland. She has won several awards for short stories, many of which share the post-World War One setting of 'Let Me Be Part of All This Joy'. Her story 'Each Slow Dusk', also set in a Belfast school, was included in the anthology *The Great War* (Walker Books, 2014). Sheena is an experienced creative writing tutor, and teaches regularly for the Arvon Foundation. She set up and runs the Belfast Inter-Schools Creative Writing Network for teenaged writers, and was the inaugural Bringing to Book writer-in-residence at the Church of Ireland College of Education in Dublin. She is currently Royal Literary Fund Writing Fellow at Queen's University, Belfast. *Street Song*, her latest contemporary novel, was published in April 2017 (Black and White) and *Star by Star*, her second historical novel for teens, is due from Little Island in October 2017.

Ann Zell (1933–2016) was born into a Mormon family in Idaho and raised on a small farm. She graduated from Utah State University and worked in publishing in New York before emigrating in the sixties to London. There she raised her daughter while working at a variety of jobs and becoming involved in community and political activism. She gained a Master's degree in Chinese language and history from the School of Oriental and African Studies (SOAS), London University. In 1980 she moved to West Belfast at the height of the Troubles. While still involved in political activism, it was here that she also committed herself to writing poetry, founding, together with Ruth Carr, the Word of Mouth Poetry Collective in 1991. Ann's poems were published widely in literary journals and anthologies. The publication of the Word of Mouth anthology by Blackstaff Press in 1996 led later to a partnership with Russian women poets in St Petersburg, involving exchange visits and readings. She initiated Word of Mouth's translation of five women poets in *When the Neva Rushes Backwards*, published in 2014. Her publications include *Weathering, Between Me and All Harm*, and *Donegal is a red door*, a posthumous collection edited by Ruth Carr and Natasha Cuddington in 2016. Ann's work has been anthologised in *Virago New Poets* (1993), *The White Page/An Bhileog Bhán: Twentieth Century Irish Women Poets*(2000) and *The Field Day Anthology of Irish Writing Volume V*(2006).

Acknowledgements

We would like to thank Dan Bolger and the team at New Island for taking on this anthology and for all the care and expertise they have devoted to it. Huge thanks also to Damian Smyth and the Arts Council of Northern Ireland for championing the book.

Many people gave us support and advice or put us in contact with potential contributors. We appreciate in particular the enthusiasm and encouragement we received from Sinéad Gleeson, Patsy Horton, and Jane Talbot.

Drue Zell, Ruth Carr and Natasha Cuddington gave us permission to reprint some of Ann Zell's final poems from *Donegal is a red door* (Of Mouth, 2016). A heartfelt thanks to Ruth Carr also for the inspiration of her edited collection *The Female Line* (1985) and for allowing us to adapt her original title.

Finally, we are grateful and proud of the superb and varied writings we have received from the contributors. It was a joy to work with them.

Linda Anderson and Dawn Miranda Sherratt-Bado

Summer 2017